"And of course you are beautiful. You cannot change that."

"I wish I could," she replied softly.

He wished he could as well—his friendship with Percy was too important to let his reaction to her change anything.

So he'd maintained an aura of indifference to her presence, except when he was surprised by it, as he was tonight.

It didn't help matters that the gown she wore was an elegant confection of lace and cream-colored satin, likely a remnant from her days as a debutante. It sloped over her shoulders to discreetly highlight the gentle swells of her bosom, which wasn't large, but also not small.

Perfectly shaped, at least as far as Thomas's knowledgeable eye could discern.

Everything about her was perfect, in fact. Her golden blond hair that glinted in the soft candlelight, the paler, almost silvery strands that made her look ethereal. Her large blue eyes, the blue of a rare summer day, her mouth with its perfectly curved lips, the upper one tilted up as though waiting for a kiss.

By Megan Frampton

The Hazards of Dukes
GENTLEMAN SEEKS BRIDE
A WICKED BARGAIN FOR THE DUKE
TALL, DUKE, AND DANGEROUS
NEVER KISS A DUKE

The Duke's Daughters
THE EARL'S CHRISTMAS PEARL (novella)
NEVER A BRIDE
THE LADY IS DARING
LADY BE RECKLESS
LADY BE BAD

Dukes Behaving Badly
MY FAIR DUCHESS
WHY DO DUKES FALL IN LOVE?
ONE-EYED DUKES ARE WILD
NO GROOM AT THE INN (novella)
PUT UP YOUR DUKE
WHEN GOOD EARLS GO BAD (novella)
THE DUKE'S GUIDE TO CORRECT BEHAVIOR

MEGAN FRAMPTON

GENTLEMAN SEEKS BRIDE

A HAZARDS OF DUKES NOVEL

AVONBOOKS

An Imprint of HarperCollinsPublishers

Untitled excerpt copyright © 2022 by Megan Frampton.

First Avon Books mass market printing: December 2021

Print Edition ISBN: 978-0-06-302310-9
Digital Edition ISBN: 978-0-06-301101-4

Cover design by Amy Halperin
Cover illustration by Victor Gadino
Cover image © Svyatoslava Vladzimirskaya | Dreamstime.com (hair)

FIRST EDITION

Printed in Lithuania

21 22 23 24 25 SB 10 9 8 7 6 5 4 3 2 1

In memory of Joan, who loved me.

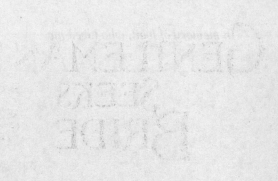

GENTLEMAN
SEEKS
BRIDE

Chapter One

Life was always easy for Thomas Sharpe.

He was witty, gracious, and unexpectedly charming. He didn't enter a room so much as owned it; women wanted to be seduced by him, and men wanted to be him. He was tall, handsome, and excelled at everything he did.

Life was easy.

Until it wasn't.

He could recall, to a second, the moment when things shifted. When his father entered the family dining room, his hat in his hands, his face ashen.

When his mother half rose from her chair, one hand to her throat.

It was a cold, dreary day; one where the idea of the sun was just that—an idea, not reality. A day when you looked outside and imagined all the ways the world could go wrong, secure in the comfort of your home and the knowledge that what you were imagining was just your imagination.

Unless it wasn't.

His father looked directly at his mother. "It's gone, Matilda. All of it. Gone."

His mother's eyes widened, and she slumped back down in her chair, her hand now clutching her heart. And then her expression changed from one of despair to one of desperate hope.

Thomas watched, a growing sickening feeling in his throat as his mother's gaze shifted to him. She had a fierce look in her eye, a look that demanded attention.

"It's up to you," she said. She nodded toward his younger sisters. "What will happen to them? To us?"

Thomas glanced at them, at Julia, who was just about to make her debut, and had been talking about nothing but for weeks. At fourteen-year-old Alice, who was excruciatingly shy because of a bad stammer, who would likely never want to be seen in public, but would need to be cared for for the rest of her life.

At his parents, who were already old. Their children had come late in life, and this investment—the one they'd staked everything that wasn't already entailed on—was supposed to see them through to the ends of their lives. Provide a dowry for Julia, who wasn't blessed with Thomas's good looks. A poor, plain debutante from a respectable family had as much a chance at making a good marriage as Thomas had of going unnoticed at a social gathering.

It was up to him. It was all up to him.

He didn't need her to explain; after all, Alice had pointed out, ladies had done the same thing for their families for centuries: marry someone wealthy to enable the family to survive. They had even joked about it, back when it seemed an impossibility that they would come to this point.

And now the joke had become reality, and it was all up to him.

How could he refuse his mother's plea? There was no other choice, not one that would provide for his family. Even though it made a fierce anger burn in his chest. The inequity of it, having to sell himself in order to ensure his family survived.

He nodded as he took a deep breath. "I'll do it."

And so, with those three words, Thomas set off on an heiress hunt.

IT WAS NEARLY two years after he'd accepted his future and Thomas was no closer to finding the woman of his dreams. Specifically, an unmarried woman with enough of a fortune to keep his family in relative comfort. His earlier dreams— dreams where someone would keep his attention long enough for him to develop a lasting affection for them—had fizzled at the same time as his family's money.

Julia had made her debut, and had thankfully married a baronet's third son, a man who had secured himself a vicarage. She seemed happy, and had one child with another on the way. She was taken care of.

But his parents and Alice were not. And things were only getting worse. Alice was sixteen now, and still painfully shy. His father now walked much more slowly, while his mother had never been able to shake last winter's cough.

Doctor visits. Upkeep for the estate, which provided land for the farmers who paid rent, the family's only source of income now that they had no investments. No money in savings. A few nice things for Alice, who never asked for anything, and who was clearly terrified at having to survive alone when their parents died.

It all cost money. Money that was just out of reach of Thomas's grasp. Money that went to other, less comely gentlemen in as desperate straits.

Despite—or perhaps because of—his undeniable charm, he hadn't been able to get a lady to commit to him for life.

He was someone with whom they flirted, or sometimes more, but take him as a permanent partner? No.

It seemed that they thought that he might be so irresistible as to be irresistible to *everyone*. That a vow of marriage wasn't enough to halt the perpetual interest he seemed to attract wherever he went.

It was wearisome, frankly, to be charming but not too much so; to be witty without being too clever; to be as well garbed as any other gentleman without seeming to make it apparent he was far better looking than any other gentleman.

Which was why he was on the hunt. Again.

The room was full to bursting with the best Society had to offer: ribald chaperones who insisted on cavorting, drinking, and gambling more than their demure charges; patriarchs who had been forced to attend by their insistent wives and then quickly escaped into a back room to smoke cigars and inhale port; the demure charges whose sole goal was to attract a gentleman they could tolerate for the rest of their lives, and vice versa; and the eagle-eyed mothers, who could sniff out, to a penny, just how much a prospective husband had. The night air was crisp and refreshing, but inside it was stiflingly warm, a testament to the party's success.

And Thomas was in the middle of it, navigating through the party's rough course, adjusting his behavior depending on who he was talking to.

"Miss Porter," he said as mildly as he could. The lady stood alone at the edge of the dance floor close to a cluster of chatting debutantes. She glanced wistfully toward them as they burst into laughter. One of Miss Porter's hands held a shaky glass of punch, while the other adjusted her hair behind her ear, feeling her necklace, scratching her nose, or simply dangling in the air as though waiting for the next task its owner assigned.

Miss Porter reminded him of his sister Alice—clearly shy, obviously in a form of mild agony at being in such a large company.

Unlike Alice, however, Miss Porter was of age to make her debut in Society, and she had, it sounded like, several sisters who needed their eldest sister to hurry up and get married so they could also make their debuts.

This evening she wore the pristine white favored by most of the young ladies in attendance, a signal to the single gentlemen that they had not yet been matrimonially acquired. Rather like waving a red cape toward a bull.

Thomas had responded to her signaling with paying her particular attention at parties, but not so much that other ladies believed he was taken.

But Miss Porter either hadn't noticed or was ignoring Thomas's gentle hints, and he didn't want to overwhelm her with his attentions or force her into anything just because she was naturally timid.

Yes, he needed a wife, and Miss Porter's family definitely came with enough money, but if she wasn't in complete agreement with his suit, if it wasn't what she wanted, then he would not pursue her.

It shouldn't matter, the lady's happiness, not if it meant he could rescue his family, but Thomas wasn't able to *completely* lose his humanity in search of a bride. In that he differed from other gentlemen in his situation; he'd lost a few potential wives to more aggressive suitors, ones who didn't seem to care if the lady they'd chosen actually liked them. And had seen as those wives had been worn down by their husbands' indifference, or worse.

He would not be that kind of husband, even if his motivations for marriage were the same.

"Yes, Mr. Sharpe?" Miss Porter spoke at last.

"May I take that? I would not want your lovely gown to be ruined." He gestured toward the hand holding the punch, which wavered even more as he spoke.

She nodded, a shy smile crossing her face.

Another burst of laughter. Another longing look.

And not at him. Not what he was accustomed to, but it was almost refreshing not to be the focus of attention for once.

"Miss Porter, might I introduce you to Lady Emily?" Thomas nodded toward the clear ringleader of the group, a young lady who was already betrothed to a gentleman back home, but was in London so she "wouldn't miss out on anything."

Thomas had deduced that Lady Emily enjoyed being admired, meaning she had something in common with everybody else in the world, but she had a very specific limit to said admiration. Thomas usually counted his compliments on the fingers of his left hand; if he reached his thumb, it was likely one compliment too many.

"Oh yes, please," Miss Porter said.

"A moment, Miss Porter." Thomas lowered his head so he could speak close to her ear. "If you want to tell Lady Emily she looks splendid, or any such words to that nature, please observe the rules."

"Rules?" she replied back in a puzzled tone.

"No more than four such thoughts. Otherwise, Lady Emily gets snappish. Rather like when you feed too many treats to a dog."

She smothered a giggle, turning bright eyes up to him. Thank goodness—she seemed much more relaxed, much less susceptible to being unfortunately judged by the group of ladies, some of whom he knew could be quite critical.

Thanks to his mission, he'd paid scrupulous attention to each of the possible candidates that might save his family.

Lady Emily was off his list, but she was a valuable asset. Miss Hemingsworth would settle for nothing less than a title, which he did not have. Ladies Thomasina and Theodora were nearly indistinguishable from one another, even though they were not related.

He'd confused one with the other too many times for either to believe he was serious in his admiration. Both were inordinately silly, so a part of him wondered if he had confused them deliberately, so as to avoid having to possibly marry one of them.

He held his arm out for Miss Porter, who took it with her hair-adjusting hand.

"Thank you, Mr. Sharpe," she said again.

"Of course." He patted the hand that rested on his sleeve.

"Ladies," Thomas began as they drew up to the group, "might I have the honor of introducing Miss Porter? Miss Porter is desirous of making the acquaintance of the most beautiful and charming ladies in London. Naturally I brought her to you." He accompanied his words with a bow, keeping his eyes on Lady Emily, knowing how she reacted would dictate what the rest of the ladies would do.

"Oh, Mr. Sharpe," Lady Emily replied with a knowing smirk, "you are too kind."

"I am not being kind, merely truthful," Thomas said smoothly.

"Miss Porter, do not believe a word this rascal says," Lady Emily said. "Come here, let me speak to you a moment. I do not believe we have met."

Miss Porter released her hold on Thomas's arm, but not before mouthing *thank you* to him as she turned toward her new friend.

"If you will excuse me," Thomas said. "I will leave you to discuss my various attributes."

Smiles all around, and then Thomas strode over to a more discreet corner than the one Miss Porter had been hiding in, taking a deep breath as he allowed himself to relax.

It was exhausting. *He* was exhausted.

He turned to see Miss Porter with a delighted smile on her face. His task was arduous, but if he could help someone along the way, it was nearly worth it.

And he'd promised himself a night off the next day.

HE STOOD AT the entrance to Miss Ivy's, a gambling club that had lately begun to host special evenings. Evenings, such as tonight, where everyone and anyone could attend, provided they had money to spend and a mask to wear.

Thomas relished the feeling of anonymity, even though he knew it was a facade; after all, there weren't many men in London who had his height and grace. He wasn't vain—it was a simple fact, a fact that was supposed to have gained him a wealthy wife long before now.

"Good evening," a voice said as he entered.

Thomas turned and smiled as he saw his friend Octavia. She ran the day-to-day of Miss Ivy's now that her sister—the titular Miss Ivy—was managing the books and the buying and all the other behind-the-scenes work.

Since that fateful day two years ago, he'd found himself to be overly cautious, at least in financial terms. He'd seen men gain and lose fortunes through gambling, so rescuing his family that way had never crossed his mind. Too risky. Much easier to marry well, he'd thought. He would rely on his appearance before he'd count on his luck.

Though now his odds on doing that were increasing. Perhaps he should just wager everything as his father had done.

Though he was already doing that, wasn't he?

Goddamn it, but he was in a foul mood.

"Thomas?" she asked, sounding amused.

"Good evening," he replied with a bow. "I need a stiff drink and a moment where I'm not obliged to make conversation."

"Poor you," Octavia replied in a wry tone. "To have to be charming wherever you go. How is the hunt going, anyway?"

Thomas shrugged.

"That well, hmm?"

He and Octavia were two of a kind: charming, gracious, and sometimes reckless. They had had a brief flirtation, one that had even included a few kisses, but they both knew their relationship wasn't sustainable. They were both flints, capable of striking sparks, but unable to manage a true fire.

But where Thomas had lost a potential lover—since Octavia wasn't wealthy enough for him to marry, and she was far too determined to remain independent—he had gained a friend. One who understood him, who knew what it was like to have fallen in status. Before she was the face of Miss Ivy's, she'd been a lady, living in the country with her older sister.

But things happened, as they did, and now she was here flouting respectability with zeal. He knew it would take a remarkable gentleman to get her to give up even a tiny measure of her independence—she was a whirlwind of forthright opinions and plain speaking.

Octavia took his arm and led him to the other end of the club to the bar.

The club was decorated in vibrant shades of fuchsia and gold, a bold testament to the Duchess of Malvern, who was one of Octavia's best friends and a woman who appreciated the value of audacious color combinations. The entire effect was both inviting and challenging. The guests, for the most part, wore masks that ranged from a simple scarf with eyeholes to a far more complicated contraption that looked as though Marie Antoinette might have donned it at the Tuileries.

"If only you had enough to afford me," Thomas said mournfully as he and Octavia walked through the crowd.

"I don't know that I'd wish to buy you," Octavia replied. "You'd be far too difficult to maintain."

Thomas paused, putting his hand to his heart in an exaggeratedly shocked gesture. "I am wounded to the core." He pointed to himself. "All I need from a wife is a healthy bank account, not too many bothersome relatives, and who is a pleasant companion." He paused. "In that order."

"As I said," Octavia replied archly. "Too difficult to maintain."

Thomas laughed, as he was meant to, as they reached the bar.

The bartender nodded at him and began to pour him his drink—whisky with a splash of water—and set it on the bar.

He was bringing it to his mouth when he heard

Octavia's intake of breath, and turned to see what had managed to startle his unflappable friend.

And then he saw her.

Dressed in a gown more suited for a court presentation than a gambling establishment, her golden hair gleaming in the candlelight, her enticing lips curling in a delighted smile, her mask barely concealing the beauty of her face and doing nothing to hide her identity.

Lady Jane Capel, daughter of the Earl of Scudamore. The sister of his best friend. A woman blessed with both beauty and wealth, who'd seemed to be on the verge of becoming a duchess two years ago—the same time Thomas's fortunes had changed so dramatically—when her sister had married the duke unexpectedly and Lady Jane had gotten engaged to her next-door neighbor.

Jane was still unmarried. Two years ago her life had been upended. Or more accurately, she had upended her own life after her fiancé had broken their engagement. She'd left her family home and taken lodgings with her half brother, Percy Waters, Thomas's closest friend, rather than hide out in the safety of her parents' home until someone else was lured in by her beauty and quiet disposition.

Thomas had met Jane over the years, of course, but Percy's sister was far more likely to spend time with a book or at the park than carousing with Thomas and Percy. Plus her occasional presence now at social events invariably caused comment, because of how she lived, and he could not afford to have anyone question his reputation by spending time with her.

It wasn't fair, but it was their world.

He admired her for her bravery, rejecting the well-trodden path of other aristocratic ladies. He wished he could do the same, but his path was what hers had been—marriage to a stranger in an arrangement that would be as transactional as it was based on any kind of emotion. A charming husband in exchange for enough money to keep her charming husband's family afloat.

"What is someone like *her* doing here?" Octavia asked, echoing the question dancing in his mind. People of all sorts came to Miss Ivy's, of course, but few of them were quietly demure bookish ladies. It was as jarring to see her in this setting as it would be for Thomas to appear at a meeting for Somber Sorts Who Much Preferred Staying at Home Reading to Going Out.

Otherwise known as the Lady Jane Club, if she had one.

Lady Jane was seated at one of the gaming tables, a half dozen or more gentlemen surrounding her. She reached out to pick up the cup of dice, shaking it with that same delighted expression on her face. As though the cup was a new book and she was just diving into its pages.

The men around her wore expressions ranging from fascinated to intrigued to plain lustful, their emotions not at all disguised by the masks they wore.

It was the last one that made Thomas place his drink, untouched, back down on the bar, turning to walk toward her. He owed it to his friend to watch out for his little sister, even though the little sister appeared to be having a wonderful time.

But Thomas knew, more than most, that appearances were deceiving.

He reached her table just as she had tossed the dice, her eyes wide behind the mask as the counters tumbled onto the green felt.

"Lucky seven!" the dealer called, pushing the stack of chips toward Lady Jane. She leaned forward to gather them toward the stack she already had in front of her.

"Congratulations," one of the gentlemen said, placing his hand on the back of her chair in a proprietary gesture. "Let me escort you to where there are other, more interesting wagers."

Thomas recognized him as Lord Joseph Callender, another gentleman on the heiress hunt, a handsome man who needed money to maintain his lifestyle of expensive horses, expensive women, and expensive wine.

In a few years, Thomas forecast, Lord Joseph's looks would have succumbed to his various vices so that now was his only chance to take advantage of his appearance.

Not that Lord Joseph likely realized that. He was just desperate for funds and, like Thomas, had recognized that his best way out of his financial hole was to marry well.

And Lady Jane was no longer an heiress, thanks to being disowned by her parents when she had moved in with Percy.

So Lord Joseph's intentions were definitely not honorable. Which meant that Thomas would have to intervene.

"My lady," he said in his smoothest tone as he

reached her side, "I believe you have promised to allow me to show you around Miss Ivy's." He caught Octavia's eye and gestured toward the door to her private office. She nodded in understanding, withdrawing a key from her bodice and holding it toward him.

Lady Jane's blue eyes blinked up at him in confusion. "I did?" she began, and then her expression cleared as she recognized him. At which point she began to scowl. "I did not," she continued, her gaze returning to the table. "You have done your duty. Thank you, Mr. Sharpe."

Thomas froze, unaccustomed as he was to being refused.

"You heard her, Mr. Sharpe," Lord Joseph added. "I'll take care of Lady Jane."

Lady Jane turned her head sharply toward Lord Joseph. "Not you, too," she said in an aggrieved tone. "I will not be *taken care of,* thank you very much." She rose from the table, dropping her chips into a small bag she wore on her wrist. "I believe I will try my luck at another table."

Instead of moving to another table, however, she walked briskly to the bar, nodding at Octavia whose face wore the same startled expression Thomas knew was on his own.

"Let me handle this," he murmured to Octavia, taking her key. She nodded, and he made his way to the bar, dropping himself beside Lady Jane, who seemed determined to ignore him.

Fine. As long as she didn't disappear to back rooms with random scoundrels, he didn't care.

His drink appeared in front of him, and he

reached toward it, only to have her snatch it away.

She lifted her chin in defiance, keeping her eyes locked with his as she began to drink.

And then broke the gaze as she began to cough, one hand going to her throat, the other one placing the glass firmly back on the table.

He suppressed a smile as well as an "I told you so," because he hadn't *actually* warned her against the whisky. He hadn't had the chance—she'd snatched it too quickly.

"Well," she said, when she was finally able to speak, "that was unexpected." Her eyes were watering, and she removed the mask to wipe them. Despite her reaction to the whisky, her expression was gleeful.

"Allow me to escort you home, Lady Jane," Thomas said, placing his fingers on her elbow as he rose.

"Home?" she replied, scowling in displeasure. "No, this"—she gestured to the glass on the bar— "means I am definitely not done here. I'll need another, please," she said to the bartender with a warm smile.

And before he could speak, before he could do anything, she picked up the glass again and drank the balance of the whisky, slamming it down on the bar with a flourish. This time with no coughing.

"There!" she exclaimed triumphantly. "That was much better."

Thomas could only stare at her, wondering what the hell had happened to turn the meek Lady Jane into this gambling, drinking flirt.

JANE HAD TO bite her lip from laughing in his face. The unflappable Thomas Sharpe, perpetually suave, determinedly pleasing, was staring at her as though he had never encountered her like before.

Perhaps he had not.

Certainly it had never seemed as though he had seen her, truly *see* her, even though they had been in the same house several times—he was Percy's best friend, his accomplice in all the disreputable ventures Percy indulged in. Jane wasn't certain just what those ventures were—Percy refused to share, irking her by telling her she was far too naive to understand—but she had gotten the impression that they involved things like alcohol, exuberant parties, and plenty of things young unmarried ladies were supposed to know nothing about.

To Jane's great annoyance, she *was* one of those ignorant unmarried ladies.

Which was why she was at Miss Ivy's, tossing dice and drinking whisky. Learning things she didn't know. Trading her naivete for something more worldly.

And unfortunately running into her brother's best friend. He was definitely going to put a crimp in her plans if she didn't figure out how to thwart his Lancelot tendencies.

"Mr. Sharpe," she began as the bartender placed another drink in front of her, "there is really no need to keep me company. I am doing perfectly well on my own." She spoke with an assured tone that she'd stolen from one of her mother's many harangues about how Jane had to marry *well* and *soon*.

Two things she would not be doing. But the tone itself was effective. At least she hoped so.

One of his wickedly intriguing eyebrows shot up from under his mask in a clear expression of doubt. Damn it, why wouldn't he listen to her when she'd insisted she was fine?

And why did he have to be so remarkably good-looking? She'd just barely learned how to control her breathing when he visited Percy, and then she'd always had time to prepare.

His arrival now was so unexpected she had no time to brace herself for the impact. Of those knowing dark blue eyes that were both intense and seductive; of the casual grace of his body; of his strong jaw and sensual mouth. Even his hair was alluring: dark brown, with a few wavy curls that brushed his shoulders and dangled impudently over his forehead.

Sometimes her fingers tingled with the urge to sweep those curls back, and she had to remind herself that it would be exceedingly odd for her to actually do such a thing.

But she certainly thought of it.

The mask he wore did nothing to hide his allure; if anything, it only enticed someone to see if she could be the one to get him to remove it. To reveal himself to her, and only her.

She should not be thinking this way about her brother's best friend. Especially not when said brother's best friend was trying to shepherd her like a lost lamb.

She was done being a lamb.

"Does Percy know you are here?" he replied, not

responding at all to her explicit request to leave her be. "Because I am guessing he does not," he continued, not waiting for her answer. Perhaps the answer to her fascination with him would be him trying to control her. That would remove any kind of curl-sweeping impulse.

"Of course he does not," Jane said heatedly. "Because," she said, jabbing an accusing finger toward him, "my brother is a perfectly grown person, as am I. I do not ask him where he is going when he is with you, do I?" She crossed her arms over her chest and mimicked his eyebrow look.

Only if she had to guess, she thought she probably didn't look as mocking as he did. Lady Jane Capel did not *mock*, after all; she was accommodating, quiet, acquiescent, modest, and well behaved.

She did not, as it turned out, like Lady Jane Capel very much. At least not that iteration of her.

"The two things are entirely different," he replied in a condescending tone. A tone that bothered her so much she did forget, for a moment at least, how handsome he was.

"Because I am female?"

His jaw worked, and she suppressed a cheer at finally getting him to notice her—even though he seemed to be noticing she was aggravating. But still.

"Could we discuss this more privately?" he said, glancing around the club. She saw his eyes narrow, and she turned to look. Lord Joseph, accompanied by a few of his friends and a look of determination, was heading their way.

"Oh lord," she said in exasperation. She tossed a few chips on the bar. "Fine."

Anything to avoid causing another scandal where she was helpless to do anything.

If there was a scandal to be had, *she* wanted to be the one doing it.

Not standing by as the man she thought she was in love with jilted her. Not standing by as people gossiped behind their hands about her, and about how she was living. Not standing by as men she'd always thought were gentlemen made inappropriate suggestions to her now that they believed her to be vulnerable.

Mr. Sharpe got up as well, gesturing toward a door to the left of the bar. She walked ahead of him, slightly placated that he hadn't taken her arm to guide her, or otherwise asserted his right to dominate.

She stepped to the side as he withdrew a key from his pocket, unlocking the door and following her into the room, then closing the door behind them.

It was a small office with a tidy desk and several bookshelves lining the walls. Instead of books, however, there were bottles of liquor on the shelves. A candle was burning on the desk, but otherwise the room was dark.

It was shockingly intimate. More so because Jane realized that this was the first time she'd been alone with a man since Mr. McTavish, the rat in sheep's clothing who'd broken her heart a few years ago. Though she might want to thank him—if he hadn't jilted her, she'd be married to him, sheep-like.

But the intimacy wasn't anything she needed to worry about. She knew full well—and felt somewhat chagrined—that Mr. Sharpe did not view her as anything other than his friend's sister. He'd made that absolutely clear on all of their previous encounters, and his motivation now was simply that: he felt some responsibility for her as she was his best friend's sister, but nothing more.

She should have been relieved at his lack of interest. After all, she'd been getting noticed by gentlemen since the age of sixteen. Her mother had assured her she would make a spectacular marriage, and that all she needed to do was appear. To stand by, so to speak.

And being the demure Jane she now so desperately wished to shed, she had.

Which had resulted in her getting humiliatingly thrown over by a man who didn't come close to deserving her.

"Well?" she said in an impatient tone.

"I am genuinely curious," he said, removing his mask as he moved closer. To see her more clearly in the dim light, she knew, though her treacherous heart fluttered. "What made you decide to come to Miss Ivy's? Alone?"

The annoying thing was, he did sound genuinely curious. Not judgmental, or lecturing, or condescending.

She paused, then lifted her chin to stare into his eyes. "I don't want to be me anymore," she said simply.

Chapter Two

Thomas frowned in confusion.

"Not want to be you anymore?" He peered into her face. "Who do you want to be then?"

She removed her mask and took a deep breath before she answered. "Anyone but me. Someone who does what she wants when she wants. Who doesn't have to ask anyone for permission to just *be*." She flung her hands out in a frustrated gesture. "Who isn't harried into some back room because she has the audacity to venture out in the evening."

Thomas folded his arms over his chest. What she wanted—it was just—"It's not possible," he blurted out, then felt remorse as he saw her face fall. "You have to be you, Lady Jane," he continued, this time in a softer tone. "You should *want* to be you. From what I hear from Percy, you are a remarkably loyal sister; you're both kind and generous." He hesitated before speaking again. He'd been determined not to notice just how lovely she was because of whose sister she was, and how inappropriate his forming a connection with her would be. And yet here she was.

"And of course you are beautiful. You cannot change that."

"I wish I could," she replied softly.

He wished he could as well—his friendship with Percy was too important to let his reaction to her change anything.

So he'd maintained an aura of indifference to her presence, except when he was surprised by it, as he was tonight.

It didn't help matters that the gown she wore was an elegant confection of lace and cream-colored satin, likely a remnant from her days as a debutante. It sloped over her shoulders to discreetly highlight the gentle swells of her bosom, which wasn't large, but also not small.

Perfectly shaped, at least as far as Thomas's knowledgeable eye could discern.

Everything about her was perfect, in fact. Her golden blond hair that glinted in the soft candlelight, the paler, almost silvery strands that made her look ethereal. Her large blue eyes, the blue of a rare summer day, her mouth with its perfectly curved lips, the upper one tilted up as though waiting for a kiss.

A kiss he could and would not allow himself to give.

"You know what it's like to be judged on your appearance," she replied, her tone disdainful. "I would prefer not to be judged at all."

Thomas snorted. "You know full well that is not

possible for either of us. It's exhausting, isn't it?" he asked in a rueful tone. "Believe me, I understand." He wished it were different for her. For both of them, actually.

Or not—because if he weren't blessed with his particular appearance, he'd have even less of a chance to marry enough money to rescue his family. So perhaps he should be grateful he looked the way he did.

"That doesn't explain why you're here, however," he said, folding his arms over his chest. He needed to maintain his distance from her. Not form a sympathetic connection because of their respective gorgeousness.

She gave him a look indicating what she thought of his analytical skills. Not much, apparently.

"Because Miss Ivy's, from what I know of it, is the one place I can go where I won't be judged. They allow anyone entry, as long as they have funds." She arched her eyebrow at him. "Which makes me wonder—how did you come to be admitted?" Her tone was suspicious. "From what I know, you barely have enough money to pay your tailor." Her gaze raked him up and down, eventually returning to his face. "I hope you do pay your tailor, he does excellent work."

Thomas gave her an exaggerated bow, indicating his annoyance. "Yes, I pay my tailor," he said sharply.

It was an investment, one that his parents were eager to make, since they expected the returns would be worth their while. But his mother's jewelry would last only so long. Time was running out, and thus far, the only returns on the investment were the admiring glances thrown his way anytime he entered a room.

And those, he knew, would happen no matter what he wore.

"I hope you know you cannot continue this course of action," he said, returning his focus to her. "It is true that Miss Ivy's is the only place you could come on your own with a reasonable expectation you would emerge unscathed." His next words held a tinge of regret. "It is unfair, I will give you that, that you cannot do just what you want to. But the reality of our world is that you cannot."

She opened her mouth as if to argue, then snapped it shut again, a look of frustration on her face.

"You are right, of course." She sounded bitter, and Thomas felt his chest tighten at the loss she was so visibly experiencing. But he couldn't concern himself with that, not if it meant she was agreeing to be safe. Secure. Herself.

He exhaled in relief. "Then, if I may, can I escort you safely home?"

"Escort me—?" she echoed, and then her expression shifted, her eyes widening as though she'd been surprised. He nearly turned around to look at what might have startled her, but he knew full well they were alone.

"You!" she exclaimed. As though he were the answer to a question that had been burning in her mind.

"Me?" he said, sounding nearly as idiotic as it seemed she'd just thought him to be.

"Yes, you! Oh, it's so obvious, I wish I had thought of it before!" She was regarding him with a look of satisfaction. He'd been the answer to ladies' questions before, of course, but he highly doubted she was searching for *that* type of satisfaction.

"Thought of—pardon me, my lady, but I must be dim-witted. What are you thinking of?"

A feeling of trepidation rose in his chest.

Which only increased when she poked him in the chest.

"You—" *poke* "—can—" *poke* "—take—" *poke* "—me—" *poke* "—places and show me things." Her expression grew even more excited. "I want to do everything, everything that Lady Jane could never do before."

The feeling of trepidation was now fully developed trepidation.

"Why would I help you?" He didn't try to disguise his distant tone. This was Percy's sister—she was not someone he wished to help. At least not the kind of help he was most able to give.

She nodded before she spoke, a satisfied smile on that lovely mouth.

"Because if you do, I will help you secure a wealthy bride."

He felt as though she'd just punched him in the stomach. The one thing he needed most in the world, and here she was offering it. As though it was as simple as giving him a slice of cake or a compliment. Offering her assistance, which nobody had done yet, even though everyone knew his circumstances.

"But how?"

She shrugged. "It would be easy. A few dropped comments about you in the privacy of the ladies' washroom, about how you try to hide your goodness behind your charming facade. Perhaps how I have tried to secure your interest, but you are focused on another"—she waved her hand in the air—"and of course I wouldn't say who, so every lady would imagine it was them." She met his gaze. "That would quash any rumors about your eventual loyalty, would it not?" She gave another careless shrug. "I would refine it as I went along. These are only the rudiments of the plan, but as I said, it would be easy."

It was such a simple idea Thomas was astonished he hadn't thought of it himself. But then again, he hadn't had a gorgeous accomplice, unless you counted Percy, who was as excessively handsome as Thomas was, albeit in a far more forgetful-poet kind of way. And Percy wasn't one to frequent ladies' washrooms.

"And in return?" he said tightly.

Her tone made it look as though what she was about to say was nothing. A trifle to be dealt with and then forgotten.

Only Thomas very much suspected that was not to be the case.

She had the same expression on her face that his mother had had when she'd pinned a mission to him. A fierce determination that would not be denied.

"You'll take me wherever you go with Percy. I want to see it all." Her eyes sparkled in the dim light. "Places like Miss Ivy's, only places where I would be safer with you as my escort." She flung her hand out. "I want to drink whisky, and laugh, and share my opinion." They sounded like such humble desires. Things Thomas did every day without thinking about it. He could do it, couldn't he? If it meant he'd finally secure a bride?

"And," she said, taking a deep breath as she lifted her gaze to his, "I want to do it all." She bit her lip and images began to speed through his brain, images not at all suitable for him to have about the sister of his best friend.

"You mean—?" he began, not sure he should say it. Because if that wasn't what she meant she would be horrified. And if it was what she meant, *he* would be horrified.

And tempted. The one thing he could not be, not with Percy's sister.

"I mean," she said slowly, "I want you to show me the things that ladies and gentlemen—that women and men—do together." She exhaled. "I don't think it is fair, having to miss out on the same experiences you have had. Just because I am not married." A shrug. "And there will be no obligations on either side when we have fulfilled our bargain." He saw her swallow in the dim light, saw how she lifted her chin and kept her eyes locked with his. "I mean I want to do all of that. Or at least most of it," she corrected quickly. "We will take precautions, of course. The one thing I know neither of us wants is to have to marry. Which is fine, since I have the feeling you could not stand my independence, and I could not tolerate your condescension."

He wouldn't respond to that. Though she was likely correct. "So everything but—?"

She nodded again, this time much more vigorously, God help him.

"Yes."

She made it all seem so simple—a bartering of talents, a trading of expertise.

But this was his best friend's sister, a lady he knew to be gentle and quiet. A lady who found pleasure in books and walking in the park. Who couldn't possibly know what she was asking of him.

But if she were able to assist him in finding a bride, how could he refuse? At least not without negotiation?

"What about Percy?" he asked.

She arched an eyebrow at him again. As though in challenge. "What about Percy?" And then folded her arms over her chest, giving him a questioning look.

His mind ran through several possible answers— *Percy was protective of his sister. Percy wouldn't want her to be exposed to danger. Percy might think it was odd for his best friend to keep company with his sister*— but all of that made it seem as though she herself was not to be trusted with her own wishes.

And that was not at all what he wanted to say. Not because he didn't want to say it, but because he could see that that would not persuade her. If anything, knowing what he had just discovered about her, it would encourage her even more.

"You see?" she said triumphantly. "Anything you might reply diminishes my choice in the matter. I am my own person, or at least I want to be. This is *my* choice."

Mr. Thomas Sharpe, the smoothest conversationalist in Society, was at a loss for words.

"Oh," she said, now sounding apologetic, "but I did not ask you if that aspect of our agreement would be acceptable. Now I am as bad as some of those gentlemen who've insisted on taking advantage—"

"You're not taking advantage of me," Thomas bit out. This was the most bizarre discussion he'd ever engaged in. Certainly nobody had ever asked him if he minded being used for his skills in the bedroom.

Her face brightened. It was a good thing she hadn't been playing cards earlier—every one of her emotions showed on her face.

"So you think you would want to—?" she asked. He could see her cheeks turn pink, even in the dim candlelight.

"Yes." The truth. Even though he would not allow himself to act on the truth. No matter how tempted he was. And despite how much she seemed to relish arguing with him.

"Oh good." She looked delighted, and it was hard for him not to share her enthusiasm—after all, she was asking him to take her to the most entertaining places he knew of in London plus show her what pleasure felt like.

Why wouldn't he be pleased?

Well, Thomas, a stern voice said in his head, *because if you do anything with her, you would likely lose your best friend. If you do anything with her, it is more than likely one or the other of you would become emotionally entangled, and there is to be no sustainable future.*

Because while she said she wanted to experience those things, he knew she was entirely innocent, and he didn't want to take advantage of that innocence, even if she was offering it.

And because if he did anything with her, he'd still end up being married for the rest of his life to a woman about whom the only thing he knew for certain was that she was wealthy.

Best not to think of that now. Better to concentrate on what she had proposed. And figure out how to delay fulfilling his end of the bargain, the scandalous part, until she realized that she didn't need him, after all. Make the decisions hers, her choice, as she wanted. And then, when he had secured his wealthy heiress, he could walk away knowing he had treated her honorably.

He held his hand out to her. "I agree to take you to places you wouldn't normally go, and you agree to help me find a wife."

"And the other thing, too," she said as she took his hand.

"Yes," he said, unable to resist a wry smile. "I will also *take you* to places you wouldn't normally go." He lowered his voice as he spoke, imbuing it with his customary seductive charm. While also desperately attempting to keep himself from reacting to her.

She shook his hand, a myriad of emotions skimming her face: delight, anticipation, and desire. "When do we start?"

Everything he'd just thought, as well as the prickles of gentlemanly conduct, the standard to which he held himself and those around him, would never allow for him to school her in passion. In pleasure. Despite how much the idea intrigued him. Tantalized him.

But he couldn't tell her he was planning not to fulfill that part of the agreement, or she would refuse to help him. Or worse, she'd find another less reputable gentleman to teach her, and he could not allow that. He owed it to Percy, for one thing, and he owed it to her as well.

So the trick would be to lure her close to the edge of safety, tempt her into the forbidden, and make it seem as though it was her idea when she pulled back.

She didn't know what she was asking for. But when she did, she would understand that this was far more than just not being herself. She would understand she could be herself without compromise—in every sense of the word.

He met her gaze. "Why not now?"

WHY NOT NOW?

Oh. Jane felt her whole body react to his words, to the touch of his hand on hers. He still held her hand, and as they stood there, looking into one another's eyes in the dim light, he slowly turned his palm so it rested underneath her hand, his fingers touching her wrist. His touch tightening ever so slightly as he tugged her toward him. So gently that if she wished to she could have resisted.

She did not wish to.

She found herself within a few inches of him, staring up into his handsome face, his eyes locked with hers, his fingers making slow swirling movements on her inner arm. She was terrified. She was intrigued. She was excited.

"The first lesson," he said in a low rumble that made her shiver, "is that the moments before are as important as the reality." His voice got even lower. "Anticipation, Lady Jane."

Her breath caught at the intensity of his gaze. And his tone.

He stroked her skin, sending shivers through her spine. His mouth curled up in satisfaction as though he were pleased at her reaction.

"Were you thinking about this when you said you wanted not to be you?" he asked, those sly fingers still touching her arm, making her wonder what it would feel like if his fingers went elsewhere. Did fingers go *there*, for example?

She had no idea. She cursed her own ignorance, but then reminded herself that she had just negotiated a means of education. She would no longer be the kind of woman who had no idea about things.

And then her future would unfurl before her with possibility—not binding her with its limitations.

She raised her chin in defiance as she answered his question. "No." He was altogether too conceited. Even though it was merited.

His smile was smug. "So you just thought of it because it was me?"

Her lips curled up into a matching smile. "Tell me, Mr. Sharpe, are you always this arrogant?"

He chuckled as though caught off guard by

her words. "Always, my lady. With good cause," he replied, shifting his position as if on display. "And with plenty of confirmation that everything I promise—that everything I've made someone anticipate—is well worth the wait."

"And speaking of that," he continued, raising her wrist up toward his mouth, "this is the end of the first lesson." He placed his lips on her inner wrist, kissing it softly, and then releasing her, stepping back as he did so.

Well. It wasn't as though she thought he would ravish her here, in the back room of Miss Ivy's.

Even though a tiny part of her—or more than a tiny part of her—wished he had.

"It's late. I'm certain Octavia wants to reclaim her office, and I want to escort you home so you can speak with Percy before he hears about you being here."

"Speak with Percy?" She scowled. "Why would I need to speak with my brother?"

He exhaled as he glanced up at the ceiling. She'd seen people do that before, but it had never been directed at her. Normally it was in response to her sister, Lavinia, who seemed to be able to nettle even the most sanguine of people.

She was definitely getting better at this making a choice thing. Because while she hadn't deliberately chosen to annoy him in advance, if she had been asked if she wished to, given what he was saying, she would have replied with an emphatic yes.

"You will want to tell him what you've planned." He spoke as if it was so obvious she was slow for not comprehending it. He truly was condescending. And conceited. And overly confident. "I will leave all the details up to you, but I would expect Percy would wish to know that you will be safe on your adventures. The adventures you've chosen to have." He paused. "Unless you wish me to speak with him?"

"No!" she shot out. She would never have another man speak for her. She'd had enough of that already, thank you very much. But he did have a point—she couldn't hide something like this from her brother. She took a deep breath. "You are right. I should let him know we have made an agreement. Not that I will share the specifics with him, you understand."

Because even though Percy was one of the most accommodating brothers, she thought even he would balk at her spending *that* kind of time with his notorious friend.

"Then," he began, gesturing toward the door, "may I escort you home now?" His tone was amused, as though she was a recalcitrant responsibility he had to take care of.

Which wasn't far from the truth, to be honest.

But she did not want to be anyone's responsibility anymore, she thought as she strode to the door. If she had wanted that, she could have married any of the gentlemen who'd offered for her even after her parents cut her off. They had wanted her to exchange her appearance for the security of a good home, protection from being a single female in London.

Just as he was planning to do, come to think of it. Though he was trading his appearance for the security of his parents' home. He couldn't afford any kind of commitment to her beyond their agreement, and she wouldn't obligate him to do so.

It was just a business proposition.

She would make certain that she owed him nothing at the end of their agreement, when he was wedded to a wealthy woman and she was finally able to figure out just who she was and what she wanted.

And in the meantime, he would teach her all the things she wanted to know.

Chapter Three

"Good morning," Jane said, keeping her tone as light as possible.

Percy groaned in reply, holding his head.

She leaned over to kiss him, then went to the sideboard and poured herself some coffee. She turned, holding the carafe. "Do you need some?"

Percy gave a vigorous nod, then winced.

Their dining room was snug, but warm and welcoming. It held a rectangular table with six well-upholstered chairs, the sideboard, and a cupboard displaying various items Jane and Percy had found since deciding to live together. Not for them the displaying of dinnerware and fragile vases; Jane kept finding books in increasing stages of decay, while Percy took great joy in locating various mathematical tools such as abacuses from China and compasses from Italy. Not to mention a variety of writing implements purportedly used by famous economists from the past.

She chuckled at Percy's continuing groans as she filled another cup. "Was it another reading?" Percy and Jane's sister, Lavinia, was the author of several salacious novels, but Lavinia had persuaded Percy to appear in public as the author for a variety of reasons, not least of which was that Percy was handsome in a tortured artist sort of way, even though he was neither tortured nor an artist.

He was, in fact, extremely adept at numbers, and worked for their father, who was a financial advisor to the queen. He was kind, and gentle, and loved to meet and speak with people. If he had been born in different circumstances, he would be the king of London Society. As it was, he was close to being its prince.

Percy, however, was only her half brother, born to an illicit liaison their father had had in between Jane's and Lavinia's births.

Oddly enough, Jane's mother adored her husband's bastard son, far preferring him to Lavinia. But it was Lavinia's marriage to the Duke of Hasford that had enabled Percy to rise to such a prestigious position—nobody would dare to scorn a duke's relative, since the duke had made his acceptance of his wife's family clear to everyone.

He shook his head. "No, not a reading. It was a meeting of the Economic Society."

"Oh, those economic rascals," she said with a wry smile.

"They don't get to go out very often," he replied in a wan tone. "And so they wanted me to take them out. All night. I got in around six o'clock this morning."

Jane glanced at the clock in the corner. "So what are you doing up at nine, then? Shouldn't you be sleeping?"

"I promised to meet Thomas to visit the Free Exhibition."

"Is he coming here?" she asked, her tone deliberately light. As though she didn't care at all, when of course she did.

"Mmm-hmm." Percy took a sip of coffee, giving a happy exhale as he put the cup back down. "He says that the exhibition is a good place to find—" And then he froze, his eyes widening in horror. "Never mind that," he continued hastily.

"To find eligible and wealthy young ladies?" Jane said. "I know what he wants. In fact," she began, trying to sound as casual as possible, "we spoke about it last evening."

"You did?" Percy narrowed his gaze at her. Not entirely the forbidding look he was striving for, given he still had a sack held to one side of his head, but she understood his expression nonetheless. "You spoke to him?" His tone was suspicious.

"He is your friend, Percy. Should I not speak with him?" Well. Now she knew for certain what he'd say about all those other things she and Mr. Sharpe had spoken about last night.

Percy's expression was reproving. "It is fine if you speak with him, just don't—"

"Don't what?"

He shook his head, making him wince again.

"You might want to stop that, given how much pain you're in. Really, I'm impressed those economics types could bring you to such a state."

"We were calculating the precise volume of liquor one could drink and still walk a straight line. We might have overdone it a bit."

"How much did it end up being?"

He opened his mouth, then sat straight up in his chair, finally achieving that impressive glare. "Don't change the subject!"

"Me?" She gave him an innocent gaze. "I am merely curious about your calculations."

"What did you and Thomas speak about? Where did you see him, anyway?" He hesitated, then spoke again. "I know he is charming and all that, but he is not anyone for you to know. I mean," he continued, as her eyes narrowed, "he is so charming that ladies can't help but fall in love with him. And I know you are still bruised from Mr. McTavish—"

"Mr. RatTavish," she corrected. "And it was two years ago." Yes, it still hurt. No, she wasn't going to admit that to Percy.

Percy waved her off dismissively. "And I don't want you to read into anything he might say. You're—and I mean this in the best possible way—you're sweet and inexperienced, and you might get hurt."

"You think that if I do something as simple as speak to your friend—your best friend, mind you—that I will fall horribly in love with him and have my heart broken?"

Percy considered it, twisting his mouth in thought. "That's about right."

"Oh you!" she exclaimed, flinging her hands up in the air. "We were at Miss Ivy's. I went for their masked evening since Lavinia said it was so much fun." She put her hands on her hips. "Do you seriously believe that I am so innocent that I will mistake a gentleman's conversing with me for something more serious?"

His silence spoke volumes. And was also why she was even more determined to continue her mission. She no longer wished to be Lady Jane Capel, Naive and Gentle Flower. She wanted to be Lady Jane, Fearsome and Adventurous Miscreant.

And Mr. Sharpe would be the one to help her. She'd prove Percy wrong—and keep her heart protected—by treating Mr. Sharpe as though he was providing a service. Nothing more.

"So I have bad news for you, then," she said. She kept her tone firm without sounding defiant. "Mr. Sharpe has agreed to escort me to some of those places you and he go together."

"He will not!" Percy leaped to his feet.

"Stop," she said, holding her hand up. He snapped his mouth shut. "And sit," she commanded, which he did.

"I told him if he would do this for me that I would ensure he gets married to a very wealthy woman."

"How are you going to manage that?" Percy sounded entirely skeptical. And she couldn't blame him—Mr. Sharpe and his vast expanse of good looks hadn't been able to manage it. How could she?

"I have a plan," she said, waving her hand in dismissal. "But the point is, he and I will be spending time together, and you are going to have to be all right with that."

"But you're my sister!"

"And he's your best friend!"

He scowled. "Fine. Just don't—" And he flung his hand up in a vague gesture.

"Fall in love with him? The gentleman whose only choice of future survival is to marry money, and I happen to have none?" She rolled her eyes. "No, Percy, don't be concerned about it. I will not." She had made that mistake before with Mr. RatTavish. She would have fun, she would flirt, she would do everything she wished to.

But she would not fall in love. Perhaps not ever again, but definitely not with Mr. Sharpe.

THOMAS HESITATED BEFORE knocking on the door to Percy and Lady Jane's house.

They lived in a respectable, if not entirely fashionable, neighborhood. Suitable, he supposed, for an earl's bastard son and his not-so-obedient half sister.

The door opened, and Thomas was greeted by one of the house's few servants, their housekeeper. She appeared to be in her midthirties, and her demeanor and accent indicated she'd been born a lady. It seemed the entire household was made up of people just outside of proper Society—a bastard son, a defiant daughter, and a former lady.

"Good morning, Mr. Sharpe," she said, holding the door wider. He stepped inside, waiting in the small foyer as she turned toward the dining room. "I'll let Mr. Waters know you are here."

"I'll tell him, Mrs. Charing," Lady Jane said, emerging from the room across the hall.

"Excellent, my lady," the housekeeper replied, reversing her steps to walk down to the kitchen.

The foyer wasn't the splendid entrance of other, grander homes, but it was exceedingly well-kept, with a few jaunty vases of flowers placed on two of the low tables set against the wall. The floor gleamed as though it had been recently polished, and there were paintings on the walls clearly chosen for the joy they'd bring to the viewer rather than presenting a gallery of forebears.

"Good morning, Mr. Sharpe."

Thomas bowed, his gaze traveling over her. She wore a simple gown printed with tiny flowers, her hair pinned up in a low bun at the back of her neck. The gown, like the previous evening's gown, was a few years out-of-date, and showed signs of wear. A reminder that while she wasn't in Thomas's desperate straits, she wasn't the solution he required.

He needed to keep that reminder firmly in his mind. He also needed her help, so he'd have to ensure she was pleased with their agreement, or it would be another year of failure.

And his family couldn't afford for him to fail.

"I told Percy you would be taking me around town." Her cheeks flushed. "I did not give him any of the specifics." She raised her chin. "He warned me not to fall in love with you. Apparently he believes you are so charming that any lady could not help herself." She arched a brow as she spoke in the driest tone possible. "I will take it as a personal challenge not to fall in love with you."

Thomas couldn't help but feel her words were a taunt. A dare to prove his irresistibility.

But he couldn't allow her to bait him. Not when he needed her help so desperately.

He took a deep breath, wishing she wasn't quite so tempting. That he wasn't so tempted by her.

"Excellent," he replied in what he hoped was a relieved tone. "I have faith in you, my lady."

She narrowed her gaze. "You sound as though you doubt me. Are you that irresistible, Mr. Sharpe?"

Now she was definitely challenging him. The urge crossed his mind to stalk over to her and give her a challenge-accepting kiss, one that would establish that he was most definitely in charge and knew precisely what he was doing. And did it well.

But he could not.

"I will leave the answer to that question to you, my lady," he said instead, sweeping into a bow.

She rolled her eyes. "You're ridiculous."

"Ah, but I am leaving the decision up to you. That is what you want, is it not? Not to allow anyone else to decide who you are and what you will do?" He bowed again. "I am at your service."

Her expression shifted as she processed his words. And then his chest tightened—and other things reacted as well—as her lush mouth curled into a sly, knowing smile. As though owning what he was saying and planning to take him up on his promise.

Dear lord, she was going to tempt him to the brink, wasn't she. And he was going to have to allow her, since if he didn't, she might not help him as she'd promised.

"And since you are at my service," she replied, "I wanted to catch you this morning because I believe you and I are both invited to the Lindens' party tonight. I thought perhaps we could attend that, and I would begin to honor my part of our agreement. I'll need to do it subtly, of course. And you can let me know which young ladies you are most interested in pursuing."

The ones with the most money. It was brutal, but it

was the truth—he couldn't afford to choose a wife based on anything but her finances. Just as in exchange his as-yet-unknown wife would be choosing him based primarily on his appearance.

But he wouldn't speak of all that with Lady Jane—she knew it already, and why admit something that made him feel so dishonorable?

Even though he would make it a point to reveal everything about his situation to whichever woman accepted his proposal. It was the least he could do, given how mercenary his decision would be. And, if he were being even more brutally honest, to ensure he would have access to her money after they wed—he wouldn't blame a protective family member for tying up a young lady's fortune if there was any suspicion that her betrothed was infatuated with her funds, not her delightful self.

He might be able to retain some modicum of respect for himself if he were honest. Just as it was crucial he not abuse his best friend's trust, or rob a woman of her innocence, even if she wished to be robbed.

"I will see you at the Lindens' then," he said as he bowed.

"Oh good." She practically glowed with excitement. "I'll go fetch Percy."

She walked toward the dining room, turning her head to give him another sly smile. As though she was very much looking forward to whatever they were going to do that evening, God help him.

He'd have to tread very carefully. He couldn't, he *wouldn't*, abuse her or Percy's trust. But he also wouldn't deny her some of what she sought—within reason.

It was difficult, he mused wryly, to be entirely pragmatic and ruthless about one's own future while still respecting everyone else's.

But at least if this endeavor was successful, his parents and his sister would have a future. If he failed?

They would have nothing. So it was crucial that he keep that in mind as he navigated these perilous waters, perilous waters meaning, in this case, a curious, ravishing woman. Who wanted to explore her sexuality with him.

Life was so much easier when he was just a rakish gentleman pursuing his passions.

THE LINDENS' HOUSE was filled with people, but the rooms were so spacious and the decorations so well planned that it didn't feel like it was crowded.

A phalanx of footmen circled discreetly, offering a wide variety of beverages. Another phalanx filled and refilled the scattering of tables holding the food, ranging from the most delicately morseled pastry to the thinnest slices of ham.

The room Jane was standing in had enormously vaulted ceilings, which were decorated with a whimsical assortment of clouds and cherubs. Chandeliers hung down just over the tallest gentlemen's heads, the candlelight casting a warm yellow glow. The long, narrow windows were flung open to allow for air circulation, while the musicians played on a small stage at one corner of the room.

It was glorious, all of it, but nothing could surpass Mr. Sharpe in presence and appearance.

"Good evening, Mr. Sharpe," she said, when she was able to breathe again.

Tonight, for the first time, Jane hadn't braced herself before seeing him. Because last night he had agreed to show her things—show her so many things—and so she could appreciate his looks with that knowledge in mind. He was going to be available to her, albeit for a limited time, and she would revel in his splendor.

So it was an epiphany of desire to see him dressed for the evening. Like every other gentleman at the party, he wore a black coat with a white shirt. Like every other gentleman at the party, he was elegantly and simply attired.

But unlike every other gentleman at the party, he held himself with a careless grace that spoke of his own confidence, of his keen awareness of how mere mortals paled before his godliness.

Not that he was falsely conceited, even though he was clearly arrogant and confident; a conceited person had little to base their own conceit on. He, like her, was better looking than anyone else. It was a relief, she had to admit, to acknowledge that fact about both of them, as he had pointed out last night. Did that make her conceited?

Possibly. But it was a flaw, and she'd been told often enough by many people that she was perfect, so she would welcome any flaws she could claim.

Perhaps she should begin to interrupt people when they were speaking, or forget to use her handkerchief when she sneezed.

Though those things were merely bad manners, not character flaws.

She'd need to work on cultivating some sort of flaw. Thoughtlessness, perhaps? But she couldn't bear to see people suffer. So that wouldn't work. Pride? But then she would seem to be proud of her appearance. Which would negate the purpose of the flaw in the first place. Jealousy? No, she had nothing to be jealous about. She was not going to care for Mr. Sharpe—she'd promised Percy and herself, so not that.

If being indecisive was a character flaw, then she could proudly claim that.

"Good evening, my lady," Mr. Sharpe said, bowing over her hand, that treacherous lock of hair spilling over his forehead. He rose, sweeping it back into place with one gloved hand.

Whichever woman he could persuade to marry him was going to have a lovely thing to look at each morning. Would that be worth a fortune?

Looking at him now, she rather thought it might.

But only if they said yes. Which meant she'd have to get her plan in motion.

"I think you should ask me to dance," she said in a low tone, one only he could hear. "But not the supper dance. That one you should save for one of your prospects." She pursed her lips in thought. "Maybe it should be soon, so I can then start talking about you, about how much I admire you, but that you were distant, as though you were thinking of another."

He nodded, an amused look on his face. "Anything else? Are there any particular points of conversation you wish me to make? Since you are directing this entire facade."

She huffed out an annoyed breath. He was remarkably good-looking, but also incredibly irritating. "Don't be absurd. We are doing this together—it is just that this part is *my* plan, so I should have the management of it."

"Of course, my lady," he replied in an ironic tone of voice, bowing slightly. He placed his fingers on her wrist—the other wrist than the one he'd held the night before—and spoke so that the people around them could hear.

"Might I beg you for the favor of a dance, my lady?" He had a mischievous twinkle in his eyes, and she felt her glower shift into a slight smile. He was charming, she had to admit, despite also being able to get under her skin. Perhaps it was the feeling of camaraderie they shared, the knowledge that they were embarking on an adventure that was altogether not suitable for a young lady.

Had she ever made dangerous plans with someone before? Plans that would ruin her irrevocably if they were discovered?

Of course not, she could answer firmly. Because if she had, she wouldn't be in need of his instruction. She'd already have the knowledge he was going to give her, and likely she wouldn't have to wonder what he and her brother did in the evenings—she would know because she was going there, too.

If she weren't so sheltered, if she weren't so protected, if she weren't so naive.

If she hadn't thought she had fallen in love with Mr. McTavish, who had done her the good fortune of breaking her heart. She wasn't certain she had a heart now, to be honest. And if she did, she was going to protect it at all costs.

That was the point of all of it. To know things. To experience things, not just watch from the side-lines as things happened. Not just have things happen to her, but be the cause of the happening.

It was damned dull to be the observer. She wanted to be the participant. And she wanted to participate with him. Because he was safe; she would not allow herself to come close to falling in love with him, nor he with her. Neither one of them wanted that, but both had goals that could be better accomplished with the other's assistance.

"Two dances from now would be quite agreeable, Mr. Sharpe," she replied, bowing her head slightly. Long enough from now to make everyone watch who else he might ask, and yet not so long that they would forget.

It was a tricky thing, navigating people's need for gossip with their short attention spans.

"Excellent," he replied. He still had hold of her wrist, and he squeezed it slightly, looking deep into her eyes as he did so. As though promising some-thing that she couldn't even possibly imagine.

Though hopefully after a few . . . *interludes* with him she would be able to imagine it.

Something in her expression must have changed, because his gaze grew even more intense, and then he emitted some sort of growl, a feral noise that made her whole body shiver in reaction. But not as if she was cold; no, it was the opposite—she was on fire, her whole body suddenly sensitive, as though feathers were lightly caressing her skin. Or fingers, the callused tips of his fingers sliding over her body. Going everywhere they wanted to.

Where he wanted them to, which would mean she would want them there, too.

"Stop looking at me like that," he murmured, his hand sliding up to grip her elbow.

"Like what?" she replied, tilting her face up to his. As though—

"As though you're waiting for me to kiss you. As though you're dying for me to kiss you," he said in a low, rough tone. "Anticipating it." Much different from his usual suave way of speaking.

She bit back a smile at the feeling of triumph that swept over her. She, Lady Jane of the Naive Flowers or whatever it was she was, had made Mr. Thomas Sharpe speak in a ragged, wanting voice to her.

No wonder these activities were so appealing. To be able to cause such a reaction with only a look was intoxicating stuff, nearly as much as the whisky she'd had the night before. Warming her through, like the whisky, burning a trail through her body to fire her up everywhere.

"Your lessons are already working," she said in a low tone. "Anticipation, remember? I will see you for our dance," she replied more loudly, shooting him a glance from under her lashes. She saw his jaw tighten, but he removed his hand from her arm, stepping back to allow her to leave.

Keenly aware that he was watching her walk away, keenly aware that she had given him permission to touch her, and that even now he might be anticipating it as much as she was. Power. It felt like power, and she never wanted to stop tasting it.

Chapter Four

$\mathcal{T}$homas had always prided himself on being able to accommodate any situation. But he had no idea how he was going to work any of this, especially if she continued to regard him with that mix of innocence and desire, a look that said, "I don't know what it is I want, but I do know I want it."

He wanted it, too.

But he couldn't allow it, no matter how tempting she was. No matter how much he wished to discover what would make her sigh in pleasure. What would make her cry out in ecstasy.

What would take her to the heights of passion.

Like the night before, she wore a simple, elegant gown she must have purchased—or had purchased for her—when she was dowried and looking for a husband.

It was several layers of sheer fabric, shot through with silver thread that highlighted the silver of her hair. A light pink ribbon wrapped around her, right under her bosom, with the ends of the ribbon trailing down her back. Her gloves were pink as well, and she wore what Thomas presumed were diamonds in her ears and around her neck.

She looked like what she was, what she no longer wanted to be: a lovely unmarried lady whose most obvious accomplishment was being beautiful.

"Thomas!"

He jumped at the voice shouting in his ear.

"Percy!" he exclaimed, clapping one hand on his friend's shoulder and reaching out to clasp his friend's hand with the other. Hoping Percy would be reasonable, even though he strongly suspected he would not.

Instead of attending the Free Exhibition, as they'd planned, Percy had made an excuse while holding his head and scowling. Thomas presumed the head holding was because of drinking the previous evening, while the scowling might have been because of what Percy's sister and Thomas had planned. Before Thomas could ask for details, however, Percy retreated back to the dining room.

Percy glared at Thomas's outstretched hand, then looked up at Thomas with a suspicious gaze. Thomas didn't blame him; Lady Jane had confirmed that she had informed her brother of her wish for shenanigans. And even though Percy had no idea the extent of the shenanigans she wished for, Thomas knew that Percy was naturally concerned about his sister.

So not only would he have to walk the narrow tightrope of assisting her without compromising her, he would have to walk an even narrower tightrope of making certain his best friend believed his sister was in good care.

Perhaps if he wasn't able to find a wealthy woman to marry he could consider a career as a diplomat.

Though a diplomat's salary wouldn't give him enough money for his family.

"She told me you're going to take her places," Percy said, still glaring. "Show her things."

Thomas hated to lie to his friend. But he couldn't tell him the truth either.

"Yes, she asked me to escort her to places such as Miss Ivy's. And in exchange, she has said she will help me in finding a wife. You know how badly I need that, Percy."

It felt even worse to remind his friend just how desperate his straits were as an excuse for engaging in the behavior she was asking for.

"I do." Percy folded his arms over his chest. "And I'll tell you what I told her, which is that neither of you is allowed to fall in love with the other."

Well. That was certainly blunt speaking. He admired Percy for that.

"I assure you, Lady Jane has no intention of that. She said as much," he replied, his lips curling up at the memory of her saying it. *I will take it as a personal challenge not to fall in love with you.*

"Jane is too innocent for all of this," Percy said, holding his hands out to indicate—the world? This party? Their society?

Likely all of it.

"And doesn't that mean she should learn more before she makes her mind up about what she wants to do?"

Odd that Thomas now found himself in the position of defending her. But it wasn't fair that she should remain so sheltered, not if she wished to be educated.

"She's just barely learning who she is, much less what the world is like." Percy shook his head. "Jane had her heart broken only a few years ago, and I was proud of her for refusing to go along with her mother's plans."

"Which were?"

"To drag her right back on the marriage market." Percy spoke in a bitter tone. "To parade her in front of all the eligible bachelors in hopes that one of them would take her."

Thomas felt a keen anger at the image—that she would have so little say in her own life that her mother would just roll past a broken engagement and try to settle her as soon as possible.

Though that was what he was trying to do for himself, wasn't it? Get married as soon as possible to the first wealthy woman who would have him?

But at least he was *choosing* to do that. Even though the choice had been forced on him by his father's feckless investments.

"It's no wonder she wants to know something else of the world, then, if that is all she thinks is out there for her."

"That's the thing, though," Percy replied earnestly. "I'm concerned she won't like what she learns. Jane isn't like us, cynical about the world and our place in it. She was badly hurt once, but that doesn't mean she won't find happiness again. I want to be certain she'll stay herself."

Who do you want to be then?

Anyone but me.

Percy had no idea who his sister was.

And neither did his sister.

"I promise I will do nothing to change who she is, who she is at her heart." Thomas spoke fervently, hoping his friend would hear the truth in these words, even though his other words had been deliberately vague. He could make the same promise to Percy, who hadn't said it in so many words, but whose romantic choices were not the usual. His friend didn't need his protection—Percy had his father and the queen at his back, after all—but he would fight anyone who tried to make Percy change.

"Thank you," Percy said at last.

Thomas exhaled in relief. At least he wouldn't have to get into a fight with his best friend this particular evening.

Perhaps later, if Percy ever learned just what Lady Jane wanted from Thomas.

But for now, he could breathe.

"IT IS TIME for our dance, Lady Jane."

Jane turned casually, as though she hadn't been aware of the precise moment when it would be time for them to dance.

"Oh of course, Mr. Sharpe. Might I introduce you to my acquaintances? This is Miss Grosvenor from Sussex. This is her first Society party." Miss Grosvenor was a fresh-faced girl with bright red cheeks and a delighted gleam in her dark brown eyes. Thomas bowed, noticing the excellent cut of her gown and the perfect strand of pearls wrapped around her neck. "And I believe you already know Lady Elizabeth?"

Lady Elizabeth offered him a wan smile as he bowed in her direction. She was one of the wealthiest unmarried ladies who was in London this Season, but she was also one of the snobbiest women he had ever met—he knew she would never deign to marry a mere mister. She was on the hunt for a titled gentleman, even if he had nothing else to recommend him.

And as if on cue, Lord Joseph arrived to join their group.

"My lady, my lady," he said, nodding to Jane and Lady Elizabeth in turn. "And I do not know your lovely friend. I am Lord Joseph Callender, a friend to these two. Oh, hello, Sharpe," he added, sounding as dismissive as he could without actually causing a scene.

Thomas opened his mouth to say something in response, but he caught Jane's eye, and she was shaking her head no as though to warn him to stay quiet.

Fine. He'd stay quiet.

"This is Miss Grosvenor, my lord," Jane said. "She has just come to town."

"And I have just arrived here! Miss Grosvenor, might I beg you for a dance?"

Lady Elizabeth's face tightened, and Thomas resisted showing his delight at the obvious annoyance on her face.

"And that reminds me, my lady, the dance is already halfway done." Thomas gestured toward the dance floor. "I don't want to miss a moment more."

"Yes, I've been anticipating it all evening," Jane replied in an artless manner. As though she didn't know entirely what she was saying.

Thomas froze for a moment as she placed her hand in his. She had actually unsettled him. Yesterday she had left him with nothing to say and today she was upending his unflappably calm mien.

Had he thought he was in trouble before?

He was in so much trouble. More than he possibly knew.

He followed her onto the dance floor, then she turned to place her hand on his shoulder as he put his at her waist. They began to dance, and within seconds, Thomas had forgotten everything he'd been thinking of.

She was a beautiful dancer, light and elegant, a slight smile on her face as her eyes met his. Of course she was good at dancing; ladies in her situation were drilled on how best to become a welcome accessory at a party. To engage in light, meaningless conversation; to be perfectly attired for any occasion; to wear a benign smile on their faces even if they were experiencing discomfort.

"Miss Grosvenor has oodles of money," she said after a moment. "And she is new here—she wouldn't have seen you make your way through all the debutantes like others have."

Put that way, it sounded vulgar. Rapacious.

Which, honestly, it was.

It was also necessary if he was going to help his family.

But for the first time, it made him feel uncomfortable inside. He didn't want to be seen, at least not by Lady Jane, as someone whose only thought for the future was finding a wealthy woman to marry.

Even though that was his only thought.

Goddamn it. He couldn't be honorable and save his family. He'd long ago reconciled himself to the latter, leveraging his appearance and manners to obtain his goal. But the longer it took to obtain that goal, the more obvious and calculated it seemed.

"She might be a bit silly," Jane continued, unaware he was currently suffering a moral crisis, "but she seems good-hearted." Her gaze went over his shoulder, and her eyes narrowed. "And I would not want to see Lord Joseph get his hands on her."

"How am I any better?"

He hadn't wanted to say that, hadn't even realized he'd been thinking it, until it burst from his mouth.

Her gaze snapped back to him, her eyes wide. "Of course you're better than he is. You're far more handsome, of course," she said.

"Of course," he echoed.

"And you are more charming, and I get the feeling you will be a decently kind husband to whomever you marry."

He snorted. "Decently kind?"

Was that all she could say about him? That he probably wouldn't treat his wife poorly? That he was handsome and able to parlay his looks into a charming facade?

Probably. Because that was all he'd ever shown the world. Was that all he believed himself to be?

"Can we—?" he said, not finishing his sentence, but guiding her toward the doors that led out onto the terrace.

"Oh!" she said in what he presumed was her delighted debutante voice—pleased, enthusiastic, and innocent. "Yes, that would be lovely."

JANE HAD BEEN led onto terraces by gentlemen before, of course. Under the guise of showing her the night sky, or a particularly intriguing bit of shrubbery, or because the gentleman was concerned she was getting too warm.

All ruses, of course. All suggested in the hope of getting her alone so they could tell her how beautiful she was or, in the case of some of the bolder gentlemen, to try to steal a kiss.

Thankfully, she'd always had her sister, Lavinia, nearby to come to her rescue. But Lavinia had been married to her duke for two years now, and Jane had had to develop her own terrace-avoiding strategies.

But for the first time, she actually *wanted* to go onto the terrace.

Her ex-fiancé, Mr. McTavish, had been far too proper to even suggest anything remotely terrace related.

Perhaps if he had, she would have realized long before she did what a wretched person he was. Or would she? She wasn't certain, not at all, that she was any kind of judge of good character. After all, she had fallen in love with Mr. McTavish, rat though he was.

"How does one know if someone else is a good person?" she blurted as they stepped out into the cool night air. Not quite the conversational lure she knew was proper, but everything about their situation was improper—except for how it appeared to everyone but them.

"Pardon?" Mr. Sharpe said, sounding startled. Of course, she'd just posed some sort of philosophical question to him, and likely she was supposed to say something about the darkness of the night, as if the daily disappearance of the sun was something to remark on. It was astonishing just how banal an unmarried lady's conversation was supposed to be.

"I was just thinking," she said, reaching the edge of the terrace and leaning over the stone wall to look at the gardens, "that we all assume someone is of good character until they do something that indicates they are not."

"Not all of us assume that," he said dryly. His back was to the wall, and he leaned against it, regarding her with an amused expression. One that also added in a touch of his usual condescension. As though her statement was naive.

"I tend to think the worst of people, at least until they do something that indicates they are not the worst." His lip curled. "Sometimes they are merely not good. A few, a precious few, are good." He nodded toward her. "I believe you are of good character, for example. As is your brother."

Her cheeks heated. "Even though I am asking for things no proper lady should?" She huffed out a breath. "And I do not mean the most scandalous things. I mean no proper young lady should want to be taken to some sort of evil den."

"An evil den?" he said, his eyebrows raised, laughter in his voice.

"Or wherever you'll take me," she replied, waving her hand.

"I think proper young ladies want to be taken to evil dens," he said matter-of-factly. "It is just that our world has said they should not. It does not mean they do not want to."

"But shouldn't young ladies know their world? All of it?" She shook her head in frustration. "Now that I think about it, truly think about it, I wonder just what our world is trying to keep from us. Are they worried that we'll refuse to follow the course we're supposed to?" She felt herself grow more irate by the second.

And it felt marvelous. Feeling angry about what she was supposed to do, and who she was supposed to be, was why she was here on this terrace in the first place.

If she had done what she was supposed to, she would have married anyone who'd asked after Mr. McTavish jilted her. If she had done what she was supposed to even before that, she'd have married the duke, when it was now so clear that he and Lavinia were the perfect match.

Thank God she hadn't done what she was supposed to. And now she was going to do even more of what she wasn't supposed to—taking control of her own life, her own destiny.

It was far beyond just going places a young lady

would not normally go. It felt as though she was fomenting a revolution, albeit a revolution of one.

He hadn't answered her question yet. Instead, he was regarding her with what appeared to be surprise—appeared to be, since she'd seen that expression on his face only a few times, all of them within the past two days.

"You should see things. You will see things." He spoke in a determined tone. "I hope you find what it is you're looking for, my lady. And that you are able to choose what you want rather than have it chosen for you."

"Unlike you?" She regretted the words as soon as she spoke. Not because it wasn't true, but because it felt unkind. As though reminding him that he had no choice in his own future, in contrast to her, was a slap in the face.

"I'm sorry, I shouldn't have said that." She took a deep breath. "I know you don't have a choice."

"Oh, but I do," he replied, his expression hardening. "I could take myself back to my family and tell them I cannot marry someone I don't love just to keep them in food and clothing." She winced at the sharp tone in his voice. "Though that is what women have done for eternity, haven't they?"

His words were softer now, as though he was being thoughtful about what he was saying. "You are fortunate enough not to have to make that choice, Lady Jane." He shrugged. "I am fortunate enough that I can choose who I will marry, although my choice is limited to women with money." He smiled as he spoke, but it was a smile without humor. She felt her chest constrict at the clear ache in his expression. "I would never want anyone to have their choice forced on them. It's not a choice at all, is it?"

From his tone, she suspected he was speaking not only about her, but about Percy. Something that made her warm toward him even more.

"But in the meantime, you and I will have a last hurrah. Before I finally persuade a lady to marry me for my pretty face."

She couldn't help but reach out to touch him. Putting her hand on his arm and giving a gentle squeeze. "You know what you're doing is noble, in a way."

"In a way," he snorted, moving away from her touch.

"Because you're not doing it for yourself," she retorted. "You're doing it for your family." She met his gaze. "Tell me about them."

HAD ANYONE BESIDES Percy ever asked him anything about himself?

He could answer that definitively. No.

People asked him if he would like to attend their gathering. If he would like this beverage or that one. If he would dance with that young lady in the corner.

But never anything about *him*.

"They—" he began, but stopped as Lord Joseph stepped out from the ballroom, accompanied by Miss Grosvenor. She held on to his arm, gazing at him with those same bright, wide eyes she'd had before. Thomas wished he could warn her against him, but what would he say? *Don't fool yourself, Lord Joseph is only interested in your money?*

It would be hypocritical to say anything of the sort, given that he was only interested in her—and every other unmarried lady's—money.

"Hello, my lady," Miss Grosvenor said in a cheery voice. "And Mr. Sharpe." Her eyes widened even more as she looked at him, and he felt the familiar spark of potential flare within him, scenting a possible target.

He'd need to find out precisely how much she was worth.

"Miss Grosvenor wanted to see the gardens," Lord Joseph said, sounding defensive. As though he had heard Thomas issuing a warning to her. "I have been to the Lindens' house a few times—they are quite splendid."

"Are they?" Lady Jane asked, stepping forward. She glanced back at Thomas. "Could we accompany them? I wish to see the gardens also."

"I don't think—" Lord Joseph began.

"Of course. An excellent idea." Thomas extended his hand toward the gardens. Which were, he wanted to point out, in the dark, so there would be nothing to see.

But that was the point, wasn't it?

Which was likely why Lady Jane leaped to Miss Grosvenor's defense. Not that Miss Grosvenor likely understood she was under assault from a desperate fortune hunter, but Lady Jane certainly did.

Miss Grosvenor glanced at Lord Joseph, whose expression had tightened. She looked as though she was considering what he might be feeling.

Don't do it, Thomas wanted to say. *Because he'll never do the same for you.*

"Mr. Sharpe," Miss Grosvenor said, returning her gaze to Thomas, "please show the way to these estimable gardens." She spoke in a dry tone, and Lord Joseph's face began to turn red.

He heard Lady Jane smother a snort of laughter, and he felt his lips twitch. "Of course," he said, taking Jane's arm and nodding toward the other couple.

The four made their way to the stairs and descended, Jane tightening her hold on him when her dress caught under her slipper.

"Thank you for following along," she said in a whisper. He could hear Lord Joseph and Miss Grosvenor conversing behind them.

"Certainly. I know what it sounds like when a lady wishes me to do something without saying it aloud."

He bit back a curse as he realized that what he'd just said could be misinterpreted, particularly in this context. And her sharp inhale told him she had misinterpreted.

"Do ladies wish you to . . . do things often?" Now she was speaking in code.

"Uh—"

"Perhaps you could earn money for your family by opening up a school of sorts. For one-on-one instruction." She spoke in a wry tone, and his tension eased.

Because while he'd have to answer yes to her question, he didn't want her to think she was just another one in a long line of ladies wishing to do things with him, even though she was precisely that. But she was also his friend's sister, and a kind, generous woman who merely wished to know more. And had chosen him as her teacher.

"Isn't that what I am attempting to do already?" he asked in a dry tone.

"Oh!" she exclaimed as they walked onto the grass. "I suppose it is. I hadn't thought of it in that way before, but that is precisely it."

"What part of the garden do you recommend, Mr. Sharpe?" Miss Grosvenor's voice called from behind them. He and Jane turned to face the other two, Lord Joseph's expression still set and sullen.

If Thomas had a school for fortune hunters, he'd instruct his pupils never to allow their pique to show on their faces. They were not allowed to be displeased with the object of their hunt, at least not until after marriage.

But he didn't, so Lord Joseph would remain unenlightened.

"I'd say the fountain," Thomas replied, turning back to indicate the fountain that lay directly ahead of them.

Thank God.

He'd had no idea what the gardens held when Jane had suggested viewing them. Perhaps they were the kitchen gardens, with a few rows of bedraggled lettuces fighting for dirt alongside various squashes.

Or maybe it was an actual flower garden, but all the flowers there were closed up for the evening, in which case they'd be looking at a whole bunch of tall plants with closed buds.

Well, he could cross becoming a gardener off his list of potential future occupations.

"Thank goodness there is a fountain," Jane murmured, and he had to force himself not to exclaim how similarly their thoughts had run.

"The fountain, then," Miss Grosvenor said, a bright smile on her face.

The four made their way forward, moving past various trimmed bushes and trees, benches at regular intervals indicating this was a place to rest, and converse, and observe.

Although usually, Thomas had to admit, during the day.

The moon hid behind some clouds, casting a faint silver glow to light their way. They could hear the fountain's gurgling now, and Thomas's sharp eyesight could see the details more clearly, a stone boy perched on top of a complicated set of shapes pouring water out of his pitcher.

The boy appeared to be a Cupid sort, a chubby angel with a riot of curls around his head, his feet lifted as though he were in motion.

"There it is," Thomas proclaimed, feeling like an idiot. "The fountain."

"Indeed. The fountain," Lord Joseph echoed, sounding as though he was blaming Thomas for the fountain's less than impressive appearance. What with being in the dark and all.

"I wonder if any fish live here," Miss Grosvenor said, darting forward. Jane released Thomas's arm and joined the lady, both of them peering into the wide moat that encircled the boy and his pitcher.

"She doesn't have anything, you know," Lord Joseph said in a low voice as he stepped to Thomas's side. "Her family disowned her when her fiancé jilted her."

That wasn't what happened, Thomas wanted to say, but it wasn't any of Lord Joseph's business, and that wasn't the point, anyway. Percy had confided what had really happened, and it would break that confidence to share anything with Lord Joseph, who definitely did not deserve the information.

"I just thought you should know since you and I are in the same game."

Thomas felt himself recoil at the words. And the truth.

"Thank you, my lord," he replied, speaking through a clenched jaw. "I appreciate your looking out for my interests."

"Not that she's not a welcome companion," Lord Joseph continued. "If only she had even some of that dowry left, I'd take her." He spoke as though there would be no hesitation on her part to take him.

"Well, then, it's good she does not have even some of that dowry left," Thomas replied in his smoothest tone of voice, "because I'd hate to see her married to an oafish dunderhead like you."

He didn't wait for the lord's reply, but walked to join Lady Jane and Miss Grosvenor. "And are there piscine creatures lurking below?" He dug in his waistcoat for a coin, holding it between the two ladies. "If either of you would like to make a wish . . . ?" he said.

Lady Jane and Miss Grosvenor glanced at one another, then Lady Jane snatched it from his hand, a look of delight on her face.

And when she smiled—it felt as though it was

midday and the sun was shining, even though of course it was nearing midnight and the moon was still behind the clouds.

Thomas felt his lips tug upward at her expression. "And what will you wish for, my lady?"

She shook her head in mock disapproval. "You know that if I tell that means the wish will not come true. And I very much wish for this wish to come true," she added, one eyebrow rising in challenge.

Thomas froze at her words, his gaze darting between her and Miss Grosvenor. The latter's expression did not change, so likely Thomas was the only person who had understood her coded language.

It was a dangerous game she was playing. And, he realized, he had started it.

Chapter Five

Jane was exhilarated. By a stroll in a garden.
That should remind her just why she was so determined to educate herself on all sorts of things.

But it felt dangerously, wonderfully delicious to converse with him when it would be clear no one else knew what they were talking about.

It was a perfectly innocuous exchange, if you didn't know the deeper meaning.

But she did. As did he.

And now her whole body felt alive, and she wanted to yank her slippers off and run on the grass in her bare feet yelling her joy.

Of course she could not do that. For one thing, the grass was slightly damp, so she'd likely slip and upend herself. An injury was not joyful.

For another, she wasn't quite so free-spirited to actually follow through on her desires.

Perhaps, after a few weeks of lessons with him, she would be.

She giggled at the thought of what her Thomas Sharpe Graduation Ceremony might look like—

her, barefoot and shrieking, romping in some aristocrat's garden heedless of what anyone might say about her. Perhaps wearing a placard proclaiming her newly learned skills: knows what happens between a gentleman and a lady when there are no chaperones about; has gained entrance to the more scandalous clubs and evil dens of London; drinks whisky without sputtering.

Skills no young lady would ever admit to having.

Unless they wished to be known for those skills.

Which would mean the lady in question was utterly and totally ruined. Yet a gentleman such as Mr. Thomas Sharpe was lauded for the very same behavior.

Entirely unfair.

"Lady Jane," Miss Grosvenor said, her dark eyes sparkling with mischief, "I hope you get everything you wish for." And she accompanied her words with a smile that seemed to indicate that she might have some sort of idea just what Jane had wished for.

Perhaps there was more to Miss Grosvenor than met the eye at first glance. Which was true of her and Mr. Sharpe, for that matter.

He was more than a gorgeous face, and she was more than a dutiful, beautiful debutante.

"Lady Jane," Lord Joseph said as he rejoined them at the fountain, "do you have plans to return to Miss Ivy's? There were some games I have not yet shown you. We were interrupted last evening," he continued, shooting a pointed glance toward Mr. Sharpe.

As though he was the person controlling Jane's actions last evening, and not Jane herself.

Hmph.

"I do plan on it," she replied. "I am not certain when that will be." She raised her chin. "And when I do go, I plan on learning my own games."

Mr. Sharpe smothered a noise that sounded suspiciously like a laugh.

"I would like to join you some evening, Lady Jane," Miss Grosvenor said brightly.

"That would be lovely," Jane replied.

"We will make a night of it," Lord Joseph proclaimed in a too-hearty voice.

She did not like Lord Joseph. But that she could admit that to herself—that she did not like someone, even though she was the Most Amiable Jane with the Milksop Opinions—felt monumental.

And she *did* like Mr. Sharpe. Even though he nettled her at any opportunity.

But that kind of sparring riposte made her feel as though he was treating her as his equal, not a lesser type of person because she was female, or innocent, or too pretty to be taken seriously.

He hadn't spoken for some time—he wasn't trying to insert himself into the conversation. Wasn't insisting he be the one to take the ladies to Miss Ivy's. He accorded her the deference she deserved as an adult person in her own right. Not an ornament, or a mirror onto which to project one's own ideas.

It was gratifying. And far too rare—only her siblings treated her like that, and she did not feel the same frisson of delicious danger that he engendered in her.

She wanted to dance with him again. She wanted

to begin her explorations with him. She wanted to—or she could end that thought right there.

She wanted.

And she was going to take what she wanted. Not wait to be given it, like a child with a treat. But take it, like a person whose wishes and desires were valid. Whose inner thoughts and feelings were just as important as what appeared to everyone on the outside.

"Mr. Sharpe," she said, giving him a direct look, "would you care to finish our dance?"

His gaze met hers, and what she saw there made her sharply inhale. A challenge, a look that declared, "I might be instructing you, but we are equals." A look of dark intent that declared he would honor his promise to her.

"I would love to, my lady."

SHE WAS REMARKABLE. He'd already known that, but he'd thought her remarkable for other things: her beauty, her quiet elegance, her loyalty to her brother.

Now he could find her remarkable for her courage and commitment to fighting for herself and for other ladies like her, innocent women who might not know what trouble they were getting themselves into.

He wouldn't teach her every kind of trouble—he couldn't allow himself to do that—but by the end of their time together, she would know more than she did before. Which would mean she could navigate her world, the world she wanted to live in, with greater ease. He owed her that kind of instruction.

And if he got to spend time with a remarkably beautiful woman of both elegance and courage?

So much the better.

Though it would make the inevitability of his marriage that much more difficult. The contrast between spending time with a person because one wanted to, and spending time with a person because one wanted something from them—it was incalculable.

No wonder she was so determined not to have to make that choice. It was just his bad luck that she was going to ensure he would, if she was successful in her campaign to find him a wealthy woman who would take him.

He held his arm out for her, and she took it, giving him a sly look through her lashes. "Oh," she exclaimed, turning back around, "Miss Grosvenor, are you coming in?"

"Yes, my lady," Miss Grosvenor replied eagerly.

Thomas and Lady Jane waited as Miss Grosvenor scurried toward them, Lord Joseph following disgruntledly behind.

"Miss Grosvenor, what sights have you seen so far?" he heard Lady Jane ask.

He smiled to himself at Miss Grosvenor's excited response.

And then they were in the ballroom, dancing again, and it was as though their bodies knew each other well, moving in perfect time to the music.

"I do love dancing," she said, as though admitting a shameful secret.

"It is one of the few pleasures of an event like this," Thomas admitted. He continued at her quizzical expression. "It is the only time when it is acceptable to just be silent and absorb what is happening. You don't have to perform beyond your movements, and if the music is good—as it is tonight—it is exhilarating to go through the steps. I don't have to be witty, or charming, or any of the things people normally expect of me. I just have to . . . dance."

"It is exhausting," she agreed in a thoughtful tone. "Which means we shouldn't speak until the dance is over." As she spoke, she shifted just a fraction so she was closer in his arms. His fingers tightened at her waist, and he heard her sigh in pleasure, which sent a spark of response shooting through his body.

They were just dancing. Merely dancing, and yet it felt as though they were so in tune with one another that it was an intimate moment, as private as if they were in his bed tangled up in his sheets. Her, warm and naked and responsive, him equally naked giving her as much pleasure as she had asked for. And more.

The image of it was so palpable he nearly stumbled, making her widen her eyes and give him a questioning look. He shook his head as though it were nothing.

It wasn't nothing.

It was want, and desire, and a yearning in his soul he hadn't felt since before that moment when his whole world shattered.

He hadn't thought he'd ever have that feeling again, much less at a Society party wearing all of his clothes.

But here he was. Dancing with the most beautiful and most forbidden woman of his acquaintance. Making him keenly aware of how much loyalty he owed to his best friend, and how he dared not jeopardize that as he weighed just how much to show her.

Because he wanted to show her *everything*. All of him, and all of them, and goddamn his future and his future wife and loveless marriage if he could have a few moments like this one.

The music stopped, far too soon, and Thomas felt as though he'd been running for miles, giving chase to something just out of reach.

Her cheeks were flushed from the dancing, a few strands of silver-blond hair had fallen out of her carefully tidy coiffure, making her look more like the naked woman he'd just imagined in his bed.

"Mr. Sharpe?" she asked after a moment of silent staring.

"Yes, my lady," he replied, shaking his head to clear it. "We should be off on the second part of our evening." He gestured toward the door. "Shall we go? I believe an evil den of pleasure awaits."

Her eyes lit up, and her lips curled into the most genuinely happy smile he'd ever seen. "An evil den of pleasure!" she repeated, clapping her hands together. "Oh, I cannot wait!"

Her words were said so excitedly he couldn't help but smile in response. He hoped that no matter what she learned, either in the next few weeks or the rest of her life, that she would never lose her honest glee and clear enthusiasm for whatever might greet her next.

JANE SETTLED INTO the carriage, waiting impatiently as Mr. Sharpe swung himself in beside her.

It was just them. Alone in the dark, the closed carriage creating a kind of cocoon from the outside world, even though they could see the party guests dancing by the windows.

And then the carriage began to move, its gentle rocking motion making her lean into him. She straightened in automatic response, but then realized she need not. Not with him, not now.

In her previous life as the Most Demure and Innocent Debutante in London, she would never have been alone in a carriage with a gentleman, much less have her *shoulders* bump into his *arm*. She giggled at the thought.

"What is on your mind, my lady?" he asked, taking her hand in his. She looked down at their hands, both gloved, his fingers curled around hers.

The holding of hands was even more scandalous than the shoulder/arm bumping combination.

"I was just thinking," she began, still looking down, "how ridiculous it is to be so constrained." She gestured with her free hand. "I mean, here we are. We have done nothing shocking, and yet the very circumstance of us being here alone together instantly means we have done something shocking."

He chuckled in reply, then released her hand suddenly.

"Oh, I didn't mean—" she began, but then he stripped off both of his gloves, and the next thing she knew, his fingers were undoing the buttons of her glove with practiced ease.

And then her glove was removed, and he'd taken her hand again, only now their skin was touching.

His hand was warm, and larger than hers. His grip was firm, but she knew if she wanted to wrest her hand away she could. He wouldn't stop her.

She did not want to.

She wanted to keep holding his hand forever, feel that connection through her whole body. And it was only their hands that were touching; what if—no, not if, but when—other parts of them touched?

Oh. The thought sent skitters of acute awareness over her skin, making her feel as though she was overdressed, too constricted in her evening gown and slippers.

"My lady?" he said in a low, questioning tone.

She didn't respond. Instead, she placed her free hand on his arm, twisting herself in her seat to manage it. Their faces were suddenly close to one another, and she gave a sharp inhale. So close.

"Did you want something?" he said, again in that low tone. A tone that made that awareness increase, if such a thing were possible.

She shook her head, biting her lip. And then she lifted her chin and met his gaze. It was dark in the carriage, but the streetlamps gave enough light that she could make out his features. The light wasn't consistent, however, so there were moments where she could barely see, but she could hear: the horses' harnesses jingling, the wheels clattering over the cobblestone roads.

Her own breath. Her heart, which seemed as though it were beating much faster than before.

An inarticulate noise from him, low and deep in his throat.

Her gaze didn't waver. Even as she let go of his hand to swiftly remove her other glove, casting it God knows where, before putting her hand back in his and returning her other hand to his arm. Now feeling the cloth of his evening jacket as she slid her fingers up to his shoulder. Swallowing hard before moving her hand across to his neck, right where his cravat ended, wrapping her fingers up into his hair, tugging gently on the strands.

"My lady," he said in a strangled tone. He tilted his head back against the carriage cushion and closed his eyes. Her fingers tugged those strands of hair again, and he grunted in response.

Meanwhile, his fingers tightened their grip on hers, and she felt a tiny feeling of triumph course through her.

She was doing this to him. She, Lady Jane the Meek, was making Mr. Thomas Sharpe utter an inarticulate noise as he surrendered to whatever she was doing to him.

She raked her fingernails on his scalp, and he made a pleasurable sound, encouraging her to do it again.

His hair was soft under her fingers, and she held her breath as she finally—finally!—swept that enticing curl up off his forehead.

"I had no idea my head was so sensitive," he murmured, after her fingers had come to rest again at the back of his neck. He sat up straight again, his eyes meeting hers. "Or perhaps it's just you," he continued in that same low, intimate tone. "I like when you touch me."

Her eyes widened. Six words, just six small words, and yet to hear him confess something so personal, something so specific to them in this moment, made her feel as though he'd just told her his darkest secret.

"I don't know yet if I like it when you touch me," she replied. Her voice didn't sound like hers—it was huskier, as though she was having difficulty catching her breath and the words were getting caught in her throat.

Which was true, she realized.

She inhaled deeply as she strengthened her resolve. "I don't know if I like it when you touch me," she repeated, then added, "so you'll have to do it more for me to reach a conclusion."

And then she froze, worried he would think her too forward, too fast, too strong.

"Oh, my lady," he replied in a warm, sensual tone that relieved all her concerns, "I already know I will like that."

He placed his hand at her waist as he spoke, holding her in his firm grasp. Lowering his mouth to hers, the warm firmness of his lips pressed against hers.

She gasped, and he chuckled against her mouth, his fingers tightening at her waist.

He was *kissing* her.

THE LAST THING Thomas wanted was to kiss her now. Though that wasn't true, was it? It was the *only* thing he wanted to do. It was the last thing he *should* be doing, but clearly he was skirting propriety and the bonds of friendship and whatever veneer of politeness he drew over himself in more public situations.

This moment was just for them. For just this moment, he wasn't thinking about what he was going to have to do, or about Percy, or the fact that this woman was deserving of so much more than him.

For just this moment, it was just them.

And he was kissing her, her warm mouth pressed against his. Opening slightly, just enough for him to tease her lips with his tongue, licking her mouth until she allowed him entry.

And then he was exploring with lips and teeth and tongue, his cock hardening in his trousers as she responded to his touch.

Her tongue met his, and she made a surprised noise, nearly making him laugh. But he was too engrossed in what they were doing to stop. He didn't want to stop, not now, not ever.

He wanted to kiss her forever, just relish this moment when it was only them, and he didn't have any responsibilities toward anyone. When they were simply Jane and Thomas. Not a desperate fortune hunter and a curious young lady.

Her fingers were back in his hair, pulling on the strands, and it was as though she was touching him all the way down to his soul, making him want to writhe in torment as she continued her gentle torture.

His hand had begun a slow ascent upward without his realizing it, from her waist to her rib cage to just beside her breast. And then she shifted slightly, moving his fingers closer to her breast, and then she moved again, making what she wanted perfectly clear without having to say a word.

He spread his fingers out over the soft warmth of her and squeezed lightly as she uttered a soft moan deep in her throat. A noise that definitely went straight to his cock, making him picture what else he could do to elicit those intoxicating sounds.

She was actively engaged in the kissing now, her tongue clashing with his as they sucked and licked one another.

Dear God, this was only a kiss. He'd had plenty of kisses before, he wasn't a scandalous rake for nothing, but he had never experienced a kiss so profoundly sensual, so exciting, before.

Only a kiss. Everything contained in a kiss, every fiber of his being focused on this moment, this interlude of delicious pleasure, just them in the dark together, exploring one another.

Her hand had found its way to his waist, and was holding him still, as if restraining him. As though preventing him from leaving.

He didn't want to leave.

He was fully erect now, his cock nearly painful as it throbbed in response to her kisses.

He wished he could take her hand and put it on himself, show her what she had done to him, beg her to touch him, to grip his aching shaft in her hand, tease him with those fingernails up and down until he pleaded for mercy. Which he would not actually want.

No mercy. He wanted her complete and unrelenting, that eager desire to learn coupled with the knowledge that she could reduce him to rubble with just a few strokes of her hand.

Just as his mind was racing with what he could do and how he could accomplish it, the carriage slowed, indicating they had arrived at their destination.

They broke apart, both gasping, their eyes meeting in the dark, his palm still stretched over her breast.

His mouth curled into a smile as he removed his hand, his skin instantly missing the feel of her.

She smiled in response as she slid her fingers out of his hair and away from his waist. She twisted away from him, picking up her discarded gloves and making short work of putting them back on.

He did the same as the carriage door swung open, and he stepped out of the carriage, drawing the tails of his jacket over his erection as he descended.

Thankfully, it was too dark for anyone to see anything.

He held his hand out to her, and she took it, her hold tightening as she stepped down.

They stood in front of where he'd instructed the carriage to take them, a nondescript building just at the edge of where respectable London began to bleed into disreputable London.

He pressed a coin into the coachman's hand, then gestured to the front door, which opened as they watched, warm golden light spilling out onto the steps of the building as two people exited.

Both were finely dressed, both were stumbling slightly, both were laughing joyously as they clutched at one another to find their balance.

She glanced at him, a satisfied expression on her face. "My first evil den!" she exclaimed. "What is this place?"

He took her arm and navigated her around the inebriated couple, walking up the steps to the entrance.

"Good evening, sir," the doorman said. "Mr. Sharpe, is it not?"

"It is," Thomas confirmed.

"Excellent. I will ask Mr. Archer to escort you to your table." The doorman gestured to someone inside, and then Mr. Archer appeared, a dapper Black man wearing an excellently tailored suit with a handkerchief in a bright blue color tucked in his pocket, his cravat made of matching fabric.

"What *is* this place?" she repeated, sounding even more enthusiastic now.

Her exuberance was contagious. He hadn't felt this excited about going anywhere since he'd first come to London on the heiress hunt.

And here he was, two years later, still hunting.

The thought made him deflate.

"What is it?" she asked in a very different tone of voice. As though she had sensed his mood, and was worried about him. He would have to keep that in mind—that she seemed able to intuit his mood. He was accustomed to being able to hide whatever he was thinking and feeling. But with her it was as though he was stripped bare.

Unfortunately for him and his base desires, he was not stripped bare. And worse was that she wasn't either.

Though thank God they weren't. He'd have buried himself inside her soft warmth long before now.

He needed to think about something else. Anything else.

He focused on Mr. Archer, the owner of the hall, who was moving through the tables, leading them to one close enough to the dance floor to make their way there easily, but not so close to the musicians that they couldn't speak.

Thomas helped her into her chair, then sat down beside her, both of them gazing out into the crowd. There were several couples dancing, and it was clear that none of the people belonged to their world. Like going to Miss Ivy's, that fact made Thomas feel more relaxed, since he wouldn't have to perform for anyone. On the contrary, people would be performing for him. And her.

"This is a dance hall?" she asked, raising her voice to be heard over the music.

He shrugged. "Sometimes. It's owned by the gentleman who saw us to our table. At other times it—well, you will see when it happens."

Her eyes widened, and her expression got even more excited, if such a thing were possible.

"Oh, I cannot wait!" she said, turning her head to drink in the view. The music was boisterous and rowdy, as was the dancing—the dancers' faces were flushed, and skirts were whirling, revealing glimpses of stockinged ankles and calves.

"We should dance," she declared as she rose

from her seat. She held her hand out to him, and he took it, rising slowly out of his chair.

"Are you certain?" he asked. "Because Mr. Archer's dance floor is not like the ones you are accustomed to."

"That is why I wish to even more," she replied in an impatient tone. "Come on," she added, leading him to the edge of the dance floor.

"I don't know this dance," he objected, but she just shook her head and turned so she was in his arms.

"Where is your spirit of adventure?" she asked in a challenging tone of voice. That same tone that dared him to make her fall in love with him.

She looked over his shoulder at the dancers. "This doesn't look so difficult, I'm certain we can figure it out."

He drew her closer so their faces were mere inches apart. "Much better," he murmured, then swept her out into the crowd.

Chapter Six

$\mathcal{J}$ane felt overwhelmed by everything that had happened in the past hour. Or less, even—past half an hour, perhaps?

She'd ridden alone in a carriage with an unmarried gentleman. And that wasn't even the most shocking part. The most shocking part, of course, was that he had kissed her. Or she had kissed him— she wasn't sure which. Just that there was kissing.

And it had felt amazing. She had thought she had been kissed before, but now, after kissing Mr. Thomas Sharpe, she knew those previous experiences had been something else entirely. Definitely not kissing, not in the way she'd just experienced.

How his tongue had slid into her mouth, claiming possession. How their noses had bumped, and she could feel his breath on her skin. How he nibbled and licked at her lips, and she had done the same to him. How his hand had moved slowly, far too slowly for her body's wishes, to palm her breast. Which had felt amazing, that part of her aching for his touch.

How everything he'd done, everything they'd

done together, had made other parts ache, too, parts she hadn't realized even were responsive beyond causing her discomfort every month.

But my goodness. That kiss was exceptional.

Or maybe not—maybe that was what kissing was, which was why so many people seemed to like doing it. She should have known already—after all, her sister, Lavinia, frequently had a bemused, starry look on her face after she'd gotten married.

Jane had just assumed it was because the duke was so remarkable under his clothing, not because of anything he and Lavinia had done together.

But while it might have been the first thing, she now could definitely say it was the second, because she knew her expression was in the bemused, starry category now as well.

And now they were dancing. It was a rollicking rhythm, an up-and-down beat that made her want to hop around in joy.

Which was actually a fairly good descriptor of what the other couples were doing—the dancers would shuffle two steps on one foot, and then two steps on the other, and repeat, so they dipped up and down as if they were jack-in-the-boxes. Or jacks-in-the-box.

And they were doing it, too. Mr. Sharpe—though she should call him Thomas, shouldn't she, given that he'd had his *tongue* in her *mouth*—was an excellent dancer, and quickly picked up the steps, guiding her gracefully around the dance floor.

"What is this dance called?" she asked him in a loud voice.

"I have no idea," he replied, shaking his head.

"It's the polka, miss," one of the other dancers answered. The woman had a kerchief tied on her head, another kerchief at her neck, and she wore a gown that looked as though it might once have been blue, but had faded to a vague gray color. Her partner wore plain clothing as well, his face well tanned, indicating he spent a lot of time outdoors. Perhaps he was a coachman? Or a mail carrier?

Whatever they were, she would never have met them in any Society ballroom.

"Thank you," Jane called when the other couple had swung back around in the dance.

The woman waved in response.

"It's the polka," she repeated to him as they continued to dance—down and up, down and up, down and up.

"I heard," he replied, his mouth twisting up in a wry smile.

"I think I like the polka," Jane declared. "Quite an excellent way to get exercise."

He laughed, but not as though he were laughing at her—as though he were laughing because he found her amusing.

People never found her amusing. Mostly because people never found her—they found Lady Jane the Quiet Beautiful Debutante. Or Lady Jane, the Jilted One who still had a Large Dowry, so perhaps one should make a go at it. And now Lady Jane the Scandalous but Still Beautiful Lady who Might Want to Bend her Morals.

But they didn't find *her*.

But he did.

They kept dancing for another few minutes, and

then the music finally wound down, and they returned to their table. Jane was surprised to see two glasses of what she presumed was ale on their table.

"Did someone leave that—?" she began.

"I ordered it," he said before she could finish. "I thought you would get thirsty cavorting in this evil den." And he accompanied his words with a wink that made her insides all fluttery.

He'd *winked* at her. As though they were both in this adventure together, which of course they were, but she had so rarely felt a part of something it was entirely unexpected. Usually the only people she had this same conviviality with were her siblings, and she felt decidedly unbrotherly toward Mr. Sharpe. Thomas. Whatever she should call him.

"Well, then, thank you," she said as he helped her back into her chair. She wrapped her fingers around the glass and waited for him to sit.

He picked his glass up and held it out to her. *"Dum vivimus vivamus,"* he said as he clinked her glass. They both drank; the ale was surprisingly refreshing, a bit bitter, but still tasty.

"What does that mean?" she asked.

"Let us live while we live," he replied, sounding rueful as he put the glass to his mouth.

Of course. She had the rest of her life to live, while he—he was going to have to live the rest of his life only half living, if she understood his situation correctly. There was the hope that he would find a woman to marry whom he got along with, whom perhaps he might love, but he didn't have much choice in the matter. Whichever woman would take him would be who he would have.

She put her hand over his and squeezed. "I am sorry, you know."

"Sorry?" he said, taking another swallow. "Whatever for?" He was being deliberately obtuse. Avoiding the topic, of course, for fear of eliciting sympathy?

Men.

"For what you have to do."

He uttered a derisive snort. "To have to marry someone with enough money to support my grandiose lifestyle?" Now he was being disdainful. As though he truly was so shallow just to want money for himself when she already knew he had to do it to keep his family afloat.

"Don't be an idiot," she said brusquely. "You are working with your assets to secure yourself a better future. It's what any good businessperson would do."

"My assets being my looks and my charm?" he replied, one eyebrow raised. At least now he sounded less cynical.

"Precisely." She spread her hands out. "You and I, we are seen as having only one redeeming quality. Because nobody has bothered to look past that quality to find the person within. You should take that advantage and leverage it to find yourself someone who is willing to pay for that quality." She met his gaze. "It's what ladies do all the time."

"So with me doing it it's a balancing of the sexes?" he replied with an amused smile.

She gave a vigorous nod. "Yes. Besides, what if you and I, what if we are secretly horrible people and our only value is our appearance? Then we will have tricked everyone into thinking we're kind and charming and thoughtful—"

"I am not kind," he said as he finished his drink, beckoning to one of the servers for another.

She rolled her eyes. "Of course not. If you were kind, you would have insisted on rescuing your friend's sister from what you saw as a dangerous situation. If you were kind, you would have become best friends with someone others might be suspicious of. If you were kind, you would have ensured that a naive debutante from Sussex was not left alone with a notorious fortune hunter. If you were kind—"

"Enough!" he said, holding his hand up to stop her. "Fine. I'm kind." He spoke as though it was abhorrent. "But don't tell anybody."

She chuckled as she took another drink. "Your secret is safe with me," she replied.

The server arrived with two more ales, and Jane quickly finished her glass, feeling the bitter liquid slide down her throat and settle warmly in her stomach.

"What do you think?" he asked.

She tilted her head to one side as she thought. "I like it. Ale?" she asked.

He nodded.

"I am not certain if I like it better than whisky," she said. "But it is easier to drink."

"Because you're not coughing?" he asked in an innocent tone.

She gave him a mockingly cold stare. "I was

merely having a bit of trouble breathing, that was all that was. It wasn't because it was my first time drinking spirits like that, I assure you."

He chuckled. "Of course not, my lady. I never meant to cast aspersion."

He leaned back in his chair and seemed about to continue the conversation when there was a loud blast of horns—trumpets or French horns or something equally cacophonous—and they turned to see a group of people at the edge of the dance floor, which had been entirely cleared.

WATCHING HER EXPRESSION as the circus troupe stepped onto their makeshift stage was more glorious than anything he had ever seen before. It made him believe in hope, and possibility, and a bright future.

Her eyes gleamed like stars, and her beautiful mouth—that mouth he'd kissed only an hour or so ago—was curled up into the widest smile, and it looked as though she were practically vibrating with joy.

"Ladies and gentlemen," the circus master said as he entered the stage, "I am pleased to introduce the most entertaining players in all of England, the Marvelous Miscreants of Mayfair, here to tempt your fancies—and your pocketbook," he said with a cheeky grin. The circus master wore a gaudy red jacket, a worn top hat perched on his head. He was close in age to Thomas's father, but was far more agile.

The players spilled out around the circus master as she gasped aloud.

She tugged at his sleeve, whispering urgently. "Do you see? There is a dog dressed as a ballerina! And a lady wearing a horse costume!"

Her enthusiasm was infectious.

The first performance was the dancing dog, its owner a red-haired woman wearing an outfit that matched her dog's. Both had pink tutus on, and the woman wore an enormous hat with pink feathers that bobbed gently with her every movement. The dog did a series of tricks, including twirling in a circle on its hind legs, jumping through a hoop, and catching a ball in midair.

But Thomas didn't watch much of the dog's antics. He was too entranced by Jane's face, by how expressive it was, how every sparkling moment of joy was reflected in her eyes.

Had he ever been so enchanted by anything as much as she was this poodle and its handler?

He couldn't recall. There had been moments, fleeting moments during particularly passionate interludes when he had lost himself to his feelings, but then he had snapped back into reality after the moment was over.

He hungered to feel that fascinated intoxication, the moment when all else fell away and the only thing that mattered was the feeling in that specific time.

He'd caught a glimmer of that when he'd been kissing her. When he, the consummate lover, had been surprised by how quickly she'd learned what to do, and what seemed to please him. Had been grateful that she was so responsive to what they both wanted.

Would she be as adept during more intimate encounters?

Goddamn it, but he couldn't allow himself to find out. He owed it to her as well as to her brother not to take advantage of her desire for knowledge—*desire* being the crucial word—and keep her at arm's length.

Even though he had done a terrible job of it thus far, since he'd barely kept her at cock's length in the carriage. The thought of which sent a prickly awareness through him. Her soft skin. Her searching tongue. The tug of her fingers on his hair.

"Are you feeling well?" she asked in a soft voice.

And damn her for being so perceptive.

"I'm fine," he said, forcing himself to put on his most charming mask, a casual smile that indicated that he was at ease and didn't have a care in the world.

"You're not," she snapped back.

Apparently she could see past his mask.

"Just watch the performance," he said, picking up his glass of ale.

She glared at him, but limited herself to one annoyed shake of her head as she returned her attention to the stage.

Next up was a trio of jugglers tossing increasingly dangerous items in the air: first a few balls, then eggs, then finally knives, making the crowd gasp in unison at each terrifying toss.

He forced himself to watch them, not her. Watching her was far more dangerous than whatever the jugglers were doing—if he watched her, he might get entranced by her generous spirit, her warmth, her palpable excitement at life and its pleasures.

He might forget for a few minutes that his course was not one he would enjoy. Or if he would enjoy it, that would be a mere benefit of what he had to do.

The reality of it stuck in his throat, as weighty as if one of the juggler's balls had gotten thrown in there, making it impossible to breathe. Making him gulp for air.

He wished he could just get up and leave, escape this room with its hope and shining possibility and endless excitement. Return to his well-worn weariness unaccompanied by anything remotely approaching optimism.

Why had he agreed to be here with her, anyway?

Of course. Because she was going to ensure he would never feel free again—because she was going to capture him a bride with her carefully chosen words, thereby capturing him in the golden web of marriage.

It was a horrible irony. Feeling free to let his thoughts wander now, which meant that he would be trapped that much sooner in the future. Which was what he wanted. No. Not wanted. Needed.

Not in the craving something so impossibly forbidden kind of way. But literally needed to maintain any semblance of normalcy.

If only his father hadn't risked everything.

If only he hadn't felt responsible for all of them.

If only he hadn't been born with most of the looks and all of the charm in his family.

If only he weren't such an arrogant, conscientious

friend. To both Percy and Lady Jane. And an arrogant, conscientious member of his family, who had the straining bonds of loyalty to deal with as well.

"Mr. Sharpe."

She spoke urgently, and he shook his thoughts away, turning his attention back to her.

"What, my lady?" he replied in his smoothest tone of voice.

"You're not having a good time," she said. "And although I am enjoying this adventure, knowing that you are not means we should not stay. We should go do something you want to. Or I should leave you be, and allow you to be comfortable, because it is clear you are not now."

Her clear, penetrating gaze seemed as though she was looking straight through him, to his traitorous thoughts that were wondering if he truly had to marry someone he did not love and might not even like just for their money. If it would be so terrible if his family were forced into more straitened circumstances.

Of course it would be. Alice would suffer the most, and she was the one he loved the most. He couldn't dare even speak it aloud. He'd have to get over whatever wishes he held for himself.

Because of course it would be terrible to marry someone with enough money to keep one in excellent style.

He emitted a derisive snort at himself. He truly was arrogant. And angry about what he had to do. Even though he was the one insisting he do it.

Her expression remained resolute, and he nodded. "Yes, fine then. I will escort you home. I—" And he, who was never without something to say, was completely at a loss for words.

Because it was talking about his feelings, and his doubts, and his flaws. He never did that, not even with Percy.

But he wanted to with her. And he knew she would be receptive, which made it even more tempting—to confide in someone else, to share his problems with someone who might understand.

It would be an act of betrayal, though, since he wouldn't admit to anyone that he was not the person everyone thought him to be.

"I will drop some coins in the basket as we leave," she said as she rose, nodding toward where the master of ceremonies stood.

He muttered something unintelligible even to himself and they left, not speaking until he saw her to her door.

And then he turned and walked down her steps even though what he wanted was to burst back in to tell her how the evening had been a series of new experiences—not just for her, but also for him.

And that that scared him. Even as it exhilarated him.

Chapter Seven

*J*ane shut the door softly, leaning against it as she bit her lip in thought.

It had been an incredible evening—her first real kiss, one with tongues and everything. Dancing the polka. Watching the traveling circus.

Incredible for seeing his mood shift as well. Getting a glimpse behind the charming mask he wore.

"Jane? Are you back?" Percy called.

She smiled as she called back, "I am."

"Come in here," he urged.

She made her way quickly to their sitting room, a small room that was overrun by books, from the economics and mathematical texts Percy liked to read to her own collection of her sister Lavinia's books—Lavinia wrote increasingly scandalous novels under the name Percy Wittlesford, trotting Percy out whenever the author was asked to speak in person.

Percy was on the sofa, both arms flung over his head, his feet dangling off the edge. She picked his legs up and swung them so his feet were on the floor, and then she sat in the now unoccupied space.

He promptly swung his legs back to rest on her lap.

"How was your evening?" she asked. She hoped he wouldn't pry too much into hers, since she didn't want to lie to her brother—but she also did not wish to tell him the truth.

"Fine," Percy said, waving his hand dismissively. "After the party I went to the club with a few friends and we discussed Carlyle's clothing metaphor."

At Jane's blank look, he continued. "Thomas Carlyle? He writes essays and pontificates on philosophy. Anyway, he says 'Language is the garment of thought.'"

Jane considered his words, nodding in surprise. "Hmm. Usually when you tell me something I have no idea what it means, but that one makes sense. For once," she added, with a smirk toward her brother, who was already rolling his eyes.

"Which friends were you out with?" she asked.

Percy's expression tightened. "Just Morton, Feltstone, and Smith. And Daffy," he added, as though an afterthought.

"Daffy?" Jane asked, her eyebrows raised.

Now his expression was even tighter. Interesting.

"The heir to Lady Stockham. She is the one with the field full of daffodils."

"Ah, hence Daffy," Jane said in understanding.

"Sharpe didn't come with us because he was with you," Percy said pointedly. He sat up, pinning Jane with an accusatory glance.

"He was."

This would be an excellent exercise for her—trying not to apologize or shrink into the background when a conversation became difficult or awkward. For most of her life, she'd had Lavinia to buffer her against any unpleasantness.

Which had caused the ultimately happy situation of Lavinia marrying the Duke of Hasford, but it was touch and go there for a bit.

Jane never wanted to put anyone in that situation again—having to rescue her because she was too timid to protect herself.

There was a heavy pause, and Jane resisted the urge to squirm, or blurt anything out, or otherwise react to what she presumed Percy was thinking.

He would have to say the words to her. She couldn't just run around thinking everyone was annoyed with her unless they were pondering her appearance any longer. It was time to stand up for herself, both with people and in her own mind.

"Where did he take you?" Percy asked, this time in a less combative tone.

Excellent. She wasn't going to have to have the "he's dangerous to you because you're so naive and he's so charming" conversation again.

"A dance hall that also seems to be where a traveling circus performs? It was wonderful." She sighed at the memory.

Percy's eyes lit up. "I've been there! Mr. Archer's hall, correct? Sharpe and I went a few months ago. There was this trapeze artist who—" And then he froze, apparently realizing he was about to say something shocking.

In which case, Jane wished the trapeze artist had performed this evening.

"You should take your friend Daffy there," she said in a deliberately casual tone of voice.

Percy's cheeks flushed red. *A ha!* She bit back a smile.

She, Percy, and her sister, Lavinia, had had a conversation that skirted around who Percy might . . . appreciate, and then she had suspected what she now knew almost certainly. That Thomas had implied as well.

She hoped Percy would be able to live an uncompromised life. Like she was planning to, actually. What those respective lives would look like, she had no idea—just that they would be what they truly wanted. And that what Percy likely wanted was far more dangerous than what she wanted.

She leaned forward and patted Percy's knee. "I am so glad we live together," she said. "Perhaps we should throw a dinner party," she said, the words bursting out of her mouth barely after the idea had come to her. "I could invite a few of the ladies Mr. Sharpe is interested in"—which meant the ones with the most money—"and you could invite some of your friends."

Percy frowned in confusion. "Those ladies, they can't attend without a chaperone, can they?"

Jane made a disgruntled noise. "No, they can't. I'd forgotten entirely. Blast the rules." Because a young lady could be married off to a man she'd barely spoken to, but she could not attend a dinner party at an acquaintance's house.

It really was unfair.

"We could do a public event," Percy offered. "Perhaps host it at one of those places Sharpe is taking you to, provided it is closed to the general public. Maybe ask the circus if they could do a private showing in an afternoon or something?" He nodded, pleased at his own idea. "And then you could further your campaign to make Sharpe seem palatable to those ladies, and we could all gather together. And you could meet Daffy," he said, as though it were an afterthought.

Jane hopped in her seat. "I love that idea!" Though she did not love the idea of Mr. Sharpe marrying. Not just because that would mean their interlude with one another was over, but also because it would mean he'd be sacrificing himself when he so clearly did not want to. But felt it was his duty.

Just like a debutante.

But unlike a debutante, Mr. Sharpe had the illusion of choice, which likely made it even more painful for him. Because he could change his mind anytime, not to proceed along the path he'd chosen. But that would condemn his family to a life of penury, and she knew he was far too honorable and responsible to take that course.

Meanwhile, she would try to ensure the woman he eventually was able to persuade to marry him was relatively kind. Though would that be even crueler to both sides? He'd be making a purely mercenary decision and entrapping a woman who might have hopes of something more than just an agreement. Might even have hopes of love.

Which wasn't at all what he was considering.

And now she felt sorry for the unknown woman.

She was as melodramatic as one of Lavinia's heroines. Perhaps, if she was fortunate, she'd have one of Lavinia's heroines' happy endings.

And even if she didn't, the ending would be happy because it would be under her control.

THOMAS HELD THE letter in his hand, desperation seeping through his whole body.

He'd spent most of the night trying to think through his situation, even though he had done the same thing continuously since his father had walked into the dining room two years ago.

There was no other solution to it.

And things were getting worse.

Dear Thomas,

I hope this letter finds you well. We are all in tolerable health, though Father is relying on his cane more than he used to. But he and I take daily walks, and I believe he is getting stronger.

Mother and Father have let more of the servants go. Thankfully, Squire Hastings has hired most of them—the lady to whom he is betrothed is quite full of herself, and she insists on a certain standard of living. The squire is so besotted with her he'll do whatever she asks. The wedding is in a month, and Mother is already in a panic about what to wear—all of her clothing is at least two years out-of-date, and she has been losing weight, so most of it hangs off her.

I don't care what I wear since I don't want to attend

in the first place. All those people together, most of them conscious of my speech, and trying to be kind by not speaking to me at all.

It is possible to be lonely in a crowd, I will tell you that much.

But I know I am already being gloomy, and my intent was to entertain you. I will say that I have had a column accepted for publication. It's a small newspaper that took it, and it details how young people might acquire knowledge when they don't have access to tutors or governesses. Not that I mentioned not having a governess—the newspaper believes I am a man studying at college, not a young lady who lives with her parents and learns at home.

I am hoping to write more—I find I lose myself when I do it. It's far easier to get immersed in the words than to live in my reality.

Wait. I'm doing it again. Being gloomy.

I am so sorry.

I hope your quest is going well, and that you will be able to rescue us before Mother is forced to take on all the cooking herself—do you remember the one time she tried to make a pie? And it managed to be both burnt and underdone?

Perhaps I will start observing Cook so that I can be the one to undertake the cooking if you are not successful soon. And then I could write another column about learning that, as well.

At least I have a plan!

I love you, thank you for what you are doing.

Love,
Alice

Thomas read the letter again, allowing himself to smile at Alice's description of their mother's pie. It was indeed inedible, and it had proven that his parents would be unable to take care of themselves if things got worse.

And it sounded as though things were getting worse.

Goddamn it.

He slammed his fist on the table, the clatter of it echoing around his room. He lived in his club, the cost of paying for lodgings here cheaper than the cost of keeping up his own household.

But he was still just barely making ends meet.

During the night, he'd allowed himself the luxury of dreaming about a future unhampered by the need to marry a wealthy woman. Perhaps explore what it might mean to have a relationship with a person whom he actually liked and found enticing.

Someone who looked a lot like Lady Jane.

But those fleeting thoughts had to be squashed by the truth of his and his family's situation.

Unless some heretofore unknown relative were to die and leave their fortune to him or his parents, he would have no choice.

And it wouldn't matter how much he longed to be able to make his own choice. He couldn't. Not without jeopardizing everyone he loved.

He exhaled, drawing a sheet of paper toward him and picking up a pen, preparing to write the list he'd been compiling in his head: the women who were possible candidates to marry him and solve his most pressing problem.

And if Lady Jane was not successful in her campaign to persuade at least one of these women that he would make a good husband, he would have to watch his family unravel even more.

He glanced at the clock, noting it was just barely eleven o'clock in the morning. Too early to drown his sorrows, too late to go back to bed and pretend none of this was happening.

He would have to make his list.

And work on being the charming, but not too charming, Thomas Sharpe.

He'd had a respite the past few days of that, even going so far as to not be charming all the time. And Lady Jane hadn't turned her nose up at him or decided he wasn't worth the effort.

Instead, she'd seen through to his emotions and asked him about them. Not only had she not run away, she had come closer to find out what was wrong.

Percy had never even done that.

Not that he had ever let Percy see all of his inner workings. Likely because Percy kept his own secrets close.

But he had shown Jane more than he'd ever shown anyone who wasn't Alice.

And she'd tried to understand him. She was truly a rare creature, a thoughtful person whose quiet demeanor didn't mean she wouldn't speak up when she felt she had to.

Her strength in choosing her own course made him want to be a better person.

If only there was a way he could do that and save his family.

Unfortunately, the two were at odds with one another, and he knew what he had to do.

He gave a weary sigh as he began to write.

"JANE!"

Jane glanced up toward the door, through which she could hear her sister's voice. She was in the sitting room with a cup of tea, Percy still abed. They'd stayed up half the night formulating plans for their event, but she had been too excited to sleep. The kiss, seeing the traveling circus, deciding to actively do something to help Thomas, all kept chasing themselves around in her head like crazed squirrels.

"In here," Jane called.

She smiled as she heard the yip of Lavinia's dog, Precious, and rose to open the door as they approached.

Lavinia was pregnant—again—and her enviable bosom was even more enviable, while her clear gaze and bright smile made it impossible to be unhappy when seeing her.

"Good morning," Jane said, stepping forward to embrace Lavinia.

"Good morning," Lavinia replied, her voice muffled by Jane's shoulder. Lavinia had the advantage, bosom-wise, but Jane was taller.

"Come in and sit down," Jane said. She rang the bell and waited as Mrs. Charing arrived with an expectant look on her face. "Could we have some tea, please?" she asked.

The housekeeper nodded. It was unusual for a housekeeper to be on call for something so menial as tea fetching, but Percy and Jane couldn't afford many servants, and Mrs. Charing preferred to be busy. Like Percy and Jane, Mrs. Charing was a Societal outcast—a baron's daughter who ran off to London with her low-born lover who died only a few months after their arrival. Instead of slinking back to her family, however, she'd sought out Percy and Jane's house, having heard about their unusual household and knowing they would have some sympathy for her situation.

Lavinia sat down with a relieved exhale as Precious went to lie at her feet. "I'd forgotten how exhausting this is," she said, gesturing to her belly. "And Thaddeus grumbles every time I want to move, and sometimes it is just easier to sit. But today I had to come out, it has been so long since I've seen you! How are you doing?" Lavinia placed her hand on Jane's knee as she spoke, squeezing it gently.

Jane put her hand on top of her sister's, but didn't speak. At least not right away.

"What is it?" Lavinia said, sounding even more enthusiastic than usual. "Jane! You have to tell me!"

So she did. She told Lavinia all about going to Miss Ivy's, and running into Mr. Sharpe, and their subsequent agreement. She told her about the party where they'd met Miss Grosvenor, and then the dance hall and the circus. By then, Mrs. Charing had returned with the tea, so they took a few moments to pour in the proper amount of milk and add some sugar, while Lavinia snuck a tea scone to Precious, who seemed appreciative.

And then—"And I had my first kiss. My first real kiss."

Lavinia's eyes widened, and her mouth opened as she gasped. "Why didn't you start with that?" She rolled her eyes. "Remind me never to let you write any of my books. You are totally burying the most fun part in the depths of the story."

Jane put her hand to her mouth to smother a giggle. "It feels as though I am in one of your books, honestly," she said. "What with asking for a kissing education, and helping a gentleman land an heiress, and the gentleman being my brother's best friend." She shook her head. "It would be altogether too much if you were to put all those things into a book."

Lavinia's expression turned mischievous. "Perhaps I should try. But only if you can guarantee a happy ending," she said, wagging her finger.

Jane gave a rueful smile. "I don't think there is any possibility of that. At least not in the usual way. He has to marry someone who is wealthy, and I am not. And," she continued, her voice getting stronger, "I have promised Percy I will not succumb to the inevitable and fall in love with him so it won't matter, anyway."

Even though she already knew she had fallen in serious like with him. Which was but a short step to the other thing.

She could not allow herself to do the other thing, because that way would inevitably lead to heartbreak, and she'd already dealt with that, thanks to Mr. RatTavish.

"What does Percy have to say about all of this?" Lavinia asked in an arch tone as she picked up her teacup. "Because I can imagine he would either be vastly pleased his sister and his best friend are spending time with one another, or he is fiercely worried that his dashing friend will break your heart." She took a sip. "I am betting on the latter," she said with a decided nod.

"And if you were to place that bet at Miss Ivy's, you would be the winner," Jane replied wryly. "He has been somewhat mollified because of our plans for an event where we'll invite all the young ladies Mr. Sharpe might possibly be interested in, but he remains suspicious."

"Did you tell him—?" Lavinia began.

Jane's cheeks flushed. "About the kiss? Heavens, no. He would have exploded. I have told him, repeatedly, that he should not worry about me, but he seems to think I am far too naive to—well, too naive in general."

Lavinia tilted her head as she gave Jane a searching look. "I would have said he was right before. But you seem different. And I don't think it was just one kiss—your first real kiss." She shook her head in disgust. "I always knew Mr. McTavish was a disappointment."

"I wish I'd known earlier," Jane replied ruefully.

"But without him, you wouldn't be here living with Percy. Perhaps you should thank him. If you see him. You don't see him, do you?" Lavinia asked in a concerned tone of voice.

"No. Now that he is married, it seems he spends most of his time at his wife's father's place of business." Jane snorted. "I wonder how his mother and her snobbery is faring with his having married a woman who comes from a working family." She paused as she thought. "Working family," she repeated. "We come from a working family, with Father advising the queen on finances and all. And Percy works, though he has to, given his birth. I wonder if I could work?"

Lavinia looked taken aback. A marvel, truly, to have startled her fearless sister. "You work? What would you do? And why? If you need more money, just tell me. Thaddeus has far too much for us." Lavinia's husband, the Duke of Hasford, was one of the wealthiest aristocrats in London, and his fortune was growing, thanks to his savvy investing.

"I don't need any more money, thank you," Jane replied, reaching over to pat her sister's hand. Lavinia provided Jane with the funds she needed to survive, though she resisted taking more, even though Lavinia was always offering. "I just want to feel useful. And I'd like to have a different future than just one where I find someone—anyone—to marry, merely because that is what women in our situation do."

"Well, we've already established you cannot be a writer," Lavinia replied in a sly tone. Jane poked her in the shoulder in response. "But you might have something there. After all, wouldn't it be better for everyone if we all worked? What if your Mr. Sharpe found himself a position rather than having to—to sell himself to the highest bidder?"

"I wonder if he's even thought of that," Jane replied. "We're all so accustomed to what we're expected to do we don't question it. But what if we did? Question it, I mean?"

Lavinia beamed. "And you have become a radical!

Jane, I am so proud." Her eyebrow rose. "And all it took was your first real kiss and a traveling circus. If only other ladies had access to such delights."

"Hush," Jane said in a mockingly reproving tone. "I am not a radical—I am merely expressing my opinion."

"That is how it begins," Lavinia replied knowingly. "Expressing your opinion one day, solving the world's problems the next."

Jane shook her head at her sister's hyperbole. As befit a writer, of course. "The event Percy and I are planning, will you and the duke attend? It would give a certain amount of prestige to have you there."

Lavinia's expression turned mischievous. "Of course. Thaddeus and I wouldn't miss it for the world. Though Thaddeus will no doubt grumble about going. But he'll go," she said. "I'll make it worth his while," she added, waggling her eyebrows.

"Stop!" Jane said, holding her hand up. "I do not wish to hear those things about my brother-in-law."

"No, because your Mr. Sharpe is going to show you himself," Lavinia replied. "I will just warn you to be cautious."

Jane blushed at the implication. "Of course, I am not planning on doing *that*," she said hastily.

Lavinia gave her a pointed glance. "Nobody plans on doing *that*, but it does seem to happen. Just be cautious."

"I promise," Jane said, her cheeks now bright red. "Not only will I not fall in love with Mr. Sharpe—as Percy asked that I promise—I will not allow myself to be compromised by him. At least not so anybody can tell."

"You are not the naive Jane you were two years ago," Lavinia said approvingly. "I look forward to getting to know your Mr. Sharpe."

He's not my—Oh, never mind, Jane thought. "Excellent," was her only reply.

Chapter Eight

$\mathcal{I}$ thought you were supposed to be courting all the money in England?" Octavia said as she gestured for Thomas to enter Miss Ivy's.

The club had just barely opened for the evening, so there were only a few patrons and the club staff milling about. Thomas kissed Octavia on the cheek, then took her elbow and guided her to the bar. "Do you have time for a drink?" he asked as they walked.

"With the most charming man in London? Certainly," Octavia replied, her cheeky smile reminding him just why he liked her so much.

The barkeep knew both their orders, and quickly set their drinks up on the bar. Thomas held his glass aloft, waiting as Octavia picked hers up.

"What are we drinking to?" she asked, her eyebrows raised in question.

"To my luck," he replied, taking a deep breath.

He tapped his glass against hers, then took a sip. The whisky burned going down his throat, and it reminded him of Jane coughing after she drank. And then doing it again, entirely undaunted by the alcohol's intense flavor.

"What are you smiling like that for?" Octavia asked, sounding suspicious.

"Nothing," Thomas replied, quickly shifting his expression to something more neutral. "I am going to try my luck at your tables." He'd been almost violently opposed to such an action, given that it was his father's gamble on investments that had brought the family to their current straits. But he was reaching the point where he had to take some sort of action to change the situation—either for better or for worse—and he'd decided to follow Lady Jane's lead and take a risk.

Octavia frowned as she placed her glass back on the bar. "Pardon me for saying so, but if you lose, you will have even less money than you do now."

"That is how gambling works, thank you," Thomas replied in a dry tone. It was what had kept him from the tables before.

"So why risk it? Why not find some safe woman to gamble on?"

Thomas paused as he thought about how to explain it to Octavia. Though she, of anyone, would understand risk, having been at Miss Ivy's since a young age.

Now, having kissed Jane and seen what an unencumbered future could look like—well, it was worth a gamble, literally, if it meant he could stave off having to woo and win a bride. Perhaps by the time his family needed more money, he would have figured something out that didn't require selling himself to the highest bidder.

The only way he knew to get a large sum of money quickly was to gamble. At least, the only legal way he knew; he wasn't prepared to start picking pockets, or engage in contraband smuggling or the like.

Not just because those things would send him to prison, where he'd be no help to his family, but also because he knew he would be terrible at both those things. He likely wouldn't be able to disguise himself enough to rob the bank, and he didn't have money to buy the contraband goods in the first place, let alone know where or from whom to buy them and then where to sell them.

He was good for one thing: being charming.

But that could also play out to his advantage at the gambling tables.

"I have positioned myself as a person who is a good companion, the dinner guest you always want to have at your table, the person you want to ask your wallflower young lady or ancient aunt to dance. I never say anything unpleasant, and I am adept at making people feel special, as though they are the only person in the room."

"True," Octavia admitted. "Which is why you are ideal for finding a wealthy bride. You'll be able to charm both her and her likely suspicious parents."

"But being that charming requires a certain effort of observing people." Thomas gestured around the room. More guests were arriving, and a few tables were already full. "If I can observe people while they play games of chance—"

"You can predict what kind of play they will make," Octavia finished in a triumphant tone of voice.

"Hush, don't reveal my secrets," Thomas said. "But yes."

Octavia gave a firm nod. "I will help. Lady Montague over there is loaded to the gills with money," she said, gesturing discreetly toward where an older lady sat with two younger gentlemen, "and she gets distracted by a pretty face such as yours."

Thomas finished his drink as he rose. "Then I will join Lady Montague's table." He paused. "I want to assure you I have the money to pay, should I be so unfortunate to lose."

Octavia made a shooing gesture. "I know, I would expect nothing less. Go. See if your powers of observation are as strong as you believe them to be."

Two hours later, and Thomas had won enough to pay his family's bills for another month. Not quite the windfall he'd hoped for, but a bit of breathing room—thirty days' worth of breathing room, in fact—so he wouldn't feel the constant dread that walked with him anytime he walked outside of his club.

And Lady Montague didn't seem at all annoyed he'd won against her. In fact, she'd invited him to join her the following week when she returned.

But the entire time, he'd been in a panic, realizing that his risk, his gamble, was jeopardizing everything and everyone he cared about. Even though he was doing it for them. He didn't think he could make a habit of it, not without having his heart in his throat every time he turned a card over. But at least he had won this evening. That would do for now.

Octavia was waiting as he made his way to the door. "Well?" she asked, holding his hat in her hand. He took it from her and placed it on his head.

"Well," he replied, "I was able to win just enough." He took a deep breath for the first time in hours.

"You can't stake your future on this, you understand," Octavia said in a concerned tone of voice. "Plenty of people have tried, and none have succeeded. The house always wins, you know. Eventually."

"I know." He paused. "I won't be doing it again anytime soon."

It was terrifying that only a few pounds stood between him and utter bankruptcy.

"Miss Grosvenor," Jane exclaimed as she saw the lady. It was evening, and Percy had wanted to take an evening off from carousing with his economics friends, so he had agreed to escort Jane to her event—tonight it was a party celebrating the engagement of an acquaintance of Jane's, a lady who had come out the same year and was now going to marry the second son of a member of Queen Victoria's cabinet.

The room they were in was festooned with flowers, vases and swaths and buckets of them studding the tables and walls. The bride-to-be wore a gown that matched the decorations, an ebullient gown with a veritable garden embroidered on it. She wore a headpiece with flowers on it, and her cheeks were, suitably, flushed a rosy pink.

There were rumors that the queen herself would attend, but there were always rumors that she would attend, and she seldom did. The guests in attendance included several other of the young ladies in Jane's debutante year, most of them married by now and a few of them clearly with child.

If she hadn't had her eyes opened by RatTavish's weak idiocy, she would likely have been one of them. Thank goodness she had not.

Though some of them had married for love, and it was obvious, from seeing them with their husbands, that they were happy.

She envied that. It would be even more difficult now to find someone to fall in love with—someone she could marry, that was. She'd already found someone she might possibly fall in love with, but there was no chance he would marry her.

He couldn't afford to.

"Good evening, my lady," Miss Grosvenor replied. She wore a lovely evening gown made of a cream-colored silk, small ruffles edging the hem, while diamonds glittered at her ears and wrist.

Jane was wearing something she'd worn two years ago, back when she had parents invested in her having a remarkable wardrobe so she could capture the best man as her spouse.

It was still a pretty gown, but she'd had to rework some of the tulle overskirt, since it was rather the worse for wear.

"I didn't realize you knew Miss Carnady," Jane said, gesturing to where the engaged lady was holding court, showing off her engagement ring and her husband-to-be. In that order.

Miss Grosvenor shook her head. "I don't, but my father is acquainted with Mr. Townshend's father." Mr. Townshend was the groom, a serious gentleman who seemed prepared to follow his father's footsteps into government.

"Who are you here with?" Lady Jane asked. Mostly because she didn't recall Miss Grosvenor having a chaperone, but of course she must have—all respectable young ladies did, even if said chaperone frequently decamped to gamble in another room or sit on the sidelines falling asleep.

"My stepmother," Miss Grosvenor said, wrinkling her nose. "My father is in London, of course, but is always too busy to accompany me to something so frivolous." She gave Jane a significant glance. "My stepmother is never too busy for frivolity."

As though on cue, Jane heard a shriek of feminine laughter, and Miss Grosvenor winced. "That is my stepmother."

They turned to view the source of the laughter— Mrs. Grosvenor was likely only half a dozen years older than her stepdaughter. She was remarkably, vibrantly pretty, and wore a stunning gown in a bright green satin.

"Ah," Jane said diplomatically.

"She is very kind," Miss Grosvenor added hastily. "She is just—well, I find we have little in common."

Mrs. Grosvenor shrieked again.

"It appears she finds things amusing, at least?" Jane offered.

Miss Grosvenor gave a pained smile. "Very often. Oh, there is Mr. Sharpe." Miss Grosvenor nodded toward the front of the room.

Jane tried to look delighted as he approached them determinedly. Because this was the whole point, wasn't it? For him to persuade some wealthy lady to get married? And not only was Miss Grosvenor very wealthy, but she also seemed to be kind, which could not but be a bonus in the situation.

"Ladies," he said as he joined them. "I am pleased to see you." Was it her imagination, or did his eyes linger on her mouth?

"Good evening, Mr. Sharpe," Miss Grosvenor said. "I am so glad you are here—I know so few people having just arrived."

"Where are you from?" Jane asked.

Miss Grosvenor uttered an aggrieved sigh. "Wessex. Far, far away from anywhere civilized. Father didn't want to bring me to London until I was prepared to make my debut. He was concerned some devious gentleman would convince me to elope with him so he could get his hands on my money."

"There are plenty of devious gentlemen about, Miss Grosvenor," Jane said, careful not to meet Mr. Sharpe's eyes. "If you have any questions about anyone, please feel free to ask me. I have been in and among Society for two years now, and consider myself a good judge of character."

There. That should lay the groundwork for later on, when she could inform Miss Grosvenor that Mr. Sharpe was extremely fond of a certain young lady, but wasn't certain his suit would be well considered.

She wished she didn't dread the day some lady would say yes. She also wished that Miss Grosvenor's father wasn't absolutely correct about several of the young gentlemen who would swarm around his daughter. Including Mr. Sharpe.

He was pursuing this course for altruistic reasons. But did that make it any better?

She wasn't enough of an ethicist to decide that, but she did know she wanted him to succeed. Even though she also did not.

"Lady Jane is indeed an excellent judge of character," Mr. Sharpe said in a mild tone. Jane shot him a sharp glance, which he responded to with an innocent lift of his eyebrows. As though he were saying, "who, me?"

Yes, you.

"Mr. Sharpe is very kind," Jane replied.

Mr. Sharpe smothered a snort of laughter.

Miss Grosvenor remained blissfully unaware of the undercurrents of conversation happening between them, thank goodness.

"There is no dancing this evening, is there?" Mr. Sharpe said as he gazed around the room. "Though I believe we will have a few speeches from the future bride's father and the groom." He paused in thought. "Why doesn't the bride herself get a speech?"

Jane gave him an appreciative look. Which, honestly, was the look she gave him most often, what with being the handsomest man in the room, but this time it was for his words, not his appearance.

"I did not realize you were aware of the frequent imbalance of the sexes, Mr. Sharpe," she said.

"I endeavor to right that balance in my own life," Mr. Sharpe replied, his tone silky. "For example, if there is something I've received, I will give that same thing back to a lady, if she desires it."

Jane's eyes widened, and he returned her look

with a slow, knowing smile. As though he was completely aware of what he might be saying, and was intent on teasing her.

"Oh," she said, her voice higher and breathier than usual. This was the anticipation portion of her learning. And now that she knew some of what might happen during the actuality of it all, her body was even more responsive.

Her breathing quickened, and it seemed as though she could feel his hand on her breast, which felt tight in her gown. Aching for his touch.

"And I often take measures to ensure the lady has more than a few of whatever she wants. Even if I go without. It is the right thing to do." He paused, his intent gaze locked on her face. "And it brings me satisfaction as well."

"Oh," she said again, more softly this time.

"I don't believe it would bring me any kind of satisfaction to engage in any public speaking," Miss Grosvenor declared. She wasn't looking at either one of them, instead looking at Miss Carnady.

Jane's heart leaped as his gaze shifted, lower to her mouth, and then lower still, traveling lazily back up to her eyes as though he was drinking her in. And was parched.

It was intoxicating to be looked at like that.

So she did the same back at him, making his mouth curl up into a wry smile.

"Equality in all things, Mr. Sharpe," she murmured.

Chapter Nine

$\mathcal{P}$erhaps it was the respite he'd gained because of his winnings at Miss Ivy's. Or because he had been so constrained in his behavior that something had to give eventually.

Or just because she was innocent, yes, but she knew full well what he was talking about. What *they* were talking about.

And that made it irresistible.

Then, when she had responded to his frank assessment of her entire person with one of her own—he knew what it was to be sorely, utterly tempted.

He wanted to undress in front of her, watch as her gaze traveled over his naked body.

He wanted to please her, give her the satisfaction he'd alluded to in their conversation. Hear her soft moans and cries of pleasure as he devoted himself entirely to her. Taste her climax as she shuddered under his mouth.

That was one of the things he knew made him a remarkable lover, at least according to the women he'd slept with; he did always strive for their pleasure as well as his, and he took care to discover what it was they liked in bed, and gave it to them. Thoroughly.

She wouldn't know what she liked in bed, of course. Not yet.

Damn, but he wanted her to find out. With him.

What he wouldn't give to have her in his bed; wrapped in his sheets, her skin warm and soft against his. Her slowly learning what she wanted, and him making certain she received it.

He imagined her curiosity would extend to everything. Perhaps she would want to touch his cock, stroke him to see what response she would get. Maybe she'd slide her lips down his skin, licking his nipples as she ran her hands over his body. Grab his arse in her hands.

And now he was hard as a rock at this ridiculous engagement party, as though he were new to fucking when he'd been doing it consistently since he was seventeen years old.

Though he hadn't fucked anyone in the past few months—too busy minding his reputation and growing increasingly desperate to lose himself in a woman's arms.

Perhaps that was what this was all about. It wasn't her—it was that it had been too long for him in general.

But the thought of doing it with anyone but her left him cold.

Goddamn it.

It was her.

"Mr. Sharpe?"

Her voice intruded on his thoughts. His thoughts about her. The irony did not escape him.

"Pardon, my lady?"

She wore an amused expression. One that was even slightly mocking. "Miss Grosvenor asked you a question."

Thomas shifted his attention to Miss Grosvenor. She was charming, but so fresh-faced and naive he felt nearly decadent even speaking to her.

"What is it, Miss Grosvenor? I apologize, I was"—*fantasizing about the other lady here*—"thinking about something," he finished, making a vague gesture.

"I wanted to know, Mr. Sharpe," she replied, her cheeks a bright red hue, "if you could recommend a tailor? My father," she said with a wry smile, "doesn't always pay attention to his clothing. And my stepmother," she added, "is just as new to London as I am."

"Of course," Thomas replied. "I will send you my tailor's card, and I'll include a note so he knows to take the utmost care with your father."

"Oh, thank you," she said, beaming. Her smile was brighter than the candles in the closest chandelier. "You are always so elegantly dressed, and I am hopeful my father will understand it is merely good business to look appropriate." Her face flushed even more. "Oh no, and I am not supposed to mention business. Please forgive me," she said, sounding flustered.

"Do not apologize," Lady Jane said, before Thomas could respond. "It seems ridiculous that you are not supposed to mention the thing that drives and pays for our world." Her tone was fierce, and Thomas felt his eyes widen in surprise at her vehemence. "Behaving the way Society prefers would mean ladies would never speak, would never share an opinion unless it is a corroboration of a man's opinion." She gave a firm nod. "I for one am glad you feel comfortable enough to mention business around us."

"Oh, thank you," Miss Grosvenor replied, sounding relieved. "My stepmother, she—" She glanced across the room, presumably to that lady's location. "She reads all the etiquette guides and shares what she's read. But neither she nor I have been in this type of Society before, so neither of us actually knows."

"Lady Jane is correct," Thomas said. "That you should speak whatever is on your mind, provided it isn't harmful and won't hurt anybody's feelings."

"Those are excellent guidelines in general, Mr. Sharpe," Lady Jane said approvingly.

"Thank you, my lady."

"And since this is on my mind, I would like to invite you both to an event my brother and I are hosting." She shot a quick, meaningful glance toward Miss Grosvenor. Saying, without saying it aloud, that the lady was a prime candidate to be his wife.

The thought left him feeling desolate.

Not because she wasn't charming and pretty and definitely wealthy enough to afford his family's upkeep, but because—because she wasn't who he would choose.

Because he didn't have a choice.

And who would he choose if he did? Perhaps best not to ponder that too long, or he would commit himself to an action he could never undo.

Like undoing her gown. Undoing her passion. Undoing himself as he found pleasure in her.

Wonderful job not pondering, Thomas, he thought ruefully.

"I would love to attend," Miss Grosvenor replied.

Both ladies turned to look at him, waiting for his response. Her with a wry gleam in her eye, as though fully aware that he had no choice—in general, but also in this particular instance—to agree.

"Thank you, my lady, I would love to join you. What kind of event is it?" he asked.

"Oh!" she exclaimed, flinging her hands up in the air. "I didn't even explain!"

"PERCY AND I wanted to invite some of our friends for an evening of entertainment." She twisted her mouth. "Or an afternoon of entertainment." She shook her head. "Anyway. The point is the entertainment, not the timing of it. We're thinking of—well, like a circus." And she lifted her chin as she met his gaze. "I was fortunate enough to see one recently, and it was so delightful, and so few of us are given the freedom to see something like that, not without any number of interfering chaperones and parents and such." She shrugged. "We thought it would allow people to be exposed to things they would not normally come into contact with." She felt her breath catch at her own words—*exposed to things they would not normally come into contact with.* Just what she was hoping for from him.

Only she wanted to be exposed to him, doing things she would not normally be allowed access to.

Just the thought of it was enough to make her body tighten, to make her glance at his mouth, at those gorgeous, full lips that she had kissed in the carriage. Wondering what he could expose her to. What she would reciprocate with.

And his return stare—intense, direct, and passionate—was the kind of look a man would give to a woman. Not the kind of look a brother's best friend would give to the sister. Not the kind of look that indicated that there was a power imbalance, both in gender and in experience.

But a look that said, "I want you, and you want me, and we shouldn't let anything impede our wants."

It made her feel strong. It made her feel as though she was able to make her own choices about her life.

Even though he couldn't.

"That sounds marvelous," Miss Grosvenor replied.

"It does," he said in a low, meaningful tone. She swallowed hard when he didn't look away. His look was a challenge, a challenge she wanted to—that she was going to—accept.

He was hers on loan in their most unusual business proposition. She needed to keep that in mind.

"Percy and I have to decide on a date," she continued. "It will be in about a week."

"What will be in about a week?"

Jane turned at hearing Percy's voice, her lips curling into a smile when she saw her brother.

As usual, he looked as though he had stepped out of the pages of *Romantic Poets Weekly*; his long, dark hair curled over his collar in what most would assume was studied disarray, but what she knew was merely being too distracted to see to his appearance entirely. Likewise, his evening jacket was elegant, but his shirt had a few faint ink stains, meaning he must not have changed beyond tossing on his jacket.

"Our party," Jane replied, tucking Percy's arm into hers. She felt him stiffen as he saw who she was with—clearly, he was still concerned she would be an idiot and fall in love with Mr. Sharpe.

Well, he was right to be concerned, given how much she wished Mr. Sharpe—Thomas—would show her what she had asked him to. Even though she didn't know the specifics of what she had asked.

Which was rather the point of asking him for guidance, wasn't it? If she knew already, she wouldn't need assistance.

"Yes, our party," he echoed. "You will both be able to attend?"

Miss Grosvenor nodded quickly, while Thomas inclined his head in his usual graceful manner.

What would it be like to see him undone? To see him lose that cool elegance because of something he felt. Someone he was feeling something with.

She wished she knew the names of everything she was imagining. Though that knowledge would lead her right back to not needing to be shown, so perhaps she was glad she didn't know.

So he could show her.

So he could be undone by her.

She wanted, no, she *craved* that power. She sensed it was possible—their kiss in the carriage had shown that—and with more instruction, and more time, and just *more*, she knew it was within her grasp.

That *he* was within her grasp.

Though she also had a duty to ensure Miss Grosvenor, or other wealthy unmarried ladies, saw him as unattached and secretly loyal to one of them.

Even though the idea of his marrying made her furious.

Whether it was because he was being forced to, or because it would mean he would be out of reach, she did not care to answer.

But she had promised.

"Miss Grosvenor, would you like to take a stroll about the room?" She dropped Percy's arm and stepped to the younger woman's side, giving her a warm smile, which Miss Grosvenor returned.

"I would, thank you, my lady."

Jane took a deep breath, her mind racing with the thoughts of what she should say and how she should say it.

Thankfully, Miss Grosvenor opened the conversation with the topic on Jane's mind.

"Mr. Sharpe seems very pleasant," the younger woman said hesitantly.

"He is," Jane replied. "Very."

Silence for a few moments. This was not what she had meant to do—agree and then stop talking. How would that possibly convince any young lady Mr. Sharpe was in earnest?

"Mr. Sharpe is so pleasant, in fact," Jane continued, "that he has said he appreciates a particular young lady, but he does not wish to approach her yet because he fears his reputation as somewhat of a rake might prejudice the young lady against him."

"A rake?" Miss Grosvenor replied. "My stepmother alluded to that, but I told her I did not see it. He has been nothing but a gentleman toward me."

Excellent. Terrible. Both.

The two continued walking, Jane giving an occasional smile toward an acquaintance until she spotted Lady Emily and her customary coterie of equally gossipy friends.

"Lady Emily! And Miss Hemingsworth and Lady Thomasina! You are all looking delightful." Jane drew her arm out of Miss Grosvenor's. "Might I have the pleasure of introducing my new friend, Miss Grosvenor? She has just arrived in town."

Lady Emily, as the leader of the group, held her hand out to the other lady, who took it with what seemed to be her usual friendly smile.

"And you are here to see some of Society?" She glanced around, as though fearful of being overheard. "Perhaps capture yourself a husband?"

"Why else does anyone go out?" Miss Hemingsworth cut in, an expression on her face that indicated just how aggravating the task was.

She and Thomas had that in common, then. Though Jane knew Miss Hemingsworth would settle for nothing less than a title, which Thomas did not have.

Thank goodness, Miss Hemingsworth was suitably wealthy, but she did not seem kind. Jane wanted Thomas's eventual wife to at least be someone she liked.

Lady Emily made a *tsk*ing sound, leaning in to

speak directly to Miss Grosvenor. "I see you have made the acquaintance already of Mr. Sharpe. Such a handsome man," she said, as though she was personally responsible for his appearance.

Jane realized she did not like these ladies very much.

But it was the perfect opportunity to spread her rumors. "Yes, I was just telling Miss Grosvenor that"—and she also took a moment to glance around so as to indicate what she was saying was confidential—"that I have heard him say he is quite fond of a certain young lady, but does not want to tell her so. Not yet, not when his reputation is so—so scandalous."

"A little scandal just adds to the allure of capturing such a prize," Lady Emily said, snapping her fan open and waving it frantically in the air. "Alas, I cannot capture him, thanks to Mr. Smythe at home"—her betrothed, whose family estates bordered her own family's—"but the lady who does will be rewarded. Though not financially, of course. It seems he needs a certain amount of money brought to the marriage."

"Oh," Miss Grosvenor replied slowly. "I had wondered why he was still unmarried."

"He's been on the hunt for a couple of years now, but never able to close the deal," Lady Emily said, her tone slightly malicious. "But if he has actually fallen in love with one of the young ladies, as you say—perhaps he has changed his ways." She snapped her fan closed again. "That will be quite interesting to watch."

The assembled ladies all murmured their assent,

and Jane swallowed her defense of Mr. Sharpe, who was, after all, guilty of everything the ladies had said.

But he was also kind and generous and thoughtful. So much more than a pretty face.

THOMAS AND PERCY watched as the ladies walked away, Thomas unable to keep his eyes off her, even though he knew that way lay danger.

"How is your campaign going?" Percy asked. His voice was tight. Thomas would have to reassure his friend that he was not likely to fall in love with his sister.

Even though that would mean lying.

Because if things were able to proceed without impediment, there would be a strong likelihood he would fall in love with Jane.

Her beauty drew him immediately, of course, but it was her kindness, her wit, her clear joy for life that kept him intrigued. If his life were unencumbered, he could very well see himself falling in love with her—even though he would have scoffed at the idea of falling in love with anybody six months ago.

But he could never reveal any of his feelings. Not to her, not to anybody. Barely to himself. If he did, he'd be risking ruining her happiness as well as foreclosing on his own. He wouldn't be that cruel. He'd have to maintain his distance, no matter what was in his heart.

"My campaign is looking brighter," Thomas replied, nodding in the direction Jane and Miss

Grosvenor had taken. "Miss Grosvenor comes from a very wealthy family, and it is an unexpected bonus that she actually seems like a reasonably nice person."

Percy folded his arms over his chest, giving Thomas a suspicious look.

Apparently he wasn't lying well enough. Or Percy was just being cautious, which Thomas had to applaud.

If he had a sister like Jane, he would be wary of any gentleman who spent time with her. She seemed so demure and naive, even though he knew now that she was intent on shedding that demeanor.

But she couldn't shed her appearance, or her status as a woman who was in Society but whose standing was less than it had been, likely attracting unscrupulous men.

Such as Lord Joseph.

He *did* have a sister, of course. Two in fact, though Julia was taken care of.

But Alice—Alice, who was far sharper in mind than a lady was supposed to be. Who was so shy she couldn't bear to be in a crowd of more than four without beginning to shake.

Who would need care for the rest of her life.

"Have you spoken to Miss Grosvenor's father?" Percy asked. "I have seen him at a few of the economics meetings the queen has hosted. He appears to be a genial man."

"It is far too early for that," Thomas replied.

"Why?" Percy spread his hands out wide. "His

daughter is obviously here for one thing, and that one thing is what you need to do, and fast. The sooner you are married—"

The sooner I will stop spending time with your sister. Your motivation is perfectly clear.

"The sooner you can protect your family."

Which was what Percy was doing as well by trying to dislodge his rakish friend from his innocent sister.

"You're right." Thomas swallowed against the sudden tightness in his chest. "I'll make certain Miss Grosvenor knows of my interest, and I will ask her to introduce me to her father."

Percy clapped him on the back. "That's excellent news."

Thomas gave an automatic nod, but his gaze couldn't help but find Jane in the distance. That silver-blond hair gleaming in the candlelight, her simple gown skimming gently over her curves.

How she appeared to be keenly interested in whatever it was Miss Grosvenor was saying, a generous smile on her mouth.

How he wanted to touch her mouth, first with his fingers, then with his lips, and then with his tongue.

Pouring out all the passion he'd lose when he was safely married to a woman he didn't love that he also didn't want to hurt.

Chapter Ten

Jane forced a smile onto her lips.

It was the afternoon after the Carnady party, and she had promised to visit several of the guests, teasing a few of the unmarried ladies with a tidbit about their favorite rake.

Her third stop was the Porter household. Two of the Porter daughters were in Society, the older one a pleasant enough lady with an unfortunate nose and a nervous disposition.

She knew that if Mr. Sharpe married the elder Porter daughter, he would endeavor to soothe her skittishness and make her feel less self-conscious about her appearance. She should be hoping for that outcome, since she did like Miss Porter.

Thomas was a rake, of course, she knew that; but he was also a generous man, which was likely necessary in order to become a rake in the first place.

After all, being selfish wouldn't endear a gentleman, no matter how handsome, to a lady interested in a certain kind of intrigue.

His responsiveness when they kissed, his easing her into everything, ensuring she was comfortable before proceeding—it made her heart melt. And other parts of her body react interestingly as well.

"And Mr. Sharpe, he said specifically he has fallen in love with a particular lady?" Mrs. Porter, the daughters' mother, scooted her chair closer to Jane's, her expression avidly curious.

Jane nodded. "He did not realize I could hear him," she confided. "He and my brother, Percy, are the best of friends, and tell each other everything."

She wondered briefly if Percy had mentioned Daffy to Thomas yet.

"And he was distraught at the thought he might lose the opportunity because it seems many people believe he will be . . ." How should she put this? ". . . convivial after marriage." She accompanied her words with a significant look.

Mrs. Porter glanced dubiously toward her elder daughter. "Do you know who it is?"

Jane shook her head. "No, he did not say." She threw a glance toward Miss Porter, perhaps a wordless indication of who it could be.

Mrs. Porter sighed. "I know Mary finds him irresistible. I have reminded her he has no prospects, and marrying a gentleman who is so charming and handsome could lead to trouble. Especially when—" She gestured toward her elder daughter.

Jane patted Mrs. Porter's arm. "I have become friendly with Mr. Sharpe, and I believe him to be loyal and kind." *Loyal to his family, and kind to anyone who needs his help. Such as me.*

"Well," Mrs. Porter replied, "that is good to hear. One worries about one's daughter, especially when she is—" Again, she gestured toward her daughter, whom Jane was beginning to feel sorry for. Miss Porter wasn't hideous to look at, and she was a good conversationalist if she wasn't beset by anxiety. Jane had spoken at length with her a few months ago about a book they'd both enjoyed. But Mrs. Porter, a mother determined to ensure the best outcome for her children, was likely focused more on the impediments to those outcomes rather than the possibilities.

Which, to be fair, was how most people viewed challenges.

Like her, for example.

She was focused on the reality that he would not allow himself to be with her once he had found someone to rescue him. But if she focused instead on what she would learn and how much she would enjoy it while she was with him, it would be far better. A business proposition, after all.

"Your brother, Mr. Waters," Mrs. Porter said, shaking Jane out of her thoughts. "Is he interested in anybody in particular? Such a handsome gentleman." She sighed.

"Oh, Percy," Jane replied, trying to figure out what to say. She couldn't betray Percy's confidence, especially as he hadn't confided in her in the first place, but she also couldn't outright lie so that a young lady might believe she had a chance with him.

She had to respond enough to placate anybody's suspicions but not so much she raised hopes.

"Percy is very intent on his work at the moment. He is helping our father in his work for the queen."

Mrs. Porter nodded. "Ah, yes, I see. I have not

seen him at many parties lately; that is likely because he is too busy for frivolity."

"Exactly," Jane replied, biting back her chuckle at Percy ever being too busy for frivolity—his excursions with his fellow economists were only the most recent proof of that. Prior, he spent as many evenings with Mr. Sharpe as possible, staying in only when he was too tired from the evening before.

But at least it meant Mrs. Porter wouldn't be actively hunting Percy down for one of her daughters.

"Well," Jane said as she rose, "I must be on my way." Now that she'd done her job and spread the news about Thomas's affections—Mrs. Porter was one of the many mothers who shared news and information about all the eligible bachelors who might propose to their daughters—and Jane had no doubt the information would be common knowledge by this time tomorrow.

"Thank you for coming," Mrs. Porter said, also rising. She took Jane's hand and held it for a moment. "I am relieved to know you yourself are not intrigued by Mr. Sharpe. Or are not searching for a husband?" The last bit was clearly her casting her net for more information, but this time, Jane would not oblige her.

"Yes," she replied vaguely. "Exactly."

Mrs. Porter opened her mouth, a puzzled expression on her face, but Jane removed her hand and walked over to Miss Porter, who had been steadily sliding her chair backward into the wall.

"Good day, Miss Porter," she said. "I am on my way, but I wanted to say hello, and ask if you would like to accompany me to the library some afternoon?"

Because what was the point of choosing her own life if she wasn't going to do things she actually wanted to? Such as spend time with a fellow book lover who was also somewhat quiet at parties?

"That would be wonderful." Miss Porter's face lit up as she replied.

Jane left the Porters, satisfied she'd done what she could to further both of their agendas. Even though the completion of one would mean the cessation of another.

But meanwhile, she would focus on what she could do and learn before it all ended.

Dear Alice,

Thank you for your letter. I am so pleased to hear about your column! I didn't realize you had writing aspirations. My friend's sister is a novelist, although few people know that—he told me one evening when he had had a bit too much to drink. Perhaps you know the author? Percy Wittlesford?

~~Anyway, I find myself wishing more and more I had not taken on this duty. And then despising myself for it.~~ I am getting help in my search for a bride from my friend's other sister. She is spreading word of my growing attachment to a certain young lady—without ever mentioning who the lady is—and she believes that the rumors will spur the ladies and their parents to action.

~~But the only lady I want is her. I crave her warmth, her kindness, her passion. I want to show her what is possible between a man and a woman, and I want to explore everything with her. Not just sex, though that is~~

an allure, but also bizarre entertainments, lively dance halls, traveling circuses, and the joy of locating a hard-to-find book in a pile of dusty tomes.

Please remind Father to walk slowly, and tell Mother she will look lovely in whatever gown she chooses for the wedding.

> *I send you all my love,*
> *Thomas*

THOMAS SEALED THE letter and rose quickly to retrieve his jacket from where he'd left it the previous day. He had had to let his valet go a few months prior, and while he missed having someone take care of his clothing—removing wine stains from sleeves was not his favorite task—he enjoyed being alone.

Though he knew from past experience that if he spent any more time at home, he would likely fall into a morose mood, his mind hunting through alternatives to his plan, as though he hadn't gone through them a thousand times already.

But he did have a reprieve, thanks to winning at Miss Ivy's. He had forwarded most of the money to his father's London bank, but kept some for his immediate expenses. He hadn't had more than a few pennies in his pocket for weeks now, what with having to pay rent and purchase new linen, thanks to the spilled wine.

He felt like King Midas today, and he wanted to do something that wasn't related at all to his heiress hunt, or think about his future.

Twenty minutes later, he was at Percy's door.

It swung open, revealing a flushed Jane holding a bucket, her hair pinned up but disheveled, her gown clearly one not meant for company.

"Oh!" she exclaimed, glancing down in dismay at what she was wearing. "I thought you were Mrs. Charing. She ran out to do an errand, and I told her to take some time for herself." She shrugged. "And I like helping out when I can—I like being busy and useful. Not just a helpless ornament," she said, wrinkling her nose.

Thomas bit back a smile. Her forehead was moist. There was a spot of dirt on her cheek and one on her neck, and he had never seen anyone so delightfully kissable than her at that moment.

"Not Mrs. Charing," he said, executing a bow. "I am here to see if you and Percy would like to go out."

"Go out?" she repeated.

"Mmm, yes," he replied. "Out meaning out of this house, and go is the action one would take to accomplish that."

She poked him in the belly as she rolled her eyes. "I know what it means. I just—I hadn't—"

"Expect the unexpected," he said. "Another lesson for you, since we skipped a day."

Her eyes sparkled. "Expect the unexpected? I think I like that idea," she said, opening the door wide so he could enter.

"Percy!" she called. "We've got a visitor."

Percy stepped out into the hallway from his office, his face more marked than his sister's, but with pen, not dirt.

"I am clearly interrupting," Thomas said, glancing from one to the other. "We can do this anoth—"

"No!" she burst out. "I mean, we could do this another time, but why not now?" She turned to look at her brother. "Percy, Mr. Sharpe just told me to 'expect the unexpected,' and I think not only should we do that, but we should embrace the unexpected."

Percy shrugged. "I always expect the unexpected. It is why Thomas and I are such good friends." He ran his fingers through his hair, creating another streak of pen, this time on his forehead. "What do you wish to do?"

Thomas returned the shrug. "Something that doesn't require our brains, our charm, our appearance, or our money. Or much money," he amended. Since everything cost money.

Stop thinking about that, Thomas, he reminded himself. *You gave yourself one day of freedom, now take it.*

Percy's eyes gleamed. "So we're going drinking?" he asked, his tone clearly answering the question himself. "I'll just—"

"You'll just go wash your face," Jane said, giving Thomas an amused look.

"And you, too," Thomas said, stepping forward to touch the spot on her cheek.

"Oh drat!" she said, dashing up the stairs.

Percy walked more slowly after her, turning halfway up. "We'll be down in ten minutes." He indicated the sitting room where he and Thomas had spent many a late night. "Go in and grab yourself some whisky or something while you wait."

Thomas grinned at his friend. This was going to be a wonderful day.

Chapter Eleven

It was the most wonderful day. And it was barely half over.

Jane had hurried to change, throwing on her least worn day dress, a gown in a color her mother had deemed not suitable for a debutante, so she'd seldom worn it.

It was in a pale blue, definitely not shocking, but also definitely not white, which was the only color, according to Lady Capel, that a young unmarried lady should wear.

Jane had grown to loathe wearing white.

It signified everything wrong about her situation—it indicated that she was available to wed, that she was planning on a future of nothing but agreeing with her spouse and bearing children. Occasionally being allowed to visit a friend for tea.

That was the future that had been in store for her when she was engaged to Mr. McTavish. At the time, she'd wanted that future, because she believed him when he said he loved her.

But his purported love didn't even withstand a

mild scandal, and she was glad she had found out the truth about him before they had married.

The day was warm enough not to need a cloak, and she had taken a few minutes to find a parasol that nearly matched the gown, as well as put in her favorite earrings, a gift from Lavinia.

The three left the house, Mr. Sharpe quickly hailing a hansom, though he refused—once again—to reveal where they were going.

Jane was beginning to realize she liked surprises. Especially when they involved Mr. Sharpe.

Though she really should refer to him as Thomas, if only in her head. They had kissed, after all. His hand had been on her breast. She had made noises she had never made before.

Surely that would indicate a certain amount of familiarity.

"Where are we going, Sharpe?" Percy asked for perhaps the hundredth time.

She didn't think Percy liked surprises.

"Patience," Thomas replied. He shot a quick glance at Jane, his wry smile indicating what he thought of Percy's continual questioning.

Thomas peered out the window of the hansom, leaning back as the carriage slowed. "We are here," he declared.

"Finally," an exasperated Percy said, even though it had been only about ten minutes.

Thomas stepped out first, turning to hold his hand up to help Jane out. She took his fingers in hers, the contact—since neither of them were wearing gloves—sending a shiver up her spine.

He gave her a knowing smile, as though fully aware of how she felt.

Because he felt it, too?

Dear lord, she hoped so.

Percy, still muttering under his breath, got out as well, and the hansom pulled away, leaving them in front of a set of gates that seemed to open into a park.

"We're going to look at flowers?" Percy said in a dubious tone of voice.

"Wait and see," Thomas said, taking Jane's arm and wrapping it around his. She was tucked in snugly against his side, and she felt her breath hitch at the contact.

"Oh!" she gasped, as they went through the gates. Percy was making similar noises behind her.

The gates' structure made it difficult to see inside, but once they had entered, Jane's eyes widened at everything she saw—it was a vast array of pleasures, from a row of vendors selling items such as foodstuffs, flowers, toys, and ribbons, to booths with signs proclaiming their owners' extravagant claims: *Fortunes Read and Guaranteed! High-Flying Acrobatics That Will Dazzle You!*

And one that made Jane's eyes widen. She tightened her hold on Thomas with one hand while pointing with the other. "Look! Over there! Balloon rides!"

He chuckled, looking down at her with what could only be described as a warm expression. "You are daring enough to hop into one of those contraptions?"

Her heart was in her throat at the thought, but what kind of determined adventurer would she be if she wasn't . . . adventurous? "Yes, absolutely," she said firmly.

"I refuse to go up in one of them," Percy said. He was walking on her other side, just as enchanted by what they were seeing. It wasn't a gathering of economics experts, but it was apparently just as enticing.

"What about you?" she asked Thomas, raising her eyebrow in challenge.

His lips twisted slyly. "Are you daring me?"

"I suppose I am," she replied, meeting his gaze. "Are you accepting the dare?"

"Yes, my lady. I am."

Well. She was actually going to do this, wasn't she? Something she didn't know was possible five minutes ago.

And she was going to do it with him.

She smothered a giggle as she realized those same thoughts could be applied to other things she was going to do with him.

"I'll wait for you safely here," Percy said, veering off the path to step up to a vendor selling ale. "Please do not die," he added, sounding only halfway joking.

"We'll try," Jane replied. "Not to die, that is," she added hastily.

Percy grimaced in response.

"Shall we?" Thomas asked, gesturing toward the area where a few balloons were landed. There was a queue, she could see, and there were a few balloons overhead, low enough so she could hear the excited exclamations from the passengers.

"Yes," she said, keeping her voice firm. She was terrified, of course, because she had never done anything like this before, but that was precisely why she should do it.

And she'd get to do it with him.

A bonus: if she was too scared to look down, she could stare at his handsome face.

"Are you satisfied thus far with where I've taken you?"

They were standing about five places back in the line, just behind a large family with several children scrambling about. The mother—a tall Black woman with an elaborate hat and a commanding way of speaking—was able to corral her offspring with just a few words. Her husband, meanwhile, was listening as someone who seemed to be his eldest son explained the mechanics behind ballooning.

"I am." She certainly never would have come to such a place on her own. She appreciated the opportunity to mingle with people who weren't the same fifty or so people—or so it seemed—that she encountered during the Social season. People who kept their distance from her, since she was now a scandal, but not so distant as to offend, since she was still a duchess's sister. It left her in an odd Societal limbo, where she was accepted to a point, but still regarded with some suspicion.

Because if she could refuse to follow along with her mother's plans, perhaps other young ladies would follow her example? Or just that it was outside of what they expected from someone they knew?

Thank goodness none of them suspected what

she was currently up to. She smiled to herself as she looked around at her surroundings.

"The gas is lighter than the air, you see, so when the tethers are undone, the balloon can rise."

"And how does it get back down?" the father asked.

Jane eavesdropped shamelessly as the son continued. "The balloonist releases some of the gas from the balloon, and the weight of it and its passengers help bring it back down."

She leaned forward to speak to the son. "Thank you for explaining—this will be my first time."

"You are welcome," the father said. "My George is very interested in science. He is always dragging us to see the newest technology." His tone indicated just how proud he was of his son, even while seeming to complain.

"My friend is very interested in trying new things herself," Thomas said, nodding toward Jane.

"Have you been to the whale bone exhibit?" George asked them eagerly.

"No, not yet," Jane said. "What is that?"

"They've found a whale skeleton, and you can go inside it and walk around, as though you are actually inside a whale!" the young man replied.

"I've never thought about being inside a whale before," Jane said with a smile.

"Which is the best reason to go, I'd think," Thomas said, glancing down at her. "There are so many things to do that you don't know about, and it is my task to show you."

She felt her breath catch at his words, at his promise that he would fulfill his task.

And that she would fulfill hers, convincing Society that Mr. Sharpe would be a good husband.

But only after he had done everything he'd promised.

THE WAIT FOR the balloon wasn't that terrible, especially once Jane continued her conversation with the family in front of them. The eldest son, George, was a budding scientist, and shared his knowledge of the balloons with enthusiasm, leaving Thomas to watch her face as she listened.

She had the most expressive face he'd ever seen—every emotion she felt was reflected in her smile, her narrowed eyes, her faint wrinkle of her nose. He had long ago learned to hide his feelings behind his smooth facade, and he envied her joy in even the little things in life—meeting new people, for example, or seeing a circus, or sharing a kiss in a carriage.

Though that last wasn't a little thing.

He hadn't stopped thinking about it since it happened, wondering just why it felt so different from all the other kisses he'd shared with other beautiful ladies.

Perhaps because it wasn't an inevitability that they would end up in bed? That the kissing was just a precursor? Or that she was so responsive, so engaged in what she was doing. Likely not thinking about anything but the kiss.

"Mr. Sharpe?" she said, sounding amused. "It is our turn."

"Oh of course," Thomas replied, digging in his pocket for the fee.

"I can take care of this," she said, holding her hand up in a *stop* gesture. "I don't think you would be going up if it weren't for my desire."

"True in more than just this situation," he replied in a low tone, watching as her cheeks turned pink. She took care of the payment, and then they were stepping inside the balloon, the engineer busy with the various ropes and bags that would help their ascent.

"Are you ready?" he asked. He wished he could kiss her now, in fact, kiss the pink in her cheeks before moving to her mouth, which was slightly open with excitement.

"I am," she replied. "I think."

The engineer stopped fussing with things to explain what they'd already heard from George—about the bags of sand, and the releasing of the gas, and that they wouldn't go too high, so the trip would be perfectly safe.

And then they were aloft.

They stood together against the edge of the balloon basket, the engineer on the other side.

They were only a few feet up, and she was already gasping in pleasure at the sights below.

It was remarkable; he'd never thought particularly much about what birds saw, for example, or how one's perspective could change based on where one was in the world.

Though he'd had to face the latter often enough since his father had lost his fortune. But at least this view was better than his own future.

"Look down there!" she exclaimed, pointing. "Percy! He's waving at us."

She waved enthusiastically in reply, so enthusiastically she stumbled. Thomas wrapped his arm around her within seconds, justifying his touch as needing to steady her, even though she was in no danger of falling.

She pressed into his side, looking up at him with a smile. As though she was pleased he was holding her.

The only person who could see them now was the engineer, and it wasn't likely he would pay enough attention to them or gossip about their behavior, so it was safe up here.

"Nobody can see us, Jane," he murmured. "Except for him," he said, nodding toward the engineer. "And he can't hear us." He tightened his grip on her waist. "Do you remember when I mentioned anticipation?" He was playing a dangerous game, he knew that. Not with her, but with himself—his cock was already hardening at the images playing themselves over in his mind, and he knew that whatever happened between them would change him irrevocably. Whether for better or for worse, it wouldn't matter. Because he'd be saying "for better or for worse" to someone else. That was the truth of it.

"Yes," she replied, her tone as low as his.

"And then we kissed. I can't stop thinking about that kiss, Jane." He spread his fingers wide at her waist, his index finger stretching to the underside of her breast. His pinky finger resting on top of her hip. "About sliding my tongue into your mouth. About how you opened for me, and how your fingers gripped my hair. I liked that a lot,

Jane. I liked how you explored. I want you to explore more. Would you like that?"

"Yes." Her tone was strained, and she had melted into his side. She was holding on to the edge of the balloon basket with her left hand, in front of his body, but she released her hold to take his hand, squeezing his fingers.

He edged his fingers up so that they were on top of her breast. The engineer couldn't see what was happening, since he was crouched down at the other end of the basket, and they were facing out. He paused, long enough to allow her to reject his touch if she wanted to.

She didn't want to.

Instead, she gave a soft moan and held his hand tighter. He shifted to put her body more in front of his, which had the benefit of placing his erection right near her arse.

He wondered what she would do if he bit her there. Right on her sweet arse as his fingers played with her soft, wet warmth. Rubbing the tiny bud of her clitoris as he licked his way toward her pussy. Savoring—anticipating—putting his mouth on her, tasting her, bringing her to climax.

Fuck, he was so hard.

"Touch me, Thomas," she urged, pushing herself back against him.

"Do you feel what you do to me, sweet Jane?"

She nodded as his fingers stroked her breast, finding the sharp, taut bud of her nipple beneath the fabric of her gown.

"Are you wet, Jane?" he asked. "Down there, I mean?"

She nodded again, pushing back harder against him. He shook her fingers off his left hand, moving it to the juncture of her thighs. He pressed the heel of his hand into her, and she made a strangled noise of pleasure. He could feel how tightly drawn her body was, as though concentrating entirely on what he was doing.

He wished he could yank up the skirts of her gown and sink his fingers into her, but the engineer would most definitely notice if there was skirt yanking. He'd have to work outside of her clothing. A challenge, but not impossible.

He ran his fingers around the shape of her, his mind's eye figuring out where every part of her was, sliding his fingers up and down her mound, pressing his hand into her.

"Do you like that, Jane?" he asked, speaking softly into her ear.

"Mmm-hmm."

His cock was so hard as to be painful, and he pressed against her, finding a tiny amount of relief at the contact of her arse and his penis.

"I am going to make you fly, Jane. More than you are already. Do you want that?"

"Yes, please," she said.

"Tell me."

"I want you to make me fly," she said, emphasizing her words with her shifting back harder against him. She learned quickly. "I want you—"

"I want you to make me come," he supplied.

"I want you to make me come. No," she said, making his heart stop for a moment. "No, I demand that you make me come."

He growled at her words, stroking her in a strong rhythm as he listened and felt her reaction—what she liked best, where she responded. He could feel her body stiffen, hear her soft moans, until she gasped and her breath caught and he knew she was climaxing, could tell by how her body shook and how tightly she was gripping the edge of the balloon.

"Oh my," she said, when she had stopped shaking.

"That was beautiful," he said. "You are beautiful. I wish I could have seen your face as you came."

"Oh my," she said again. Her breathing was ragged.

"Do you like flying?" he asked, shifting slightly away from her. He could feel that the balloon was descending, and he wanted to make sure they looked nearly appropriate when they reached the ground. That meant he'd have to think about some of Percy's economic theorems, or recall what the young man had said about balloons and gas and how it all worked.

Not about how responsive she was, and how much he wanted to break her apart again.

"I do," she replied, twisting her head to look at him. She wore a satisfied expression, one more knowing than he'd seen on her face before. Because he was teaching her, instructing her just what pleasure could be had, even through layers of clothing and a random man doing scientific-type things behind them.

What could he do if they were alone?

The balloon bumped the ground as they landed, jostling them together. He steadied her, wrapping his arms around her back and holding on to the edge of the basket so she was effectively trapped in his arms.

"Thank you," she said in a soft, low voice. She met his gaze again, smiling as though she was a cat who had just had all the cream. "That was most instructive."

"It was." And for him as well—he hadn't known he would want, so desperately, to make a woman climax until her. He did it, of course, because he was an unselfish lover, but it had never felt like such a need before.

He needed her.

Which was the last thing he needed, honestly. He'd have to make certain she didn't know anything about his deepening feelings—he owed it to her to keep his distance so her future wouldn't be tainted like his.

The engineer swung the door to the balloon open, and Thomas stepped out, wishing they could have just flown up into the clouds and never come back.

But he always had to come down to earth, didn't he.

It was all worth it, though. To bring her that pleasure now was worth every moment of agony at knowing her pleasure wasn't his future.

Chapter Twelve

*J*ane stepped out of the basket of the balloon, wobbling a little as her feet made contact with the ground.

Everything she looked at seemed just a bit brighter, as though she was seeing everything through a Mr. Thomas Sharpe–visioned lens. She had never felt anything like what she had just felt before—not even a hint of it—and to experience it while up in the sky over London was quite possibly the most exhilarating, ludicrous thing she'd ever heard of. If Lavinia wrote it in a book nobody would believe it.

Then again, Lavinia couldn't write precisely that in a book because she did not write those kinds of books—the kind where people did things that were normally not done, much less spoken or written about.

"How was it?"

Percy joined them as Mr. Sharpe—Thomas, for God's sake, she'd experienced a shattering climax under his fingers—guided her to a small open area just outside where a row of booths offered a variety of experiences—bearded ladies, strong men, and at least two mesmerists. There was one empty chair, and she sat abruptly, while Percy and Thomas flanked her on either side.

"It was—" she began, not certain how to say it. Or honestly how to speak more than a few words at the moment.

"It was wonderful. Wasn't it?" he asked, shooting her a sly grin. Taunting her.

Of course it was the best possible way to snap her out of her post-bliss reverie, which he had to have known, but it was also so much him to sneakily refer to something between them that nobody could know about.

Like a secret language only they knew. But not, she assured herself sternly, the language of love.

"It was wonderful. Though far too short," she added, sending him a pointed glance.

There. That was satisfying. As was—damn it, at this rate she'd never think of anything else.

But she could be forgiven for losing herself in it for just a moment, couldn't she? It was, after all, the first time.

"I believe that Lady Jane will find that such experiences only seem short because of how much one is enjoying them," Thomas replied, his lips curled in a smirk.

She had thrown down the gauntlet, and he was picking it up and tossing it in the air.

"I enjoyed having two ales while you were up there floating amongst the clouds, so perhaps you have a point there," Percy said.

"You drink quickly," Jane retorted.

"I do! And I find I am parched yet again," Percy replied with a winsome smile. The smile that always made Jane's mother, the Countess of Scudamore, melt. Jane had to admit it had nearly the same effect on her. "Shall we?" he said, gesturing toward the collection of food vendors.

"I believe we shall. Lady Jane is always open to new experiences. Aren't you, my lady?" Thomas asked, holding his hand out to help her rise out of her chair.

She met his gaze as she stood. "New experiences can be rewarding. But it is crucial that everyone is allowed to share the experience." She lifted one eyebrow, then dragged her gaze down his form and back up again. Feeling incredibly, remarkably powerful and brave to taunt the lion in his lair, so to speak.

His eyes had widened, and he appeared—for just a moment—to have lost the power of speech. *Bravo, Jane,* she cheered.

"If there is an opportunity," he began.

"Could you two stop jabbering?" Percy asked, glancing between them. "It sounds suspiciously like flirting, but I know you're not doing that." He accompanied his words with a sarcastic roll of his eyes.

"Of course, friend," Thomas said smoothly. "Your sister and I were just examining the ramifications of trying new things."

"Whatever." Percy spoke in an exasperated tone. "I came here to find pleasure, not to listen to you two discuss whatever it is you're discussing."

"That is why I came also," Jane said, giving

Thomas a significant look. Holding her breath at just how bold she was being.

Was this actually Lady Jane the Naive? The one speaking in coded language to the man she might almost say was her lover, if there was love involved?

There is not love involved, she remarked sternly to herself. Though she did like him a lot, even when he was teasing her.

"Well, then, the ale is waiting," Percy replied, marching across to the vendors, Jane and Thomas trailing behind.

HAD HE JUST brought Lady Jane to climax while hovering above London in a hot air balloon?

Apparently he did still engage in some risky behavior—what if someone had seen? What if Percy had figured out that something more than air travel was happening while he was watching from below?

But it was entirely worth it. Her gasps, her body responding to his touch, her playful teasing after—each one of the actions alone would have been enough to encourage him. But put all together, they were intoxicating. He couldn't wait to do it again.

And, judging by her reaction, she likely couldn't either.

The trick would be to figure out what to do that would satisfy her desire and his need to maintain some semblance of distance. Although that concept was laughable, given what he'd just done.

But it was just sex. Just pleasure shared with one another.

Keep telling yourself that, Sharpe, a voice said inside his head.

It doesn't matter what I feel about it, another voice retorted. *Because she can never fall in love with me, nor can she know how I feel about her. That my feelings might be starting to go beyond a mutual exchange of favors to something more.*

That was why it was good to spar with her—to keep her at a distance, albeit a playful distance. So she would not take any of this seriously.

"Ale for you, Sharpe?" Percy asked. "And—Jane, do you want lemonade? Or an ice?"

"Ale," Jane replied firmly.

Percy looked as though he wished to argue with her, but wisely kept his mouth shut. Thomas knew firsthand the lady would not be thwarted when it came to her enjoyment of things. And people.

"Three ales, please," Percy said.

They took their beverages to sit in a communal area, mismatched wooden tables and chairs providing seating for the various vendors' customers.

The sun was now straight overhead, and was warmer than Thomas was accustomed to—while he did go outside during the daytime, it wasn't a habit. It felt strangely pleasant, as though the sun was sinking into his bones and invigorating him.

Or perhaps it was just her.

"We'll be sending the invitations to our event out soon," Jane said, taking a swallow of her beer. It left a foam mustache behind, and Thomas tried not to laugh.

But failed.

"You've—you've got something there," he said, gesturing to her face.

She scowled as she took a handkerchief from her pocket and wiped it away. "Better?" she asked as she held herself still. Even now, even after knowing her for as long as he had, he was still struck by her appearance. She looked as though she could have stepped out of a Renaissance painting, the dramatic blue of her eyes contrasting with her pale, silvery hair.

Beautiful. "Yes, you've got it," Thomas replied.

"We've compiled a list of possible ladies for you," she continued. "And I've added some that are probably not on your list, but are too often left out of such events." She spoke fiercely, clearly championing those young women not fortunate enough to be the most desired at a gathering.

Unlike her.

"I'm going to invite some of my economic acquaintances as well." Percy shrugged, as though it wasn't a shocking thing to mingle actual working people with an aristocratic group. Though he was a working person and an aristocrat, albeit an illegitimate one. So it made a certain amount of sense.

"The temerity," Jane said, speaking in a mocking tone. "To think that young people of any class might want to come together to enjoy simple entertainment."

"You are quite a radical thinker, Lady Jane." Thomas raised his glass to her before taking a deep swallow.

Her expression lit up, and he wondered what he'd accidentally said.

"I was thinking about that," she said excitedly. "I mentioned it to Lavinia, in fact, just the other day."

"Thinking about what?"

"About working." She spread her hands out to indicate all three of them. "Percy works."

"I have to," he muttered.

"But you like it," she retorted. "You can't deny that."

Percy nodded.

"And I am thinking about trying to find an occupation myself. Something that will be useful to myself and others." Her expression turned rueful. "It is not as though standing around being decorative is precisely *work*."

"You mean what I do?" Thomas asked, feeling oddly defensive.

"You are doing it for a good cause." She glanced away from him, up toward where the hot air balloon was taking another group of adventurers. "I want to do something that would be for a good cause also. Not a cause where I end up supporting a husband in his work either." She straightened in resolve. "I've seen what that gets you, and it is not satisfactory. To me, at least."

"Be careful, Jane," Percy warned as he finished his ale, "if anyone hears you they'll suspect you're trying to foment a revolution."

She grimaced. "If wanting to do something useful is revolutionary, then yes, I am a revolutionary." She raised an eyebrow. "Even though that is the last thing anyone would say about me. Dutiful, polite, quiet, agreeable . . ." she began, sounding as though she was condemning herself with her words.

"Adventurous, spirited, and stubborn," Thomas rejoined.

"Not to mention bossy," Percy added.

She glanced between them, a clear expression of surprise on her face. "Do you really think so?"

"Absolutely."

"Yes."

Thomas and Percy spoke in unison.

"Well!" she exclaimed. "That is excellent to hear."

"It shouldn't be a surprise to you," Percy said. "A nonrevolutionary person would not have rejected her mother's plans, instead shockingly setting up her own establishment with her scandalously born brother."

"Nor would she want to go up in a hot air balloon. Or visit a dance hall to see a traveling circus." Thomas finished his glass, then rose. "Can I get us another round?"

"Oh, let me," she said, standing also.

He opened his mouth to tell her he could damn well afford to get them a few ales when she spoke again. "I have never had the opportunity to purchase ales at a fair. Let me add to my experiences." Her cheeks flushed as she met his gaze, and he knew she was recalling the other experiences she'd added recently.

He wanted to give her so many more. Even though *that* was the thing he could least afford.

"I'll help you," Percy said as Thomas sat back down. Keenly aware that this was a temporary respite from what was certain to be the unsatisfactory trajectory of his life—bartering his appearance and his standing in Society for the knowledge his family would survive.

Something he was willing to do, but that didn't mean he had to like it.

There were things, however, in his immediate future that he did like. Very much.

"Percy," Jane said as they walked toward the ale seller's stand, "do you really think I am all those things?"

"You're definitely bossy," he replied in a teasing tone. He put his hand on her arm to stop her walking. "But yes," he continued in a softer voice, "I do. I know that the past few years have been difficult, and perhaps you needed time to decide things for yourself. But you do seem different. Even though I will still be a protective brother."

"I promised I wouldn't fall in love with him," she reminded him, knowing she might be lying to both of them now, "and I just need you to trust that I won't do anything that will put myself in danger." That she knew was not a lie—she was apparently adventurous, but she was not foolhardy. She would never do something she thought might be risky.

Which meant she should try very hard not to fall in love with him—she knew there could be no happy ending, despite how Lavinia might write it. This was reality, not fiction. He needed to marry to save his family, and she needed . . . not to marry him so she could save herself. Not that he would be the problem, per se; just that she didn't think she could

trust that she would keep herself independent—
"bossy," according to her brother—if she was de-
pendent on a husband.

He released her arm, and they continued to walk
as she thought.

"Percy," she began abruptly as they reached the
stall, "what do you think happiness looks like?"

He signaled to the server for two ales, then
turned to look at her. His handsome face was set
in a serious expression. "Do you think I have any
idea?" He glanced away from her, a whirl of emotions playing across his face—longing, regret, and
a tiny bit of hope. "I thought when I was younger
that if I just made myself pleasant to everyone,
and tried not to cause any trouble that eventually
I would be happy. Mostly because nobody would
be actively cruel." He met her gaze again. "Your
mother made certain of that."

"You do have a champion there," Jane agreed.

"But then I realized that the lack of cruelty and
of sadness didn't necessarily mean a person was
happy. Happiness might be something a person
has to hunt down and capture for themselves."

"No matter what the cost?" she said gently.

The truth shone in his eyes as he nodded slowly.
"Yes. No matter what the cost."

His hand rested on the bar, and she put hers on
top of his, squeezing it in sympathy. "So does that
mean I have your permission to hunt my happiness down?" It was an involuntary response to
glance over toward Thomas, who had tilted his
face up to the sun, his eyes closed. Looking like a
resplendent Greek god.

His eyes followed her gaze as he took a deep breath. "I suppose it would be hypocritical to deny you what I hope to find for myself. No matter how unsuitable both of our choices are." Now his voice held a lighter tone, which she was gratified to hear—a somber Percy was not something she was accustomed to, nor did she like it.

"Which means you are inviting Daffy to our event?"

He exhaled. "Yes. I suppose it does."

She shared a smile with him before he spoke again. "But all this," he said, gesturing between them, "still does not mean you should go and fall in love with him. You know what he is honor bound to do, even though that course of action wasn't for you."

"If I had to choose between marrying someone I didn't love and jeopardizing my family? I hope I'd make the same choice."

And she did. His course of action wasn't necessarily honorable—women had been marrying men to keep themselves in food and clothing for centuries, after all—it wasn't viewed as a sacrifice when they did it, just a necessity of life—but he did have the choice, given that he was a man and could presumably choose any kind of wife he wanted.

But it did matter that he was making the choice to sacrifice his future happiness to ensure his family's. Which meant . . . if they could share happiness together for a short time, wasn't that better than no happiness at all?

Which meant she should ensure he get some pleasure—some happiness—out of their arrangement as well. She presumed it was somewhat pleasurable to escort her to various places, take her up in hot air balloons and . . . well.

But that wasn't enough; she wanted to give him the same kind of intense feeling he had given her in that hot air balloon. When he had kissed her in the carriage, truly kissed her, so she felt tingles throughout her whole body and wanted more.

She wanted more. With him.

And there was nothing preventing her from getting it.

Except the requirement that they parted from one another no more hurt than before they had met. Which meant no love. No feeling beyond a warm kindness.

Just a friendship that was far more than friendship, and shared experiences that would teach both of them.

Chapter Thirteen

$\mathcal{T}$homas hadn't expected to have as good a time as he had. He certainly hadn't had as good a time as *she* had—she was up on the pleasure count by one orgasm—but he had thoroughly enjoyed himself, forgetting for a few hours all the worries that usually dogged him when he was awake.

Her enjoyment of everything, not just that, was infectious. And he found he liked sparring with her, teasing Percy about his love of ale, or daring his friend to have his palm read by a fortune teller.

The day passed quickly, and all too soon he was back in his rooms, the feeling of joy, of conviviality, being slowly replaced by his ever-present feeling of dread.

He'd arranged to meet with her the next day, at their house, to go over the guest list for the event she and Percy were going to host—part party, part exhibition, all a ruse to endear him to as many single wealthy ladies as would fit in Mr. Archer's hall.

The money he'd held back from his winnings still jingled in his pocket, and he was tempted to go risk it in search of another windfall, but he knew that would be foolish. Luck, as Octavia was fond of saying, did not favor the unlucky. And he and his family had proven themselves to be unlucky, given his father's bad fortune.

Of course, that was balanced out by the luck of his possessing a handsome face, but that was a fortune he begrudged, even though he knew it was ludicrous. To be upset that one was profoundly attractive was as ridiculous as wishing one didn't have so much money, because it was difficult to keep track of.

He shook his head as he began to shrug out of his jacket, catching a glimpse of himself in the glass. "You're preposterous," he said. He didn't need to hear her saying it—he could say it himself. Though he liked it when she called him on things—such as when he was being presumptive, or judging without knowing all the details.

He liked her.

"You can't fall in love with her," he reminded himself. His fingers slid the buttons out of their holes, then he yanked his shirt out from his trousers and over his head before carefully folding it and placing it on his chair. Long gone were the days when he could undress with impunity; now he was the only one who took care of his clothing, and he needed to ensure he was always carefully and spotlessly dressed.

Next were his boots, followed by his trousers, until at last he stood naked in his room, all of his clothes placed neatly where he could examine them later for possible stains and repairs.

He slid under the cool sheets, leaning over to

blow the candle by his bedside out. He should go to sleep, but his mind whirled with images of the day—Percy enjoying his ale, the three of them bantering as they walked through the crowd.

The two of them in the hot air balloon, his fingers sliding over the cloth of her gown to find her soft mound. His fingers rubbing her skillfully until she came apart.

Goddamn it.

He got out of bed again, his hand reaching to grasp his cock, which was starting to harden. Would this be one of the things she'd want to be taught?

If she even knew a gentleman could reach pleasure with a hand as a woman could.

"Hold on," he murmured, feeling only slightly ridiculous. But talking out loud made it seem like she might be in the room, and he'd want to practice what to say before attempting it.

He'd never had to teach a woman how to stroke him before. His previous partners were always experienced, since he wouldn't have risked a sexual encounter with someone who didn't know the rules. Didn't know that this was all just playing.

She had established the rules by asking him for his help in the first place. He couldn't risk it all—he would not put either one of them in that position—but he could skate as close to that edge as possible.

"There," he said, sliding his hand up and down his shaft. He was fully erect now, thinking about how engaged she'd be, how her expression would shift with every new discovery. As though he was a treat she couldn't wait to explore.

Goddamn it, but he wanted her to explore him.

She'd laid waste to his earlier promise to hold back as soon as she responded so avidly to his kiss. Had pressed herself close to him, moaned in the back of her throat as he'd kissed her deeply and passionately.

"Stroke it, Jane," he said, closing his eyes as he imagined her hand on him—her fingers just barely able to wrap around his thickness, her palm sliding on his flesh, gripping the top of his cock before going back down again. "Just like that." He twisted his grip and shuddered, the sweet ache of it growing as he held back, imagining her touching him, her hair unbound and falling down her back, her face flushed, her eyes sparkling with interest and desire.

He placed his other hand on the pillar of his bed, leaning against it as his rhythm increased and intensified, his fist squeezing almost painfully around his penis. Faster, and harder, and tighter, and through it all he thought about her, and how she sounded as she came, and how quickly she would learn what undid him until—"Aagh," he groaned as the climax hit him, spread through his body like a ravaging storm, his breaths coming fast as his hand tightened even more, the orgasm pulsing as he spent.

His chest was heaving, and he collapsed onto the bed on his back, his eyes closed, allowing the rush of feelings to flood him. He usually kept most emotions at bay—he couldn't afford emotions, both literally and figuratively, but tonight he would allow himself this fantasy. This fantasy that might become reality, but would then be taken away as swiftly as it was given. His purpose was the same, after all, regardless of who he thought about as he pleasured himself.

But that truth could wait until tomorrow.

He crawled back under the covers, wishing she were lying next to him, her warm body curled up against his. Knowing it would have to be someone else. Eventually.

"I'LL TAKE THE biscuits up if you can put them on a plate," Jane said to Cook, who gave a curt nod.

Jane had barely been able to sleep the night before, the images of everything that had happened that day—everything she had felt—flooding her senses. But she didn't feel tired; on the contrary, she felt as though she'd been electrified, as though something was powering her from the inside. Like lightning, or a coal-burning furnace, or a rotating windmill.

Thomas said he'd be by at teatime, and she'd spent the morning cleaning the shared rooms and had gotten underfoot in the kitchen until Cook had exasperatedly told her to go away. She'd been back, however, to check in on how the biscuits were doing, sneaking a too-hot one just out of the oven and burning her mouth.

"Serves you right," Cook muttered.

Jane wrapped her arms around Cook, laying her head on her shoulder. "But if they weren't so delicious I wouldn't have been tempted," she said.

"Get away with you. Take those up if you're going to." Cook—whose name was Mrs. Singh—often scolded both her and Percy, but she was loyal to a fault, since Percy had hired her on the spot as she arrived on a boat from India. She'd cooked for an English family over there, but had been left with nothing when the gentleman of the family had gotten transferred unexpectedly.

Instead of searching for a position there, Mrs. Singh had taken her savings and headed to London, which was where her daughter lived, having married a clerk working in India a few years earlier.

Percy had met her ship as it docked, having become acquainted with Mrs. Singh's daughter through her husband, who was another of Her Majesty's workers. It would have been difficult for her to find work, since she had no references and most aristocratic homes preferred their cooks to be male and French for some reason. Jane strongly suspected a reverse sense of snobbery and a dash of patriarchy, but she didn't think that deeply about it, since Cook had fit into their odd household so well.

And her biscuits were glorious—Jane snuck another into her mouth as she walked up the stairs to the main floor.

"I'll bring the tea in when Mr. Sharpe arrives," Mrs. Charing said as she took the plate from Jane. "You should go change, it's nearly time."

"Oh!" Jane exclaimed, glancing down. She was wearing a worn day gown, but of course she wanted to look as good as she could when Thomas arrived. "Thank you, Mrs. Charing, I'll be only a few minutes." She scampered upstairs, quickly choosing a gown that was less worn than the one she was wearing.

She heard the knock at the door as she was finishing dressing, followed by Thomas's low rumble as Mrs. Charing let him into the house.

"There you are," she said, feeling her face flush as she saw him. He'd handed his hat to Mrs. Charing, and stood at the foot of the stairs looking up at her.

"Here I am," he replied in an amused tone of voice. "Just as I said I would be."

She rolled her eyes as she walked downstairs. "It is customary," she said reprovingly, "to make some sort of remark to a guest when he arrives at one's home. Such as 'welcome,' or 'so good to see you,' or 'there you are.'"

By this time she had reached the downstairs, and now stood face-to-face with him. Mrs. Charing had wisely retreated.

"It is very good to see you," he said, his gaze drifting down her body. She felt his look like a physical caress, and shivered in response. "Very good." He paused. "And there you are," he added in a low voice.

Her mouth felt dry, and she licked her lips, which made him focus there. The look in his eyes was hungry, and she wanted to feed him.

But not out in the foyer.

Nor did she want the tea and biscuits she'd worked so hard to obtain. She wanted something else entirely.

"I've been working on the lists upstairs, if you care to join me?" She didn't wait for his reply, but turned and walked back up, conscious that if he followed—when he followed—he'd be eye level with her arse.

Not something she'd thought before, certainly not with a teasing anticipation, but she was on the hunt for new experiences, wasn't she?

She smiled to herself as she heard his step behind her, heard him mutter a soft oath deep in his throat.

"Are you sure we should be going—where are we going, anyway?"

She paused on the stairs, turning to face him. "Anticipation, Mr. Sharpe. Wasn't that your first lesson?" She gave him a wickedly knowing smile—at least, she hoped it was wickedly knowing—and turned back around, hastening up the final few steps, then to the left toward her bedroom.

He growled as he followed her, and she felt her heart leap in, yes, anticipation.

SHE WAS A temptress.

She knew full well what she was doing, and how he would react to it. He kicked the door shut behind them, placing them alone in her bedroom. Which would be entirely scandalous if anyone discovered it, and if her reputation wasn't already sullied by her living situation.

She turned toward him, her hands on her hips, her gaze now traveling as lazily up and down his body as his had on hers in the foyer.

He spread his arms out and turned slowly in a circle. "Do you like what you see?" he asked.

"I do. But you don't need me to tell you how gorgeous you are. You've been telling yourself that for years, haven't you?" Her lips curled into a smirk.

"I have, I will admit," Thomas said, giving her a mocking bow. "But it is so much better when a lady such as yourself says it."

"And what kind of lady am I?" She spoke in a challenging tone.

"The kind," he said, "who isn't afraid to ask for what she wants." He gestured to himself as she smiled in response. "The kind who wants to be useful, who refuses to follow the path set out for her." His tone softened. "The kind who rushes to offer help to someone even though most would say he didn't need it."

"Thank you." She picked up a sheet of paper from her desk, which was to the left of where they stood. Her bed was on his right, while an enormous armoire was in back of her against the third wall.

He had been looking at her too intently to notice much about the room, but now that he had a chance to look around, he could see how she had made it her own—a collection of Percy Wittlesford books were on a shelf over the desk, their spines well-worn, while a silver brush and comb rested on a tray on top of the desk, as though it served as both workspace and beauty space.

Of course for both of them, their beauty was their work.

"Before we begin," he said as the thought struck him, "do you suppose I could be useful?"

She frowned in confusion. "Useful? How?"

"That's just what I mean. You are planning on doing something useful—I wonder if I could. Besides educate young ladies in the pursuit of pleasure," he added slyly.

Her cheeks flushed. "If you could manage to make a living out of that I am certain you would do very well."

But he didn't want to do any of that with anyone but her.

Not that he could let any of his feelings for her slip—he couldn't entangle her in his messy emotions, just because they'd decided to emerge at the worst possible time.

And he couldn't say precisely what they were in the first place. Just that he wished they had more time together, even though having more time together would mean that his family would suffer for longer.

So he couldn't wish for that.

He had to forget all of this, forget how her smile made his breathing relax, how talking with her made him feel alive in a way he only did late at night with Percy.

And Percy didn't make him feel all the other things he felt with her, that was for certain.

"You know," she said, tapping her index finger on her mouth, "I had forgotten, but I was talking to Lavinia about this a few days ago."

He blinked in surprise. "About me charging fees for my . . . service?"

She huffed out an annoyed breath. "No, not that. You're ridiculous. Tell me what you were thinking of."

"Well, I haven't been thinking all that much about it, to be honest," he admitted. He sat on the edge of her bed, and after a moment, she joined him. "But you got me wondering if there was something that would allow me to provide for my family without having to barter my freedom?"

"How much do they need?" she asked.

He was relieved she hadn't laughed at him. At the thought that someone who was him, who'd only been a useful ornament in Society, would want to be useful in a different capacity.

"More than I can likely earn, I suspect." He exhaled. "The positions that pay well enough require training, and I don't have the funds for that, nor does my family have the time." He should have thought about all this two years ago. But two years ago he would have scoffed at the idea that he would still have not captured his heiress. Two years ago he would have been happy to eschew love for commerce.

Now that he was two years older, and what felt like decades wiser, he knew he valued himself—himself, not his appearance—too much to want to compromise.

But he wouldn't put his own wishes, his own values, ahead of saving his family. And perhaps it didn't matter he hadn't thought of it before—perhaps there was nothing he could do beyond look elegant at social gatherings.

Be charming at parties.

Dance with young ladies of varying heights and weights.

"I have no skills," he said at last, collapsing onto the bed.

"Don't give up," she admonished. She lay down beside him, glancing over with an encouraging smile. "You are charming and people always want you at their parties." Just what he'd been saying to himself.

"Nobody will pay me to go to parties, Jane," he remarked dryly.

"No," she said, nudging him with her shoulder, "but you could use your charm to persuade people to do things." Both of them were silent. "Like be a diplomat or something?"

It was so odd to be here, he mused, discussing his employment prospects as though they weren't companions in a hunt for pleasure—or him her guide, if he was being accurate. Though he suspected she would show him a few things eventually.

He felt more relaxed now, alone with her, than he had in a long time. Even when he was with Percy, he was usually on his guard because Percy was often unguarded, and Thomas didn't want to see his friend taken advantage of. Or worse.

"Those positions normally go to gentlemen from influential families," he said. "My family lost its influence the same moment we lost our wealth." He gave a rueful snort. "Odd how it always seems to work out that way."

"Just as all those gentlemen who insisted they were besotted with me scampered as soon as my mother cut off my dowry," she replied in amusement. "I'm grateful to them all, honestly. It showed me what value I truly have."

He pushed himself up on his elbows to look at her. "You mean nobody has offered marriage since then?"

She waved her hand in the air. "A few, to their credit. But they implied I should be grateful to them for having me, despite my scandal and lack of money." She paused. "When I marry. If I marry, I will only marry because I actually want to."

"Ouch," he replied, leaning back onto the bed.

"Which is why you should investigate as many possibilities that aren't selling yourself to the highest bidder," she pointed out.

"If anyone bids," he said ruefully.

She nudged him again. "Don't be foolish. Of course they'll bid. Just look at you!" She turned on her side to set her words to action.

He did the same so they were lying on their sides facing one another. He reached forward to slide his hand on her cheek, then moved it to cup her neck. He paused, feeling the pleasant tension build inside, hoping she was feeling the same.

Her gaze was on his mouth, and she licked her lips, exhaling a soft breath that he felt on his skin. Then she leaned forward and pressed her mouth to his, wrapping her arm around him so her hand was at the small of his back.

And they were kissing. Frantically, urgently, passionately. Their mouths locked together, tongues exploring and licking and tasting.

Making him forget everything but what was right here right now.

Her. Him. *Them.*

Chapter Fourteen

Jane felt a low curling of heat in her belly as they kissed. Her hand clutched his back; her mouth opened to his; her breasts felt tight and heavy.

As though he was reading her mind, his palm came over her breast, kneading the soft flesh, making the low warmth burn hotter.

That part of her he'd touched in the balloon tingled, aching, and she unconsciously shifted closer to him, her fingers tightening their grip on him, splayed out over his back. She got what she thought was an incredible idea, and tugged at his shirt so it wasn't tucked into his trousers anymore, sliding her hand under the fabric to touch his skin.

The contact made her gasp, and the breath caught in her throat.

"Yes, Jane," he urged, his lips kissing her jaw, her neck, licking at where her pulse beat. "Touch me. Anywhere you want, sweetheart. Please." That last word broke hoarsely, and she felt the power of it, felt how desperately he wanted it.

Well, she wanted it, too.

Slowly, her hand went up his back, sliding along

his smooth skin, then back down to his waist, the heel of her hand catching on his hip bones. So different from her; he was all muscles and ridges and bone, and she was made of soft roundness. She liked the contrast, liked both of their shapes. They'd fit together like two parts searching for their mates, his hardness pressing into her softness, his power melding into her passion.

"Please," he said again, his mouth now at the neckline of her gown, his fingers tucked underneath the fabric. Her nipples strained hard against her gown, and she ached for him to touch her, so she knew how strongly he felt. She wanted his hands everywhere, all over her, without regard to propriety or what was done or who did it.

She wanted.

She stretched her fingers long across his lower belly, and she could hear his breathing get faster, a groan strangled in his throat.

She held her breath as her palm made contact with him there, the matching place where she burned, and he grunted his pleasure as her fingers outlined the shape of him through his trousers.

"Does it work the same as it did with me?" she asked, wishing she weren't so ignorant, but knowing she wouldn't be here with him if she weren't so ignorant in the first place.

He laughed against her skin. "Somewhat. I need a different kind of touch, but the theory is the same." He drew back for a moment, meeting her gaze. "Can you undo your gown? Or let me undo your gown? I need to taste you."

The sheer, primal desire in his gaze made her

shudder, and she gave a quick nod, twisting so his fingers could reach the back of her gown.

Of course he was as adept at undressing her as he was at everything else, and soon her gown was down her shoulders and at her waist, leaving her in her chemise from the waist up.

The blue of his eyes seemed to crackle with intensity as he stared at her. At her breasts. She knew the chemise was made of thin fabric—he could see her nipples, see how they were taut, aching points. She bit her lip as she shifted, wanting the ache to go away, but never wanting it to be assuaged—never wanting him to stop looking at her like that, at anticipating how he would touch her and where.

Anticipation, she thought, and smiled.

"What is it?" he asked. His voice was gruff and ragged. Not at all the smooth, silky tones of Mr. Thomas Sharpe, beloved Society fixture.

This was only Thomas, him of the rough desire and fierce urgency, the one whose gaze crackled hot, but his hands were gentle, never giving her more than what she wanted. What she needed.

"Anticipation," she answered. Her own voice was soft and breathy.

His gaze narrowed and she felt her whole body tingle at his expression. Like he was a lion about to pounce. But not on his prey; on his lioness, a creature as strong and powerful as he was.

"What are you anticipating, Jane?"

His hand was back on her breast, caressing its fulness. "Are you thinking about my fingers finding your nipple, stroking it?"

She shivered.

"Or perhaps you want my mouth on your breast, sucking it into my mouth, licking your nipple as my fingers find somewhere else to touch?"

"Oh," she moaned. That place between her legs ached—for him to touch her, for anything that would ease the delicious pain she felt there.

"Do you want me to touch you as I did in the balloon?"

His hand left her breast and traveled down her body, dragging the skirts of her gown up, his fingers now on the bare skin of her leg, now on her thigh, and then—

"Ahh!" she cried out as his fingers touched her there.

"You like that." It wasn't a question.

"Mmm," she moaned.

"You're this wet for me, Jane. For me." His voice was roughly proud, and she met his gaze as she nodded assent.

"I can feel how slick you are." He was touching her there, where it ached the most, and then another finger slid into her, and she gasped at the sensation. "So tight, Jane."

"Is—is that good?" she asked.

He shrugged. "If it feels good for you, it's good. That's the only rule. There are no judgments in bed, Jane. Just two people doing what feels good together."

Just two people doing what feels good together. The simplicity of it, the elegance of such a short statement, took her breath away. As though he hadn't just done that already.

"How can I make you feel good?" she asked.

He chuckled as his fingers worked their magic, and she nearly forgot her own question. "I feel good when I make you come, Jane. Like I did in the balloon."

"Oh," she said on a sigh, feeling each one of his touches through her whole body.

"Tell me what you like." His fingers continued rubbing and stroking her, and then he stopped talking because his mouth was at her breast, and the sensation was almost too much—the hot warmth of his mouth around her nipple, the rhythmic pressure of his fingers, even the odd feeling of being literally half-undressed and lying on her bed with him contributed to how her emotions flooded, until—

"Ahhh," she cried, the release suffusing her whole body with pleasure.

She was panting now, gasping as he kept his hand on her, pressing her mound as she continued to shudder.

He raised his head from her breast and met her gaze, a satisfied expression on his face. "I love making you come, Jane," he said in a low voice.

She shifted on the bed, her mind settling down again, her thoughts turning to ideas about equality and trading favors and reciprocity.

"How do I make you come, Thomas?"

HIS BREATH CAUGHT at her question. Because of what she said, of course, but also because of how she said it—as though she were invested in the answer. As though it was important to her.

"This isn't part of your education," he began,

only to stop speaking when she put her finger on his mouth as she shook her head.

"Oh, but it is," she replied with a warm smile of satisfaction. A reminder that he'd just brought her to bliss only a few moments ago. "I want to know everything about all of this, and I want to be a fair and equal and enthusiastic partner." She shrugged. "Pleasure is pleasure, regardless of who experiences it firsthand, is it not?"

He raised a brow as he nipped at her finger. Her eyes widened, and then she took his hand and brought his finger to her mouth, wrapping her lips around it slowly. Then sucked it into her mouth, licking it. Making his cock even harder than before.

God. Damn. He hadn't taught her that; she'd thought of that all on her own.

What else lurked in her imagination?

"I suppose it would help your education if I were to share how to elicit a strong sexual response from your partner."

She nodded, still with his finger in her mouth. Still sucking gently, sending shivers down his spine, directly to his throbbing erection.

Should he teach her—?

At the very least he owed it to her to tell her what some women—not all ladies, certainly—did with their mouths and their partners' cocks.

She released his finger, then her hands went to his shirt, and she began to unbutton him. "I want to see you. I've never seen—" And she blushed, even as her fingers continued their bold undressing of him.

"You've never seen a naked man? Of course you haven't," he replied. "Allow me to remedy that."

He rolled off the bed, standing at its foot, then drew his shirt over his head, tossing it to the floor. Not caring, for once, if it wrinkled.

This was far too much fun to fuss about one's wardrobe.

She leaned up on her elbows, an intent expression on her face. Her gaze traveled hungrily over him, her lips parted, her breath coming faster.

"Do you like what you see?" he said as he turned slowly in a circle.

She gave a vigorous nod. "Yes. The rest, please," she commanded with a haughty gesture. As though she was a queen and he was her servant.

He wanted to serve her. With his hands, as he had already. With his mouth and his tongue.

With his cock, though he knew that wasn't within the realm of their agreement. It was too tempting, however, to think about burying himself in her sweet warmth.

"Now, please," she said impatiently, making that imperious gesture again.

"Of course," he replied. His fingers went to the placket of his trousers and he began to unbutton them, keeping his eyes locked with hers.

She licked her lips and he felt himself tremble. With desire. With want. With *need*.

And then he was sliding his trousers down his legs, stepping out of them, leaving him in his smallclothes. His cock jutting out from the fabric.

Her gaze went directly there, and her eyes widened even more.

He resisted the urge to preen.

"That is—?" she began.

He allowed himself to reach down and give himself a quick tug, then removed his smallclothes as well, leaving him completely and entirely naked.

As before, he turned slowly, his hand at the base of his cock, aware she was looking at every naked inch of him. Wondering what her response would be to seeing him unclothed.

When he was standing back in front of her he was gratified to see her fascinated and passionate expression.

"Oh," she sighed in pleasure. "You are truly spectacular. I had no idea—that is, I knew you had to be handsome under all of that, but this," she said, extending her arm out to indicate his body, "is more than I had dreamed of."

"Have you dreamed of me, Jane?" he asked, lazily stroking his cock up and down. Resisting the urge to use a tighter grip or move faster. He wanted to see what she wanted to do, not just bring himself to satisfaction.

She tilted her head. "I haven't yet, but I suppose that now you mention it, I will be. I'll need something to keep me warm after—"

After he was married. After their agreement was over.

"But let's not speak about that," she added, gauging his expression correctly. She lifted her chin toward him. "Come back and show me what to do. With your—" Again that tilted head. "What do you call it?"

Thomas thought fleetingly about feigning ignorance to tease her, pretending he didn't know specifically what she was referring to, but more than that, he wanted to hear her say it.

"It's my penis." He stroked it again, her gaze on what his hand was doing. "My cock."

"Cock," she repeated, savoring the word as she popped its final *k* from her lips.

He stalked toward her, putting his knees on either side of her body and holding on to one bedpost to kneel on the bed. His cock was just over her pussy, though under the yards of fabric of bunched-up gown and chemise.

"Are you going to take that off?" he demanded. He gestured to himself. "It's only fair and equitable, after all."

Her hands went to her waist, and she began to shove the skirts of her gown down, wriggling on the bed and nearly making him lose his balance. He held on tighter to the bedpost as she kicked the gown off, sending it to the floor.

"And that," he said, indicating her chemise.

"So bossy," she said in a mocking reproof.

"I could tell you to do some other things, if you like," Thomas replied.

The thought was incredibly appealing. Especially if she decided she'd like to turn it all on its head and tell him what to do.

She bit her lip as she managed to wriggle out of her chemise, leaving her as naked as he was.

He still knelt above her, one hand at the base of his shaft.

"Well?" she asked, a sly lift of her eyebrow accompanying the clear challenge of her tone.

"Well," he said, maneuvering so he was again lying on his side facing her, "what do you want?"

"I told you before," she said in an impatient tone. "I want to do whatever I need to your cock to make you come."

"I know," he replied. "I just wanted to hear it again."

JANE FELT EXHILARATED by—by *everything*. By the languorous feeling she had after she'd climaxed, by how startled he'd seemed when she demanded she return the favor. By watching him undress, seeing his long, elegant fingers undo buttons as she anticipated what she might see.

Knowing it would be glorious.

Which it was, but it was even more than she'd imagined, as she'd told him.

His chest was firmly muscled, a light sprinkling of hair over the upper part. There were ridges in his abdomen where his stomach muscles were, and a very intriguing V that went down into his legs.

His shoulders were broad and muscled as well, while his legs were dusted with the same hair and were also long. Even without a stitch of clothing on, his stance still managed to be arrogant.

And then there was his penis. His cock. His man part.

It stood boldly out from the thatch of hair he had there, bulbous at the head with rippled veins on it.

It was the embodiment of masculinity, and she wanted to touch it. Was that—?

"Can I touch you?" she asked, trying not to overthink.

"I will die if you don't," he replied simply.

She held her breath as she reached down to grasp it.

He shuddered, and she paused, hoping she was doing it right. But he'd tell her if she wasn't. That was the point of education, after all—to be told how to do things correctly, and receiving instruction if one wasn't quite getting it.

The thought occurred to her that they could do all this again if she wasn't quite getting it now. Which would be marvelous.

"What are you smiling at?" he asked.

She shook her head. "Tell me what to do."

He placed his hand over hers, moving both of their hands up and down. His penis was hard, but felt as though it was covered in velvet. It was an interesting contradiction, the intersection of hard and soft.

"Like that," he said, taking his hand away. "Up and down in rhythm. Hold it tighter—yes, that's it," he encouraged as she intensified her grip. "Ungh," he groaned as she continued her movement.

She hadn't expected it to be exciting for her, but she felt that part of her that had responded so enthusiastically to his touch begin to tingle again as she thought about what she was doing. Interesting.

"What do you call my—that is," she said, feeling her cheeks turn pink. Ridiculous to blush at that, given that both of them were currently naked and she was stroking his cock, but there was no predicting anyone's behavior, was there?

"Your—?" he said, reaching down to touch her there. She couldn't help but emit a soft moan.

"Stop that," she said reprovingly. "You've already taken care of things, this is your turn now."

"Oh, but Jane," he said in a ragged voice, "I like to touch your vagina. Your pussy. Your cunt."

He said the last word as if it were both an expletive and an homage, and she shivered in response, unconsciously increasing her grip and her rhythm.

"Yes, like that," he urged. He thrust his hips closer to her, meeting her stroke so her fist jammed down to the base of his penis, her hands tickled by the hair there. "Just a little more," he said. His chest and stomach muscles were flexed, and his eyes were closed, his expression strained and intent.

And then—"Aagh," he said in a strangled tone, liquid warmth spurting out of his cock and over her hand.

He placed his hand on top of hers, slowing her rhythm as he panted, the sticky liquid coating her hand, the scent of it enveloping her with an unfamiliar and extremely intimate smell.

"Thank you." He opened his eyes as he spoke, his mouth curling up into a crooked smile. A smile she'd never seen on his face before. A smile that was entirely genuine, not imbued with any of his usual Thomas Sharpe charm.

She felt the impact of that smile through her whole body, her whole naked body, as she lay on her bed with him. As though they were truly partners, and not just friends who'd entered into a temporary arrangement exchanging mutual favors.

"We should get to that list, hmm?" he asked, rolling onto his back. Despite his words, he just lay there, that same smile on his face.

She propped herself up on her elbow and gazed down at him. "Your wife—whoever she ends up being—is going to be very lucky."

He arched a skeptical eyebrow. "Because of this?" he said, gesturing to include both of them. He shook his head. "I wish I could agree, and I know that many gentlemen don't have the same . . . skills I do"—at which he waggled both brows—"but the lady who agrees to marry me will enter into our arrangement knowing it's not a love match." He paused, taking a deep breath. "I don't have the luxury of falling in love."

Jane's chest tightened at his words, a timely reminder that none of what they were doing could result in anything permanent. She knew that, of course. It was good to be reminded of that fact when one was still reeling from such a satisfying and intense experience.

"Let's work on finding someone you can live happily with," she said in a soft voice. "That's more than many."

He nodded. "You're right, Jane." He placed his hand on her arm, sliding his palm down to find her hand, squeezing it in his. "Thank you for all of this."

"Thank *you*," she said, feeling her words choke in her throat. "You are helping me as much as I am helping you."

"A mutually beneficial relationship," he said in amusement. "So much more than what I expected when you presented the idea at Miss Ivy's."

"And you are more than I expected." It was true, which made it that much more painful to look ahead to when he was settled and she was figuring out what she wanted to do with her newfound knowledge and her future.

But at least she knew her choice would be hers. A luxury, as he'd said, that he didn't have.

Chapter Fifteen

Thomas wished he could just lie there on Jane's bed for the rest of the day. The week.

His life.

But if he did, not only would he be foregoing the wearing of clothing and the eating of food—the latter of which was, at least, necessary for survival—but he would also be denying his family the chance to live, even modestly.

After a few moments, he sat up and located his clothing, which was strewn on Jane's floor. He eased off the bed and collected it up, placing it on the spot he'd been lying.

She still lay back on the bed, her arms under her head, a warm, relaxed expression on her face.

At least he'd held up his end of the bargain—he was definitely showing her things of which she was not aware previously.

"We should compile our list," he said as he drew on his smallclothes.

She nodded, her expression faltering. As though this meant—no, it couldn't. He wouldn't let her.

If she went and fell in love with him, despite her assurances to the contrary, it would be devastating for both of them.

Because he already knew that if given a nudge, a hint that it would be all right to do so, he would absolutely fall in love with her.

Her kindness, her curiosity, her gentle spirit. Not to mention her sheer beauty, which overwhelmed him even now.

With that in mind, he steeled his resolve and spoke again. "It will be good to be settled, to be able to stop frittering my time away at parties and other things."

He saw her frown, precisely the reaction he wanted, but also the last one he desired.

If only he could be as cruel as some other men were, reminding their lovers that whatever they had didn't affect their hearts.

But he'd always been a kind lover and he wouldn't stop now, especially with this woman, one of the few he knew who could affect his heart. Had affected his heart.

"I am optimistic about Miss Grosvenor. I imagine we would get along well together. And her father is certainly wealthy enough to afford me."

"Yes," she replied as she sat up, brushing her hair away from her face. "You do come with a cost."

The bitter taste of her words made his stomach clench. It was only what he deserved, though, wasn't it? And she was speaking the truth.

She hopped off her bed and found her own clothing, donning it with an efficient speed that spoke of going without a maid for some time.

A reminder that he could not afford her. Because she could not afford him.

"I've already got a list started—let me just get it," she said. She sounded more like herself, and his tension eased. Perhaps this wouldn't be as wretched as he thought.

He sat on her bed to don his boots, the familiar task at odds with his unfamiliar setting.

Meanwhile, she was gathering her papers, laying everything out on her small desk.

"Or we should go downstairs?" she asked in a skeptical tone. "It is rather cramped in here for this."

"Good idea," he said shortly. The less he was reminded of what complete comfort and happiness felt like, the better. He felt a pang at leaving the refuge of her bedroom, but it wasn't as though he could stay here forever—he'd just reminded himself of that.

She led the way, clutching her papers in one curled arm and her writing tools in the other.

"Let me?" he said, gesturing to the hand that held her pen and ink. They looked precarious, and he didn't want them to fall, staining either one of their clothing—he knew neither one of them could afford new items if their current ones got ruined.

"Oh yes," she said, meeting his gaze. "I forgot that I was not alone—I am so accustomed to doing things for myself."

"You can, you know."

"What?" she said with a puzzled glance.

"Do things for yourself." He nodded toward her now-empty hand. "All you need is your imagination and some privacy."

Her eyes widened and she turned bright pink as she understood his meaning.

"I can teach you that as well," he replied in his smoothest voice.

This felt much more comfortable, much more familiar—flirting with a lady with whom he had no future, but plenty of attraction.

"Well," she said, still pink, "we could put that on our list of things to explore."

"Indeed."

Her response was exactly what he'd hoped for—the promise of more, the reminder of their mutual exchange of favors. And that armed with that knowledge, she would be able to take care of herself, regardless of what her romantic situation was.

Perhaps she would remain eternally unwed, since she clearly chafed at having anyone assert control over her.

They reached the downstairs, and she continued on to the sitting room where he usually drank with Percy.

Instead of liquor on the small table, however, there was a tea set, including biscuits. It looked so cozy, just what a wife might prepare for her husband after a day of work that he felt that horrible grip on his chest again, his breath catching.

If things were different, this could be his life. His tea. His biscuits.

"The tea will be cold by now, I'll just—" she said, going to pick up the bell on the table.

"Don't," he interrupted. "I'm fine with no tea. I'd rather just be here with you to take care of this task, if you don't mind."

She hesitated, and then her eyes got softer and warmer, as though she understood and felt sorry for him.

For God's sake, he wanted to shout, *don't feel sorry for me. I don't deserve it.*

"Please sit." She sat on the sofa, indicating the seat next to her.

He leaned over to read the paper she held. Her scent was warm and lightly floral. Fresh.

And now he was even more angry at himself. Noticing how she smelled? That was the final step before admitting one was completely besotted with someone. Goddamn it. He knew it well: first, the gentle intrigue; then the verbal sparring, which they'd done even before they'd made their agreement; then the various sexual encounters, starting from a kiss and ending up with the exchange of orgasms; and then, finally, imagining her pouring tea for him as he inhaled her scent.

Goddamn it.

This was not what was supposed to happen.

"Thomas?" she said, nudging him in the side with her elbow. "We should review this, unpleasant though it is." Again, she sounded as though she sympathized with how painful it must be, and he wanted to shout again—*don't care about me! I don't deserve it!*

But she would merely point out that he was doing all this for his family, and therefore his mercenary pursuit of an heiress was entirely noble.

That was the problem with kind people. They could see the good in everyone else.

And why he'd gone and fallen—

"After Miss Grosvenor," he said, interrupting his own thoughts. "Who do you think is likely to accept me?"

She frowned in thought, pursing her lips. She tapped the paper. "Miss Porter admires you already."

"Miss Porter?" He searched his mind in an effort to remember her. "Oh yes, the lady who rarely meets one's eyes."

"That is because she is bowled over by your beauty," Jane replied matter-of-factly. "I used to behave the same way—really it is ridiculous that you are allowed to walk around like that."

"You did?" Thomas said, surprised. "I thought you found me frivolous because I was always taking Percy off to carouse."

"That too." Her reply came far too swiftly for Thomas's taste. "But it turns out that I required someone frivolous to show me all of this," she said, gesturing to the space between them, "and you are horribly good-looking, so it is a pleasure to spend time with you at these places. I never expected you to be so—so . . ." Her words trailed off, and Thomas leaned closer to her.

"So what?" he asked.

He saw her swallow before she replied. "So considerate. So kind."

This was veering dangerously close to real emotions again. He had to stop it, but he wouldn't—he couldn't—hurt her.

"So horribly good-looking?" he said in a wry tone.

She rolled her eyes as she laughed, exactly what he'd wanted.

"Let's return to the list of women who are going

to have to suffer your insufferable vanity for the rest of their lives."

"Suffering for beauty is always a righteous cause," Thomas said, making her roll her eyes even harder.

It was better than having her fall in love with him.

As he was with her.

THEY WORKED TOGETHER, compiling their list into three columns: "likely," "possibly," and "about as much chance as two consecutive sunny days in London." The last was only a list of names because he'd asked her about inviting her sister, Lavinia, and the duke, which had led to a discussion of the rest of her family.

"It's been long enough, hasn't it?" Thomas asked in a gentle voice. She wasn't accustomed to this Thomas, the one who was thoughtful and considerate. She'd only just gotten to know him over the past few weeks, and yet she found herself responding to him as if they were old, dear friends. Friends who did much more together than friends usually did, of course.

Her body still tingled from where he'd touched her, where the sparks had sizzled and caught fire. Until him, she hadn't known such feelings were even possible, though she had suspected, given how her sister, Lavinia, often looked.

But she thought that just might be because Lavinia and her husband were in love, which she and Mr. Sharpe most definitely were not.

Because they couldn't be.

No matter how her heart fluttered annoyingly when he was near.

"Long enough for my mother to forgive me?" she replied at last. "You don't know the Countess of Scudamore if you think I will be that easily forgiven."

"You might have to be the better person in this situation, then. Invite her," he urged. "And you can see the rest of your family as well. I can't imagine Lavinia, once she discovers you've asked all of them to come, will allow them to stay home."

Jane chuckled in agreement. "Lavinia is strong-willed. It is one of the aspects of her personality my mother most deplores. But she's married to a duke, so—" she said, shrugging.

"So all is forgiven?" Thomas asked.

"Mmm," Jane agreed. "I imagine if I were to announce my engagement to someone my mother found suitable she would welcome me back into the family immediately." She couldn't help speaking in a tone indicating how distasteful she found the idea. "But inviting her to a party where she can pass judgment on everyone else there and find a way to order me around might also do the trick," she continued in a more normal tone of voice.

"Perhaps we should bribe the medium to predict that your mother will find great happiness if only she resolves a difference in her life."

Jane flung her hands up. "That could be applied to so many of my mother's relationships. She enjoys conflict—I do not."

Which was an understatement. Not only had she never engaged willingly in conflict, until Mr. Rat-Tavish had jilted her, she had never even spoken up for herself.

The countess had been so stunned she'd sat there

without a word as Jane announced her plans to move in with Percy.

By the time she'd regained her composure, Jane had been packed and on her way. Jane had relented and spoken with her mother after she'd received pleading notes, but the conversation had always turned to how ungrateful and rebellious Jane was, and how it must be Lavinia's fault, though it was Lavinia who had initially saved her from a terrible situation in the first place, by flinging herself into the duke's path, when it seemed as though he wished to marry Jane.

"I think you should invite her. What is the worst that could happen?" he asked.

"My mother attacks the medium for daring to suggest her life is not already perfect? My father buttonholes one of the jugglers and explains, in excruciating detail, the physics behind their work?"

Thomas's lips twitched up into a smile. "That sounds as though it could be quite amusing."

She scowled as she crossed her arms over her chest. "Try being related to them."

He nodded in understanding. "Family is difficult at times," he said.

She clapped her hands over her mouth as her eyes widened. "Oh my goodness, how incredibly self-absorbed I am! To complain about my mother when you are shouldering all of your family's burdens."

"How is that self-absorbed?" He shrugged. "How you feel about your family doesn't negate what I am doing for mine, nor is the opposite true." His mouth curled up into a gentle smile. One Jane didn't think she had ever seen on his face before. "I do wish my sister Alice could come to the party. She would enjoy seeing the circus."

"Why can't she?"

He shook his head. "She is not—she's not comfortable in company. In crowds."

"Have you asked her?"

He paused, his expression turning puzzled. "No, actually. I haven't."

"You should. If I should invite my mother, you should see if your sister would like to come. Why not give her the opportunity to say no instead of deciding for her?" She couldn't help her fierce tone.

So many people—including and especially her mother—had tried to decide for Jane, had tried to force her into a box of convenience. Jane throwing off the yoke of control had been one of the best and most powerful things she had ever done—and she wanted every woman to have that chance.

"I will write her tonight," he promised. "Meanwhile, we have to send the invitations. Are you certain all these ladies will attend?" he said, gesturing to the "likely" list.

She gave a firm nod. "They will. Every one of them wants to be the one who captured your attention, now that I've spread the word of your secret fidelity."

"*Secret Fidelity* sounds as though it is the title of one of Percy's books," he commented, a wry smile on his face.

"And something that will have you married before you know it," she replied. Wishing those words didn't strike a pain in her heart.

Chapter Sixteen

Dear Alice,

~~My lover~~ My friend has encouraged me to ask you something that I would have normally assumed I knew the answer to—but she is determinedly revolutionary, wanting every female to have their own choice in life, despite the impediments thereof.

That sounds ominous, doesn't it?

It's not. It's not as though ~~I am writing to tell you I have fallen in love with my friend. My lover. Who is not the heiress we've been waiting for.~~

The thing is, I—along with my friend and my best friend, her brother—am hosting an event, a party, with entertainers from the circus, a medium, a unicyclist, and doubtless some other types of amusements.

Would you like to come to London to attend?

I haven't been able to visit you and the parents as much recently, and it would be lovely to see you. Please don't if you have any trepidation at all.

But I was thinking that if you would like to come, I could come down to collect you the evening before, and we could travel to London together in the morning. I

will find a respectable ladies' hotel for you to stay in
that evening, and then I will bring you home.

Don't automatically answer no. Consider it thoroughly.
If you still want to say no, of course I understand.

I love you,
Thomas

Thomas reviewed what he had written, his mouth tightening as he thought about everything he hadn't said.

That he was falling in love with Jane.

That he could not allow her to know his feelings were deeper than pure desire.

That he definitely could not allow her to fall in love with him.

It was bad enough that his future was already going to be loveless. That his wife, no matter who she was, was not going to be her.

He could not allow himself to taint her future as well. She deserved to make her own choice, as she was determined to do.

But she could not be allowed to choose him.

Goddamn it.

He folded the letter and slipped it into the envelope, calculating when he might have Alice's reply. Obviously not today.

Jane was busy, sending out the invitations to the party from the guest list they'd completed the day before. After he'd brought her to bliss and she'd done the same to him.

Which, he recalled with a wry grin, she'd chosen to do.

"My revolutionary," he murmured. He could see her leading a phalanx of women to Parliament to demand they be given the opportunity to decide things for themselves—things like marriage, and wealth, and even something as simple as choosing not to wear a specific type of gown for an event.

They were going to meet that evening to go to another club, one that catered to people who wanted to do more than gamble.

He wasn't certain if he should expose her to that kind of knowledge, but even thinking that meant that he likely should. So she would know everything she needed to know after they parted ways.

After his future was secured.

In the meantime, however, he had several hours before he would go collect her. Normally, he would have gone to find if Percy was available to do some carousing, but Percy had been less available recently, and Thomas found it didn't have the same kind of appeal.

He only wanted to be with her, damn it.

He gritted his teeth and swore to himself that he would not think of her for the next hour. Not think of how gently curved she was, how responsive she was to his touch. How she gasped when she came, how her cheeks flushed, and her eyes sparkled.

How quickly she learned what would make him lose control. How she stroked his cock as they lay naked on her bed.

His hand drifted lower, to where he was already hardening, and he shook his head as he succumbed to the inevitable. Grasping himself, giving a firm, hard stroke. She wouldn't know he thought of her when he touched himself. It would be these memories of their brief time together that would sustain him through a loveless marriage.

Yes, he would provide sexual satisfaction to whomever he married—it would be part of the unspoken agreement, after all. Not part of the wedding vows, though perhaps it should be.

But the part of him he hadn't known existed before, the gentle, thoughtful part would be locked away, with her holding the key.

Even though she had no idea.

He pushed that aside as he anticipated the evening—entering the innocuous-looking club, then venturing further into its depths.

Would she be shocked? Or would she want to know more? Do more?

Likely both.

He gripped harder now, his mind's eye conjuring how she'd looked on her bed—all soft and sated, a smile of satisfaction on her face. Satisfaction for having climaxed as well as for being an equal partner in his climax.

What he wouldn't give to fuck her. Thrust his cock into her warmth, take hold of her hips as he moved in and out, finding what rhythm she preferred, if she liked being taken from behind or wanted to ride him.

Dear God, he wished she would ride him. Move up and down, sliding her deliciously wicked softness onto him and back off again, controlling the motion with her body.

It wouldn't be long now. Just thinking of her made him hard, and letting his mind drift to the possibilities made his climax imminent, especially when his hands were recreating her movements up and down his shaft.

He closed his eyes, thinking of her silver-blond hair wrapped around his fist as he fucked her mouth. As she drew him deep inside, learning what to do with her tongue as he gave himself over to the pleasure.

And then—"Aagh," he groaned as he came, the release already tinged with regret that their time together was coming to an end. Soon, if only to give his family assurance that they would be all right. That they would be able to continue their lives without worry that they would be destitute.

It was all worth it, he assured himself. What was his own happiness compared with the happiness of his family? His parents and Alice? His father's tenants, who needed his father to make necessary repairs?

It was all worth it.

He just wished it didn't hurt so much.

"MISS GROSVENOR!" JANE exclaimed as Mrs. Charing opened the door.

Miss Grosvenor gave her a smile as she removed her cloak. She wore the absolute latest in fashionable attire, a bit fussy for Jane's taste, but clearly expensive.

And the lady herself was so kind. Jane should be relieved that Thomas might end up married to her. There were worse choices—many worse choices—that he wouldn't have the benefit of not choosing, if one of those choices made their willingness to be Mrs. Thomas Sharpe apparent.

But Miss Grosvenor was undoubtedly the best of the bunch, and Jane had to admit the two would likely get along well enough together—Miss Grosvenor had a sly wit, as did Thomas, and he would definitely be appreciative of his wife's fortune. He'd ensure she felt comfortable as his wife, he would pay her the most attention so she wouldn't be worried he was straying, and he would eventually be a good father. Joining in with his children's adventures, but still keeping an eye out for possible trouble. As he'd done with her.

"Please come in. I'll send for tea." Jane met Mrs. Charing's eyes, and the housekeeper nodded in response, turning toward the kitchen.

Jane led Miss Grosvenor to her study. She had invited the lady to visit not just to gauge whether or not she was interested in Thomas, but also because she was missing having a friend. Now that Lavinia was off blissfully married, with one baby and another on the way, she didn't have as much time to spend with Jane.

Percy, while lovely, wasn't the same as swapping gossip and light talk about the latest amusements and fashion with a female. And if Miss Grosvenor did end up marrying Thomas, it would be pleasant if Jane was friends with her brother's friend's wife.

Pleasant and painful.

"How are you, my lady?" Miss Grosvenor asked. "I was so pleased you invited me. My stepmother ran to Debrett's and was horribly impressed." Her eyes widened and she clapped a hand over her mouth. "Drat, I probably shouldn't have said that. I apologize."

Jane shook her head, laughing. "It is fine. If you can use my name and family to placate your stepmother, by all means do so."

"Thank you, my lady." Miss Grosvenor removed her hand, and now her eyes had an amused glint in them. "As I mentioned, she means well, but she can be—" She paused, obviously searching for a mollifying word. "Eager."

"Believe me, your stepmother is not nearly as eager as my mother," Jane replied ruefully. "And call me Jane, please."

"Oh, call me Millie. Short for Millicent," she said. "Though I am not here merely because of your family," she added hastily, her eyes achieving maximum roundness again.

Jane patted Millie's hand. "I would not believe that for a moment. I am glad you are here, regardless of the reason. I live with my brother now, and he is often busy, and my sister—married to the Duke of Hasford, I'm certain you know," she said wryly, "is busy as well." She shrugged. "I find myself lacking in conversation. I am not looking for a husband, and I have had a few London seasons already, so the usual activities aren't as interesting to me any longer. But then I met you, and you seem so pleased to be out, and then I did go to some more unusual places, and I had an idea to introduce those places to those of us who wouldn't normally encounter them."

"Such as going to Miss Ivy's?" Miss Grosvenor said enthusiastically. "My father is too busy to take me, and my stepmother doesn't want to miss a single one of the parties."

"Yes, my brother and I are planning a party ourselves that will have entertainment from some of those places we aren't able to go to on our own."

Millie clapped her hands together in glee, and Jane couldn't help but smile.

"You're bringing the joy to us! That sounds wonderful."

"I'll be sending the invitations out later today, but I wanted to personally invite you because—" She hesitated, wishing she weren't so reluctant to broach the subject. "Because Mr. Sharpe will be there as well."

"Mr. Sharpe?" Millie tilted her head. "Yes, he is quite handsome, though I have heard he can be"— again, her expression indicated her desire to be diplomatic—"popular."

"He is indeed," Jane replied. "But I do know he is growing tired of his . . . popularity, and is hoping to become more domestic." Was there a cagier way to say he wanted to settle down and get married?

Jane didn't think so.

"I have heard, at least my stepmother has said, that Mr. Sharpe has to marry money." Millie's tone of voice was matter-of-fact, not at all judgmental.

Jane took a deep breath. "It is true that when Mr. Sharpe marries, from what I understand, he will need funds to support himself and his family, including his wife. But it is also true that Mr. Sharpe hopes to find someone who will be a good partner in life with whom he can forge a deep, true relationship."

Jane's throat grew tight as she spoke. Wasn't that

what anyone wanted from a marriage? Wasn't that what she had hoped for with Mr. McTavish?

If only she had enough money to—but no, she didn't wish that. She would never know if he loved her or he merely needed her. Best that she couldn't afford him.

"You are a good advocate for him," Millie said. "You do him credit."

"Thank you, but—"

They were interrupted by a tap on the door, followed by Mrs. Charing bringing in the tea.

They resumed talking when the tea had been properly dispersed, and each lady had two sugar biscuits sitting on a plate.

"You were saying?" Millie prompted, taking a bite from her biscuit.

"Yes, I was saying—oh, yes. I speak in admiring tones of Mr. Sharpe not just because he is my brother's friend but because there is more to him than meets the eye. And as you have said, what meets the eye is impressive already."

Millie grinned. "He really is remarkably handsome."

You should see what he looks like naked.

"He is, indeed. Imagine waking up to that face every morning, and seeing it before you go to sleep." Both of them sighed at the thought.

"Of course if there is someone else you prefer—?" Jane asked delicately.

Millie shook her head. "No, not at all. I know that marrying me off is why my father and stepmother brought me to London. I just can't see myself as a wife and a mother when I've barely seen anything at all." She sounded as mournful as Jane used to be about her situation.

Perhaps Jane should suggest Millie procure her own Mr. Sharpe to show her . . . everything.

But that would be far too tempting. Why would any young lady compromise in marriage if they had been exposed to the glories of a traveling circus, or a balloon, or what a handsome gentleman looked like without any clothes on?

Perhaps that was why parents were so adamant their daughters remain firmly protected—so they wouldn't realize everything they were missing.

Thankfully, Jane knew precisely what she had been missing. And she was going to make certain she never missed out again.

"You definitely do not want to be forced into anything. I am merely mentioning Mr. Sharpe because I do know he is kind and honorable. Unlike some."

"Such as Lord Joseph?" Millie said in a sly tone. "Do you know, he tried to lure me into the shrubbery telling me he wanted my horticultural advice?" She rolled her eyes. "I know I am new to London, but I am not that naive."

"Heaven help the poor lady who gets ensnared in his net," Jane replied.

Millie straightened. "Do you know, I believe I should warn people about him. You can tell he would not be kind, not with that kind of duplicity."

"Where were you when I was engaged?" Jane asked in a rueful tone.

Millie demanded to know all the details, and Jane told her, admitting her own ignorant culpability as well as her ex-fiancé's self-righteous rigidity.

THE AFTERNOON HAD been pleasant, reminding Jane that the life she had chosen—that the life she was planning to lead—would be entirely satisfactory. A life filled with friends, and conversation, and biscuits. A life not filled with blackguards and pedants.

But first, she had more adventures to go on. She cast a critical eye at her reflection in the glass. Thomas had told her they would be going out that evening to a club, but he hadn't said what type of club. She knew it wasn't Miss Ivy's, because she had been there already, and he had promised to show her new things.

So she wasn't certain what to wear, just that she wanted to look like the confident, assured woman she hoped she was becoming.

She wore a gown of sea-foam green, a gauzy overdress making it look as though she was floating.

Possibly floating in algae, but she wouldn't think too much about that.

She had wrapped a matching green ribbon in her hair and wrapped two more ribbons around each wrist. It made her look like a package, one she hoped Thomas would want to open.

Not that she knew if there would be package-opening hijinks this evening, but she was optimistic—with the party only a week or so away, there was limited time for him to show her everything he'd promised.

She sighed as she recalled the day before, when he'd shattered her right here on top of her coverlet.

And then she'd done the same to him.

She smiled at her reflection, then went downstairs.

It was an hour or more before Thomas would arrive, but she wanted to be ready.

For their evening, for him, for them.

"Jane, there you are," Percy said, emerging from his workroom.

She rolled her eyes as she walked down the last few steps of the stairs. "Yes, here I am. Because I wasn't hanging about in your own private room interfering with your work, was I?"

Percy had made it clear when they had moved in together that he was not to be disturbed if he was in his study—he often worked on complicated mathematical equations, he'd said grandiosely, and he couldn't let his concentration slip.

Jane suspected that he often snuck in a quick nap, but she would never test her theory.

"Are you busy? I am going to Lavinia's house this evening. She says she is too exhausted from her forthcoming special event"—her pregnancy—"to keep up with the baby."

"And the duke is busy?" Jane asked, lifting her eyebrow.

"It's just an excuse for me to go play with her, you know that," Percy said, waving a dismissive hand. "Besides, nobody expects dukes to actually interact with their offspring."

"Hmph," Jane sniffed. She'd be more appalled by Percy's words about their brother-in-law if they hadn't both seen how besotted he was by his daughter.

"Well?" Percy said, looking impatient.

"I am going out with Mr. Sharpe this evening." Her cheeks felt hotter than they had a few moments ago.

"Thomas?" As though there was another Mr. Sharpe she might be spending time with. But he didn't sound suspicious, for which she was grateful.

She could barely explain how she felt about Thomas to herself, much less to Percy.

Though she did know she felt more strongly about him than she'd promised herself—and him, and Percy—she would.

"I suppose going out with Thomas is more entertaining than visiting with a baby," he conceded. "And if all goes well, he'll be engaged, and that will be the end of all that." Now he sounded practically enthusiastic. Not that she could blame her brother; she knew he continued to have justifiable concerns about her involvement with his best friend, and she also knew he wanted Thomas to resolve his situation so he could resolve his family's financial problems.

And she would not stand in his way. "We compiled an invitation list yesterday, and I mailed the invitations out today," she told him. "We have several promising young ladies on the list."

"Oh good," he replied, sounding not at all interested.

"And I've invited the parents."

"Oh?" Percy's eyebrows shot up. "Aren't you—?" he said, his words trailing off as he gestured vaguely in the air.

"I am," Jane said. Not sure precisely what she was agreeing with, but knowing it was likely true. "Thom—Mr. Sharpe suggested that I resolve our differences, and we all know Mother isn't going to be the person to begin."

Percy tilted his head in thought, his eyes scrutinizing her intently. "You have changed," he said at last. "I hadn't realized it, but you're different, somehow."

Jane stood straighter, conscious of Percy's assessment. "Thank you. I won't try to deny it, I do feel different than I used to. I think I'm behaving like one of Lavinia's heroines, to be honest."

Percy groaned as he covered his face with his hand. "Please don't say that. Her heroines are always dashing off to behave impulsively, not thinking beyond the next minute."

Jane considered that. "True," she agreed, "but they also know their own minds, and they won't have anyone tell them what to do. That's what I mean more than the impulsive bits."

"Thank goodness," Percy said with a grin. "I wouldn't want to have to chase after you through a dark forest, or into a castle, or any of the other places Lavinia's heroines go."

"I could rescue myself, I assure you," Jane replied in a mockingly haughty tone.

Percy held his hands up in a gesture of surrender. "Of course you could. I would not dare suggest otherwise."

"Though I would like it if you came after me," Jane said, wrapping her brother in a tight embrace.

He squeezed her back, and they stood there together for a moment. Long after Thomas had spoken his vows to another woman Jane would have this: her brother, her sister, and herself.

That was all that mattered.

Chapter Seventeen

Thomas jogged up the steps to Percy and Jane's house, feeling an unfamiliar sense of excitement. He would have thought, prior to spending time with her, that he was far beyond such basic reactions, but now he knew he was capable of pleasant anticipation, and the simple warmth of an excellent and unexpected companion, and of course there was desire and passion all mixed into it as well.

The door opened as he was raising his knuckles to knock, and there she stood, looking like a beautiful summer breeze, dressed in a simple evening gown that accentuated her figure and her coloring.

"I heard you so I—" she said, gesturing to the door.

"So you let me in," Thomas finished, smiling down into her face as she stood aside to let him enter the house. "Very wise of you, leaving me on the doorstep would cause comment."

Her cheeks pinkened, and all he wanted to do was kiss her.

Well, that wasn't *all* he wanted to do.

"Thomas!" Percy called, striding toward them. His hair was even wilder than usual, meaning he must have been working, and he was wearing what appeared to be random clothing that had gotten caught in a very strong wind. Or a person who was practicing folding garments into tiny packages.

Of course, wrinkles and wild hair just made Percy look even more like a Romantic poet.

"Have you been rolling through the house?" Thomas asked, gesturing to Percy's clothing.

"What? No," his friend replied, a confused look on his face.

"I think he was napping," Jane said in a stage whisper.

"I was not!"

"It's a good thing I am taking your sister out, and not you. I don't think you'd be let in anywhere, not looking like that."

Percy struck a proud pose, his chin lifted and his hands outstretched. "As it happens, I am busy this evening."

Jane nodded in confirmation. "He's going to Lavinia's house to be the best uncle ever."

"Ah, so that explains your attire. Wise not to wear anything you care about—or that anyone would care about, honestly—with a baby in close proximity." He glanced at Jane. "Are you ready to go?"

"Yes," she replied with a smile.

"Keep her safe," Percy said in a more serious tone than usual.

"I promise." Thomas suppressed a wince at the

thought that he'd already broken a promise to Percy—*Neither of you is allowed to fall in love with the other.* And here he was, completely and entirely smitten.

Though he couldn't reveal that to either of the two siblings.

"And I will keep him safe," Jane added.

"Go on. Have fun. You'll be a somber married man soon enough."

"Soon enough," Thomas echoed as he opened the door. He tried to keep his tone light, but he felt the weight of the words catch in his throat.

She stepped past him, and he caught her scent, as light and fresh as her appearance. He wished he could bury his face in her hair, forget about everything but her.

But if he did that, he would be the most selfish person ever, threatening his parents' ability to survive, Alice's freedom, and also making Jane aware of his deeper feelings when she herself had promised not to fall in love with him.

All he could do was enjoy this time with her, make certain she came out of their agreement a stronger, prouder, more confident woman. Which he had little to do with—but that she was able to satisfy her curiosity safely and easily was something he did.

He took her arm as they began to walk down the sidewalk.

"No hackney?" she asked. "I can pay, if you need."

He snorted. "I am not completely impoverished." He paused, then added, "Only partially."

"So we are going somewhere nearby? I have my evening slippers on, I won't be able to travel very far, at least not comfortably."

He stopped walking to scoop her up into his arms, the froth of her gown spilling up into his face as she laughed.

"Put me down, you idiot," she said, whacking him on the shoulder.

"You mentioned not being able to comfortably walk. I am merely solving the problem," he replied in a matter-of-fact tone. *And getting to hold you.*

"What if one of your young ladies sees you?"

He felt his jaw tighten and he hesitated, then lowered her back to the ground. He couldn't say what he wished—that if they saw him, then they'd know he wasn't sincere. Likely none of them would treat his attentions with any more seriousness than they had in the past two years. And he would be secretly relieved that he'd exposed his true feelings because then he wouldn't have to live a lie.

But that would deny his family their lives. It would place her under more scrutiny. It would mean he'd have to acknowledge what he wished he could do.

Selfish, selfish, selfish.

"It's just up there," he said, pointing to a narrow building on the next block.

"Oh good," she replied. "I am looking forward to seeing whatever it is you wish to show me."

His mind raced with all kinds of images at her words, and then she gasped as she too caught the potential meaning. "Oh my goodness!" she exclaimed. "That sounds so salacious! Not that I wouldn't look forward to seeing all of that, but that is not what I meant!"

He burst into laughter, and she joined in, leaning against him as she laughed.

He had never laughed with a lover before. Usually, he split his amusements so his laughter was shared with friends such as Percy, and the lover-like behavior was with his lover, naturally.

He had never thought of it before, but having both possibilities wrapped into one package—her—was even more alluring.

Plus she could, and would, debate him on his character, their daily lives, and seemed to question all the norms.

Perhaps the result of not doing what was expected of her.

They were merely giggling as they approached the front of the building—deliberately nondescript, its windows were covered with dark curtains, and the house itself was nothing out of the ordinary.

But what happened inside was.

"Mr. Sharpe, welcome," the doorman said. He was a large, muscular man who exuded menace. Thomas hadn't seen him ever have to actually use his size and form, but the threat was always there.

A good thing, given what risks people took in visiting the establishment.

The door opened, and they stepped inside, Thomas smiling as he heard her surprised intake of breath.

The hall was lushly and extravagantly decorated, the walls covered with burgundy silk and pictures everywhere, while gold chandeliers dangled from the ceiling every three feet.

The hallway was wider than the average London house, allowing for visitors to settle themselves before deciding on their choice for the evening.

Thomas usually chose for his partner, but he knew how important choice was to Jane, so he was going to explain everything, and then let her decide.

Already his body was thrumming in anticipation of what she might choose.

And the intoxication of telling her just what people got up to behind closed doors. Some of which she knew about firsthand already.

"What is this place? A gambling establishment?" she asked as he took her hand and escorted her to one of the gold chairs rimming the edge of the room.

"It can be," he replied. He sat next to her, drawing his chair close.

A door opposite to where they sat opened, and one of the proprietors entered, a servant girl following behind with a tray of beverages.

The proprietor held her hand out as Thomas stood.

"Welcome," she said, glancing between the two of them, "I am Mrs. Rochford. I believe I have seen you here, sir, but this is your first time?" she said, addressing Jane.

"It is."

Mrs. Rochford nodded. "Well, then, let me assure you that everyone who works here is choosing to do so. The house takes a percentage of their earnings, but we are not like some other places."

Jane's eyes were round. "Like those other places? And what do the workers *do*?" she asked.

"I will explain what happens here," Thomas interrupted. "If you can spare a menu?"

Mrs. Rochford's lips curled in a faint smile, and she held out a menu printed on sturdy paper. "Everything is available this evening except for the dungeon. Water leak," she explained.

"The dun—?" Jane said.

"We are not here for that, thank you," Thomas said swiftly.

"I will leave you, then. Sarah will leave refreshments should you desire any. I believe I have your information—you can expect a bill tomorrow morning." She nodded toward Jane. "A pleasure," she said. "I hope you find yours here."

And then she left as the maid began to place a variety of drinks on the table to the right of Jane's chair: a full tea service, two wine glasses, a carafe of some sort of alcohol, and another carafe of water.

The maid nodded, then left also, leaving them alone. Thomas got up to pour two glasses of whatever the alcohol was and brought them back, handing one to Jane, who took it with a raised eyebrow.

"Looking forward to seeing me choke again?" she asked, eyeing the liquid.

"You're a woman of the world now, Jane," he replied. "I have every confidence you will be able to swallow anything that is given to you."

And then he gulped from his glass himself because the images those words brought to mind made his mouth go instantly dry. And his body feel as though it had been shocked with an electric current.

But this wasn't his time to choose. Nor would he choose anything she wouldn't also choose herself.

Thankfully, she didn't seem to notice his reaction, too engrossed in looking around the room and sipping from her glass.

It was sherry, as it turned out, a remarkably ordinary beverage for such an extraordinary place.

He drained his glass and drew the menu between them.

"This is The Center for Delightful and Unusual Events," he explained. The name was printed across the top of the menu, and the various items were listed in three columns as though it was offering a soup course, a fish course, and a meat course instead of a sapphist course, a convivial society course, and a godeminche course.

"What is 'tipping the velvet'?" she asked, her finger pointing to the phrase. "And what is 'horizontal refreshment,' and why would we want to watch anyone doing that?"

Well. He'd brought her here, he was going to have to explain . . . everything.

Which would make her a far more knowledgeable lady than she was before. She'd asked him to "show her things." So he would show her things. And do things that would show her things. And so on.

Until they inevitably parted when he achieved his goal.

JANE FELT A frisson of excitement as she sat in the remarkably opulent room sipping her sherry. First, there was how his eyes had glittered with a predatory anticipation when he'd picked her up. Then, how his expression had changed, just now, as he was about to explain whatever was on the menu to her.

She did not think this was a restaurant. At least, not a restaurant for food.

Which meant it would be delightful, enormous, and delicious fun to hear him explain it all to her.

And even more fun when she got to choose what she wanted.

"There are a few things that are not worth considering here," he began, scrutinizing the paper between them. "The dungeon, because of the leak, the sapphic play, because—well, it's just not an option here, and the fellatio fellows for the same reason."

She didn't think she had ever seen him blush, and yet there he was with heightened color on his cheeks. This menu was something indeed.

"So the horizontal refreshment is either participatory or observational," he continued. He ran his finger around his collar as though it was too tight. "Which means we can have the privacy to do whatever we want, or we can watch as someone else does those things."

Jane's eyes immediately widened. She knew precisely what he meant, thanks to his instruction.

"And tipping the velvet," he said, "is when kissing is applied to a vagina." He cleared his throat as she sharply inhaled. She had no idea. "When I would kiss my way down to your pussy and lick you until you orgasmed, to be specific."

His color had returned to its ordinary hue now, even though his words were absolutely not ordinary. Extraordinary, certainly; exciting, yes; incredible, yes also.

"Why not both?" she blurted before she could allow Lady Jane the Meek to respond. "I'd like to watch, and then I'd like to do. Or have you do that."

"Tipping the velvet?" he asked, his voice lowering to an intimate tone.

"Yes." She lifted her head as she replied, meeting his gaze so he could see her confidence, her passion, in her eyes. Or at least she hoped he'd see that.

A slow, sensual smile spread across his lips. And her heart fluttered in response.

Not to mention the response of her breasts, which felt heavy and tight, and her pussy, which felt as though it needed to be stroked.

"And later you can explain all these other things," she went on. She might as well get all the education she could until he was engaged.

Which, if the party was a success, would be in a little over a week.

Her heart sank.

"What is it?" he asked, his tone changing. He put his fingers to her chin and lifted it—she hadn't even been aware she had dropped it.

"It's nothing," she replied, shaking her head to emphasize her words. "I'm just—"

I'm just mourning the loss of you in my life, she thought. *I expected to spend time with someone who would educate me on things young unmarried ladies are not exposed to in their normal course of life. I didn't expect you to be so sensitive, so attuned to what I might want, so respectful of who I am. Of who I hope to become.*

What was she going to do when this all ended? When she could no longer spend time with him?

"Jane? Talk to me," he urged.

But he was here now, and so was she, and there were horizontal refreshments to be enjoyed, and velvets to be tipped.

"I am fine," she replied, reaching out to take his hand. "Let us continue my education."

Chapter Eighteen

"Who will it be tonight?"

They had left the waiting area and gone into a smaller room where a woman dressed in a gentleman's suit stood behind a counter.

Behind her was a small stage, and up on the stage were seated a variety of young men and women. They appeared to have been chatting, but as Jane and Thomas entered, they stopped speaking and turned to face them.

"Well?" Thomas said, turning to Jane.

"Well?" she echoed.

He gestured toward the group. Each person on the stage was attractive, though they differed widely from one another in size, shape, and skin color.

"Who do you wish to watch?" he asked.

She felt her cheeks heat. "You want me to choose who I wish—?"

He met her gaze. "I want you to choose everything, Jane."

Oh. The thought of that, just the idea of it, was enough to make her want to melt. But she wouldn't waste this evening, this moment when she was going to be able to make all the choices she could, when she was going to experience things she could safely assume no young lady of her station ever had.

Or if they had, they were not speaking of it.

"I want . . ." she began, her gaze traveling over the group in front of her. "The gentleman there, and the lady there."

The woman behind the counter nodded in satisfaction. "They will be a pleasure to watch, my lady," she said, beckoning to the two, both of whom rose and disappeared behind a curtain.

"You can go into Room 12," the woman said, pressing a key into Thomas's hand. "Your seat is the sofa, naturally."

"Naturally," Thomas repeated.

And then they were out of that room and walking down the hall to Room 12, Jane's heart beating faster with anticipation.

What would she be seeing? Would he be pleased with her reaction? What else could she possibly choose tonight?

"You are still fine with this?" he asked, pausing before the door.

She gave him a small smile as she nodded. "I am," she replied.

"Thank goodness. I might have died if you had said no," he replied in a matter-of-fact tone of voice.

He put the key into the door and flung it open.

And then they stepped inside.

JANE HAD SURPRISED him, yet again, with the choices she had made—the male of the two she'd chosen was a heavily muscled dark-haired gentleman who looked as though he'd come straight from the docks. His features were strong and fierce, his dark hair and eyes making him look like a brigand or a pirate.

The female was a lushly appointed redhead, with pale skin, brown eyes, and freckles. Her hair was unbound, and streamed down her back, while her gown was cut low enough to see the valley between the curves of her full breasts.

The two of them sat on the enormous bed that dominated the room as Jane and Thomas entered, both nodding but not getting up as Jane and Thomas lowered themselves onto the sofa that faced the bed. The sofa was small, made for just two people, and their thighs touched.

"Good evening," the woman said. Her gaze flicked between Jane and Thomas, settling on Thomas. "Tell us what you want to see."

Her tone was sultry, and she put her hand onto the man's thigh, giving it a squeeze as she spoke.

Thomas gave a wolfish grin in response, his eyes on Jane, who shifted beside him.

"What do you want to see?" Thomas said to Jane.

She looked back at him, her eyes wide and sparkling, her mouth still curled in that faint smile she'd worn before. "I don't know what to ask for. Perhaps—" she said, her eyes getting even wider. "Perhaps we can see the velvet thing?"

"Tipping the velvet?" the woman said, sounding pleased. "I like the way you think, my lady."

"What are your names, if you don't mind?" Jane asked. "I am Jane, and this is Thomas."

"I'm Hattie, and this is Miles," the woman said. "He doesn't like to speak much. He uses his mouth for other things," she continued.

The man—Miles—gave another of those wolfish grins, aimed directly at Jane.

"And then we want to see all of it," Thomas added.

"Thank you, sir," Miles replied in a growl.

"Do you have any instructions for how we get to everything?" Hattie asked.

Thomas turned to look at Jane, who shook her head.

"No, however you wish."

"Excellent," Hattie replied, getting up off the bed. She nodded toward Miles, who also got up. "I will tell him what to do. If you wish anything done another way, you can tell me." She looked over at Miles. "Is that clear?"

"Yes," he said in a gruff tone.

Thomas could see the man's erection already straining against his trousers. Presumably Jane could see it, too.

"Take your shirt off." Hattie shot a quick glance toward Jane. "You'll like what is underneath, my lady, I promise."

Miles yanked his shirt over his head, tossing it to the floor, then straightening his shoulders and placing his hands on his hips.

His chest was broad, covered with dark hair, and his arms were thickly muscled, making him look even more like a dock worker. As though he had been hauling boxes and pulling bowlines for hours a day.

Hattie stepped behind him to kneel on the bed, wrapping her arms around his upper body and kissing his neck. He responded by tilting his head back to allow her better access, and his hand began to travel down.

"No," Hattie ordered. "Not yet. That is mine to touch."

He grunted, instead reaching behind himself to put his hand on her waist.

She slid her hands over the planes of his chest, glancing up at Jane and Thomas every so often. Her fingers were splayed over his skin, the whiteness of her digits a sharp contrast to the dark hair she stroked.

"And now your trousers," she said.

Thomas heard Jane gasp, and turned to her. "If you want to stop—" he began.

"No, not at all," she replied. She swallowed, and then put her hand on his leg, squeezing it as Hattie had done to Miles at the beginning of the show.

Her eyes were dark with what Thomas had to assume was passion, and she was breathing more heavily beside him.

He put his hand on top of hers, stroking her skin. Idly pulling on the ribbons tied around her wrist as though he was undoing a package.

Miles undid his trousers and let them drop to the floor.

He wore nothing underneath, and his erection sprang proudly out from the thatch of dark hair.

Hattie got off the bed to stand in front of Miles, who had a fiercely hungry expression.

"Now undress me," she said.

Miles made another one of those inarticulate growls, his fingers going to the back of her gown, undoing it as he pressed close against her. He slid the garment off her shoulders, and she wriggled to get it past her hips.

She wore a very thin chemise underneath her gown. Her nipples were large and dark red, and the hair covering her pussy was dark red also.

"Take this off however you like," she said, an anticipatory smile playing on her lips.

Miles didn't hesitate, but put one hand on her belly, still behind her, then put the other hand to the front of her chemise, yanking it down with a loud shredding noise as the garment tore.

The fabric fell onto the floor, leaving Hattie also entirely naked.

"Kiss me," she commanded, still keeping her gaze on Thomas and Jane.

Miles stalked to stand in front of her, his back to them, grasping her jaw and pulling her face up to his, then lowering his mouth to hers.

They couldn't see the actual kiss, but they could see the two heads moving, see how her hands had come around to rest on his back, to go lower and squeeze his arse, see how his back muscles flexed as he shifted.

And they could hear the smacking of lips, the soft moans and rustles as they kept kissing.

Her hand had tightened its grip on his thigh, and her breathing was more intense.

"How does this make you feel, Jane?" he asked in a low rumble.

She breathed out before replying.

"I—it's exciting," she said.

Before Thomas could add anything, Miles had stopped kissing Hattie, and was instead hauling her onto the bed, spreading her legs wide so they could see her pussy.

"I didn't say you could do that," Hattie protested, but it didn't sound like a reprimand.

He growled in response, then got onto his knees at the end of the bed and put a hand on each thigh, holding her wide for him.

"Do you see how wet he makes me?" Hattie asked. "And he'll make me wetter still, won't you? With your tongue and teeth and mouth."

Another growl, and then he bent his head to her, his dark hair stark against her pale skin. Her hands went to his head to clasp him there, and she inhaled sharply at whatever he was doing.

"Just like that," she said, writhing with pleasure as her breasts jiggled in response.

Thomas held himself rigid, not wanting to do anything that would seem as though he was taking command—he wanted Jane to know she was in charge here, could ask for anything, and he would give it.

But watching the two on the bed, hearing the sucking and licking noises Miles was making as he devoured Hattie's pussy, was more arousing than anything he'd seen before. His cock throbbed in agony in his trousers, his body felt as though it needed to be touched.

But only by her.

And then her hand was sliding up and down his thigh, so close to his erection, and he held his breath as she moved her palm closer, closer, until she had her hand resting on him, making him long to shuck his trousers as Miles had so she could stroke him skin to skin.

"Is this—?" she asked, as though to seek his permission.

He cut her off with a short huff. "Goddamned right it is," he said. "Touch me as much as you want, Jane. I want all of it." Both of them were still facing toward the bed, their gazes riveted on what Miles and Hattie were doing.

Hattie moaned just as Jane grasped his shaft, rubbing him through the fabric of his trousers.

And then Hattie was crying out, her body undulating on the bed as Miles continued to grip her thighs, the muscles of his back flexing as he kept her from closing her legs.

Hattie screamed as Jane gripped him tightly, his cock aching from being so close to her and yet not nearly close enough.

And then, as soon as Hattie's cries ceased, Miles was up on the bed on his knees, twisting Hattie so she now lay sideways.

His cock was even more erect now, and he held it with one strong hand, the other holding him up over her body.

"Now?" Hattie asked, looking over at Jane.

Thomas felt her nod quickly, and then Hattie smiled.

"Fuck me," she commanded, and Miles pushed into her as she wrapped her legs around his body.

The two began to move together immediately, him thrusting in and out as she clung to his shoulders, her body shaking from the intensity of his actions.

Miles grabbed the leg that was closest to them and raised it up so they could see flashes of his cock as it went in and out of Hattie's pussy.

His hand gripped her thigh as he moved even faster and harder, now shoving Hattie up the bed with his movements.

And then Miles froze, flinging his head back as he groaned, a long guttural noise that seemed as though it had burst from him.

He collapsed onto Hattie immediately afterward, and she wrapped her arms around him.

The silence was sudden, and Thomas could hear Jane's panting breaths beside him, feel how she shifted as though uncomfortable.

Likely her body ached to be touched as much as his did, and he couldn't wait for her to allow him to do so.

"Thank you," Jane said at last, her voice lower than usual. Her hand was back on his thigh.

"It was our pleasure," Hattie replied, lazily stroking her hand through Miles's dark hair. "Wasn't it?"

He grunted in reply, and Hattie shrugged, a little smile on her curved mouth.

Thomas rose, adjusting himself before offering his hand to Jane to assist her.

She stood, a bit unsteady, and Thomas put his hand on her elbow to prevent her from stumbling.

She gazed up at him with passion-darkened eyes, her cheeks rosy, her mouth redder than usual, probably because she'd been biting her lip.

He wanted to bite her lip, too.

"Take me somewhere private," she said, her tone urgent. "Now."

JANE HAD NEVER felt more exhilarated, more alive, than she had in the past half hour. Watching two strangers perform intimate actions in front of her was far more than she had expected—just watching them had set every nerve ending on fire, made that part of her ache with want.

And now they were going somewhere so he could do the same thing to her.

She'd had no idea that men did that to ladies before. That ladies would like it as much as Hattie clearly had.

That the man would like it as well, judging by how aroused Miles had been, how he'd been intent on his task, had brought her to that pleasure.

She hadn't intended, of course, to touch Thomas there. On his cock, which had been hard as iron in his trousers.

But she'd needed to, had been desperate to touch him, had wanted to kiss him, and more, but knew that that would be coming later.

Now, in fact.

They paused in front of another door, and Thomas turned the knob and opened it, allowing her to step inside first, following quickly after and shutting it behind them.

She heard the distinct sound of a lock being slid, and then his hands were on her arms, stroking up and down, and she leaned back against him, tilting her head against his upper chest, wiggling her body so her arse could feel his erection against her.

"You'll be the death of me, Jane," he murmured, kissing her temple.

"You'll be the little death of me," she retorted smartly, delighted at her own wordplay.

He snorted, burying his face in her hair, his hands clasping each other as he embraced her.

Like the first room, this room was dominated by the bed, a massive four-poster made of some sort of dark wood. The bed covering was a lush fabric in shades of cranberry, gold, and navy blue, and there were multiple pillows strewn on the bed and, intriguingly, on the floor in front of the bed.

Assistance for someone's knees, perhaps?

She wouldn't have had that thought an hour ago. But now she knew, and that knowledge was kindling her from the inside out.

"What would you like first?" he asked.

She knew he wouldn't let her demur to his suggestions. It was clear this was her night, her choice, her desire.

"I want you to undress." She jutted her chin toward the bed. "Right in front of the bed, right in front of me."

"Gladly," he replied, biting her shoulder gently before disengaging from the embrace.

He strode past her, removing his jacket as he walked, placing it on a nearby chair before turning back to face her.

He met her gaze as his hands went to his collar, loosening his shirt. He yanked it out of his trousers, then drew it up over his head, flinging it on top of his jacket.

He was leaner than Miles, with more sharply

defined musculature. He was much less hairy—
Jane hadn't realized that men could come in such a
variety—and a line of hair ran from his belly but-
ton down into his trousers as if it were tantalizing
signage.

And then he'd removed his trousers, stepping
out of them adroitly as he put them over his shirt
on that same chair.

His erection thrust through his smallclothes,
and she swallowed at the sight. He was aching for
her as much as she was aching for him.

And he had to wait longer to reach his release
because this was her night, her choice, her desire.

As if he was following her unspoken wish, he
reached for his cock and grasped it, sliding his
hand up and down it as he kept his eyes focused
on her. "You do this to me, Jane. Your soft, sweet
body. Your delicious kisses. Your aching pussy.
Tell me how it feels, Jane."

"Not until you're naked," she ordered, surprised
at her own audacity. Though she shouldn't be—he
had brought this forth in her; he had encouraged
her; he had helped her give voice to what it was
she wanted.

Which was . . . *him*.

But she couldn't think about that now, about the
inevitability of their parting.

Now was for now, and she would savor every
drop of this experience to remind her later of
everything she'd done and felt.

"And then you'll tell me?" he coaxed, his hands
at his waistband.

She nodded.

He slid the smallclothes off, stepping out to stand proudly naked in front of her.

She let herself look her fill—though she could never tire of looking at him like this—her gaze running over his strong shoulders, his lean abdomen, his erect penis, and his muscled legs.

Even his feet were attractive.

"I think about you when I'm touching myself," he said, putting his hand back on his cock and sliding it up and down.

"What do you think about?" she asked.

He nodded toward her. "How you'll undo your gown and let it slide slowly off your shoulders. How it'll pool at your feet and then you'll be wearing only your chemise, your stockings, and your shoes. How I can see the outline of your breasts through the sheer fabric. How you might raise the hem of your chemise inch by inch, showing me more of your leg, your thigh, until you show me what I am dying to kiss."

She gasped at his words, then reached around to undo her buttons so she could suit her actions to his words.

Thankfully she'd gone without a maid for long enough she was able to undress herself. There was a benefit to being a scandalous lady, after all.

Not to mention being able to do all this without worrying someone would find out. Because if they did it wouldn't matter. She had already caused gossip when Mr. McTavish had jilted her—likely many already believed her capable of such behavior.

And now she knew she *was* capable of such behavior, and she was proud of it. She wished every young lady could have this kind of experience, to know how their bodies felt, and what their bodies wanted to do, and what was possible between two people. Or more, she thought, thinking of Miles and Hattie.

"Show me, Jane," he said in a ragged voice. His hand still stroked his shaft, his gaze was hungry on her, and it was as though he was touching her, he was regarding her so intently.

But he wasn't touching her, and she would have to change that.

She put her gown on top of his clothing on the chair and went to the bed, passing him to sit up on it. She folded her hands in her lap, straightening, biting her lip at how exposed she felt.

She still wore her chemise, stockings, and shoes, as he'd requested.

And then he got down on the floor, kneeling on the pillow, his hands on her thighs spreading her knees apart. As Miles had done to Hattie.

Her breath hitched. "Will you be—tipping the velvet?" she asked.

"Yes, indeed," he replied, and his words were a promise, a vow, a dedication.

He lowered his head to one knee and kissed it softly. It wasn't nearly enough.

But before she could say anything, his lips moved up her thigh, kissing every few inches, his fingers spreading her wide, drawing the hem of the chemise up so it rested around her hips. So she was open to him.

"Beautiful," he murmured. He glanced up at her, a wicked smile on his mouth. "I am going to kiss you there, Jane. And you are going to tell me what you like. If you don't like something, just let me know, and I will try something else."

"Oh," she breathed. He made it sound as though she would know what she would like, and she supposed that she would—after all, she was a woman who was exploring, and who had more knowledge than she had the day before, and likely she'd have more knowledge tomorrow.

He returned his fervid gaze to there, to her pussy. Just knowing the word made her feel stronger.

And then he blew softly on her, and she shuddered.

And then he pressed his mouth there, and she started in surprise.

"Too much?" he asked.

"No—I just—go on," she said.

"What do you want, Jane?" he demanded. "Tell me."

"I want you to—I want you to keep doing that," she replied. "Kiss me there until I come."

He chuckled in response, then gave her a strong, fierce lick that sent shivers through her whole body. His hands were gripping the globes of her arse, his elbows tucked into her knees holding her wide for him.

She leaned back on her arms, closing her eyes as she surrendered to the feeling.

His mouth was warm and urgent, kissing her in a variety of ways, clearly listening to her response because he did more of what made her sigh, and less of the things that didn't cause as much of a reaction.

His tongue licked there, where he'd rubbed her to climax in her bedroom, and while both feelings were marvelous, they were also entirely different. This felt as though she was losing her consciousness, lost over to sheer pleasure with each swipe of his tongue.

When he'd touched her there, she'd been so very aware of her entire body, of how it ached. Now everything felt blissful, as though she were half asleep and lying in a lily pond or something equally whimsical.

And then something shifted, and she began to feel a drive toward the peak of pleasure, a suffusing of her entire body as she headed toward the inevitable orgasm.

One hand reached up to caress her breast, and then his palm was rubbing over her nipple. His other hand was now on her pussy, his fingers caressing her as his tongue kept up its wicked assault.

She tilted her head back more as everything came together in one mad rush, and she screamed as she came, shaking and crying as the climax flowed through her.

She'd never felt so boneless in her entire life. So satisfied.

She allowed herself to fall back onto the bed and he got up to lie beside her, placing one hand on her stomach.

"Did you like that?" he asked, his expression smug.

She huffed out a breath as she gave him a mocking glance. "I think my scream at the end there might answer that question."

"I like to hear you scream," he said softly, then leaned forward to kiss her.

She could taste herself on his lips.

"Thank you," she murmured when they drew apart.

"Thank you for letting me see that. It was a pleasure."

His fingers strayed up to her breast again, feeling their fullness. His erection was hard against her leg.

"Doesn't that hurt?" she asked, nodding toward it.

He shrugged. "It's fine. I'm an adult—I can handle a little excitement."

She arched her brow. "Just a little? Don't be so modest, Thomas."

He let out a snort of laughter, and then he was kissing her again, and she didn't want it to stop, never wanted it to stop.

Only it would have to. Eventually. If eventually meant as soon as next week.

But she would have these moments to savor forever.

Chapter Nineteen

$\mathscr{A}$re you ready to go?" Thomas asked, stroking her hair away from her face.

She was always beautiful, but she was absolutely glorious now: her cheeks were flushed, her eyes were lidded, and her lips were swollen from her biting them and his kissing her.

Not to mention the rest of her, which was tantalizingly outfitted in a sheer chemise, stockings, and her shoes.

"But what about you?" she replied, her eyes darting down to where his cock pushed against her leg.

"Tonight is for you," he replied.

And it was. He had enjoyed her orgasm nearly as much as she had, and his current uncomfortable state was a sweet agony that heightened every emotion, every shift of her body against his.

Yes, he'd go home and pleasure himself with his hand thinking of her. Eventually. But right now he just wanted to savor her, her reaction. To give himself over to her pleasure, literally.

And only too soon it would be over.

Well. That was one way to calm himself down.

He exhaled, suppressing the urge to tell her precisely how he felt. Because it would be selfish. It would be wrong.

And it wouldn't matter.

Even if she felt precisely the same way, she'd never allow him to swerve from his chosen course, to put his happiness over that of his family's.

Nor would he, honestly.

But he wished he could tell her, if only to let her know how special the past few weeks had been. How special the time leading up to his betrothal would be.

Not just these moments, but the times when she was embracing the unknown—flying in a balloon, or in a dance hall, or trying whisky for the first time.

She might believe herself to be hesitant, but she was truly fearless. He admired that quality. It wasn't the recklessness that other young men of his class adopted as proof that they were sufficiently devil-may-care; it was a thoughtful weighing of the risks, balancing the outcome versus the potential losses.

And each time the new experience won out.

"What are you thinking about?" she asked. She spoke in a dreamy tone, likely still in postorgasmic bliss.

You. "I'm thinking about our journey here," he replied. So he could answer somewhat honestly, though he wouldn't tell her just how much or what he was thinking of her. "We met for the first time just after you and Percy set up house together. But it wasn't until—"

"Until I went to Miss Ivy's," she finished. "And

got so angry that you were trying to take Percy's place, if Percy was the type of brother to frown disapprovingly when I merely wanted to have fun."

"I did not frown disapprovingly!"

He felt her shoulders shrug. His hand was still on her belly, his legs tucked against hers.

"You frowned as you chided me for not knowing what I was doing. When I knew perfectly well what I was doing."

"Such as when you drank my whisky?" he teased.

She pulled his hand off her stomach and placed it exaggeratedly back on his body. "I knew it was going to be an adventure. And it was," she replied in a haughty tone.

He smothered a chuckle, but not nearly well enough, since she got up to put her knees on either side of his body and lean over him menacingly.

If she was at all menacing instead of alluring, her silver-blond hair hanging down and tickling his bare skin. Her chemise still rucked up around her waist, her breath soft on his skin.

"If I'd known you would react like this I would have mentioned your inability to hold your whisky before," he said in a laughing voice, his hands going to her waist.

She arched a brow. "And if I'd known you could show me all of this I would have drunk your whisky sooner."

And then they were both laughing, and she tumbled onto his body, and he wrapped his arms around her, and it was joyful, and companionable, and perfect.

She was perfect.

But he was not. Because he had to marry someone else.

"I should get you home," he said when their laughter had subsided.

"Because of Percy?" she said in a suspicious tone.

"No, I would never dare suggest you answer to anybody but yourself, my lady," he replied. Sounding as though he was taunting her, but truly meaning what he'd said.

"Exactly so," she replied.

She got up off the bed and was quickly dressed again, Thomas already mourning the loss of her nearly naked self.

Already mourning the loss of her.

HE DIDN'T ALLOW himself to think about her, about how hopeless everything was, for the next few days. Alice had replied saying she very much would like to attend the party, and he'd been engrossed in planning her visit.

And then he was on the train to his parents' village with plenty of time to think.

Something he did not want to do.

What if—what if he could figure out some way to make enough money to prevent his having to sell himself to the highest bidder?

Though if there was any other way out of it, he would have thought of it before.

What if he found some ancient wealthy woman to woo and hope—

No, that was both cruel and macabre.

And it wasn't what he truly wanted. Because

though his first priority was to marry a wealthy young lady, he also wanted a family. A home that was more than a glorified boarding house.

A person to care for. Even if he knew he might never love her.

"Mr. Sharpe?"

Thomas snapped out of his reverie to see an older gentleman addressing him. He searched his brain to remember the man's name—

"I'm Mr. Grosvenor. I believe you know my daughter?" And then the man smiled in a knowing way, as though he was aware that Thomas might be interested in his daughter matrimonially, and he was fine with that.

That was the most encouragement he'd gotten in the two years he'd been on the heiress hunt. Jane had clearly been holding up her end of their bargain. It should make him feel relieved.

It did not.

"Ah, yes, Mr. Grosvenor." Thomas rose, gesturing to the seat opposite him. "Would you care to join me?"

Please say no.

"Yes, thank you." The gentleman nodded behind him and a servant appeared holding a leather case, which he set above them on the wooden shelf. "That is all for now. Come back when they announce the station."

"Yes, sir," the valet replied.

Mr. Grosvenor made one of those older gentleman noises as he sat down, adjusting his jacket so it wouldn't wrinkle. He had thinning white hair with a bald patch on top, a full white beard, and light blue eyes. He looked like St. Nicholas, if St. Nicholas was wearing a bespoke suit.

"My daughter says you've been very kind to her."

"Yes, well, she is a kind person." Thomas gave an easy smile. "Not difficult to be kind to one such as she."

"She's the apple of my eye, I have to say. She and my wife—my second wife, you understand, not Millie's mother—get along well, too. But I know Millie wants to have her own home someday."

And then he gave another knowing look at Thomas, who was increasingly beginning to feel as though this perfectly nice older man was tying a noose around his neck.

A noose he wanted tied around his neck, to be fair.

But still a noose.

And how was he to answer that? *Yes, we all want our own homes someday.* That wasn't really Mr. Grosvenor's point. And he couldn't very well reply, *Well that is a lucky coincidence, I too am hoping to have my own home today, a home funded by Miss Grosvenor's dowry.*

Instead, he asked what he imagined Jane would ask if she was in the same situation.

"Have you asked her about that?"

Mr. Grosvenor's expression drew puzzled.

"About her own home, and if that is what she truly wants in her future."

Jane would be proud of him. At least he had that certainty to hold close at night.

"It's what all young ladies want," Mr. Grosvenor replied easily. As though it was a truth along with "Queen Victoria is quite short," and "London never has two sunny days in a row."

"I am not certain about that," Thomas said. He met Mr. Grosvenor's gaze. "I have come to realize that what we believe about young ladies in our world is not necessarily so. They seldom get the opportunity to speak for themselves."

Mr. Grosvenor opened his mouth to reply, but Thomas couldn't stop speaking, not now that he'd started.

"They answer when they're asked about the weather, or if they want tea, or do they want to dance. And even then they're discouraged from answering honestly—what if it's raining, and they are upset because they had planned to walk to a bookstore and purchase a book to enjoy during a rare evening alone? Or if the person wanting to dance with them smells too much like his favorite horse?"

"I never thought about that," Mr. Grosvenor replied in a thoughtful tone.

At least he wasn't insulted.

Mr. Grosvenor got a quizzical expression. "Do you think my Millie wants to buy a book in your scenario?"

Thomas shrugged, offering a wry smile. "I couldn't say. I haven't asked her." He took a deep breath. "I do know that she is intelligent, and capable of looking after herself, though some of Society's norms make that more difficult." Lord Joseph's attempt at high-handedly whisking Miss Grosvenor off to the gardens was one such circumstance. If he and Jane hadn't been there—well, likely Miss Grosvenor would have handled the situation, but it could have been so much more scandalous.

Mr. Grosvenor nodded thoughtfully. "None of us has spent much time in Society. I've always been too busy with work, and then I got married again, and my wife insisted we take Millie to town. That she deserves better than the country squire down the road. Nothing but the best for my girl," he said proudly.

It was obvious how much Mr. Grosvenor loved his daughter, though it was also obvious Mr. Grosvenor wasn't the type to question whether someone was making the right choice. The country squire, for example—

"Miss Grosvenor hasn't mentioned anybody from home, not that I recall," Thomas said, as tactfully as he could manage. Which was exceedingly tactful. "Is there someone she was especially friendly with?"

Mr. Grosvenor shrugged. "Not for me to say. I mean, Squire Andrews's family lives down the road, and he does have a son a year younger than Millie. But I don't think—do you know, I've never thought about it."

Thomas waited as Mr. Grosvenor turned the new ideas over in his head.

"Do you know, I'll have to ask Millie."

Thomas nodded, exhaling with a sort of relief. Hopefully, no matter what happened, Mr. Grosvenor would consult with his daughter about what she might want.

Jane would be proud of him.

"But what are you doing heading to Halston? Aren't you supposed to be in London making certain every young lady sees your handsome face?" Mr. Grosvenor spoke with the kind of gruff bonhomie Thomas hoped to achieve when he was Mr. Grosvenor's age.

"I am collecting my sister to bring her back to town." He smiled as he thought about Alice, about how her eyes would get huge at some of the things she would get to see. "She is with my parents now, but I am bringing her up to attend a party." He paused. "A party I believe your daughter will also be attending."

"Oh, well that is excellent. Wouldn't want to deprive the London ladies of your company."

"And you?" Thomas asked.

Mr. Grosvenor's chest puffed just a bit before he spoke. "The queen has asked me to run down to one of her smaller estates to review the inventory. Seems there was a discrepancy and she knows I have the most knowledge of the product."

"Ah, inventory discrepancy," Thomas replied, sounding as though he knew exactly what Mr. Grosvenor was talking about.

Even though he absolutely did not.

"Yes, that's right. You're as sharp as your name, hmm?" And then Mr. Grosvenor laughed at his own joke, and Thomas smiled, because the gentleman's easy affability was infectious. If it meant he could stop thinking about his own problems for just a moment and focus on someone else—well, perhaps he wouldn't feel as though he had the worst situation in the world.

Because it truly wasn't awful. It was something young ladies did every day, marry for money instead of love. That it was now he who had to do it didn't make it any less common.

"Perhaps I will accompany Millie to this party. Mrs. Grosvenor is always complaining I work too hard. Says I should go out and enjoy myself once in a while."

"And you should," Thomas replied. He thought about having fun with Jane—dance halls, and circuses, and balloon trips. Walking through a fair. Spending time together at parties.

Simple things that were profoundly enjoyable because of the company.

"What do you do when you're not going to parties and the like?" Mr. Grosvenor asked. "Not meaning you have to work for a living—I know you come from a good family."

The words hit Thomas as though he had been punched in the gut.

He came from a good family so clearly he couldn't actually work for a living? Even though Mr. Grosvenor here did work, and was striving to give his daughter a better position in life than he had?

"I have to say I wish I did work," Thomas replied honestly. "Having purpose to my days would be preferable to going from party to party. That is," he continued, drawing his brows together as he thought, "if I had the skills to earn my living, I would do that, most assuredly. It's no secret that I require a certain amount of funds to help my family." He inhaled, a lightness in his chest at saying aloud what everyone knew already. He could hear Jane again, remarking that few people seldom said what they felt. That she had vowed to speak her mind, and had been doing just that during their time together.

I want to do whatever I need to your cock to make you come.

Kiss me there until I come.

Take me somewhere private.

But he couldn't share his honest emotions with her, not the most important one. The one that began with *I* and ended with *love you*.

Because it would ruin everything.

His throat got tight as Mr. Grosvenor began to discuss the details of his inventory discrepancy. Thomas listened with half an ear, the rest of him pushing against the anguish of knowing it would be over soon.

Chapter Twenty

Alice was flying out the door when Thomas had just opened the gate.

He grinned, dropping his valise on the ground as he spread his arms wide to catch her.

"Thomas!" she yelled before barreling into his chest.

He wrapped his arms around her, noting that she had grown quite a few inches from the last time he'd hugged her.

"That is a wonderful welcome," he said after a few moments.

She looked up at him, a huge smile on her face.

Alice shared his coloring, but was stockier, like their father. When she wasn't shrinking away in the corner, she was wonderfully personable, a curious bookworm who wanted to know everything about everyone.

"Come inside, the parents are nearly as excited to see you as I am."

Thomas bent down to pick up his valise with one hand, then extended the other so Alice could lead him to the door, even though of course he knew the way.

But the simple family contact felt so good he welcomed it, gripping her hand tightly in his.

One of the few remaining servants—Tudsworth, their butler—opened the door, a broad smile on his face. "Welcome home, Mr. Thomas," Tudsworth said. "Your parents are in the sitting room."

Thomas put his valise on the floor, nodding at Tudsworth. "I'll go right in."

"I'll make sure we've got tea on the way," Alice said, nearly skipping off to the kitchen.

Thomas made his way to the sitting room, an uneasy anticipation in his gut. He knew from Alice's letters and what his parents didn't say in theirs that they were both in ill health. That they were terrified they would die and leave Alice with nothing to live on.

The weight of what he had to do was always heavy, but faced with the reality—seeing the peeling wallpaper, the worn rug, the scuffs on the baseboards—brought the weight crashing down around him.

How could he even envision a life without trying to help them? Just because he had had the audacity to fall in love?

He couldn't. He wouldn't.

He put his hand on the knob and flung the door open, pasting a smile on his lips.

His mother and father were on either side of the fireplace, a wanly flickering fire casting shadows on the floor. His mother rose, her gown hanging around her thin frame, her face worn and tired. But she was smiling broadly, so much so that her eyes were crinkling as well, and she'd stretched her arms out toward him.

He hastened forward, clasping her gently as she hugged him.

"We're so glad you came for a visit," she said.

Thomas glanced toward his father, who remained sitting, his cane in his hand. His father looked as though he'd aged ten years since the last time Thomas had visited.

"Hello, Father," he said as he disengaged from his mother.

He knelt down by the side of his father's chair, placing his hand on his father's.

"Hello, son," his father said. It sounded as though even those two words were difficult for his father to speak. Clearly his lungs were giving him even more trouble than before. "We're glad you're home," he continued, speaking jerkily.

"Tea is on the way!" Alice announced as she burst into the room.

Thomas turned and smiled at her.

Her smile faltered as she glanced at first their father, and then their mother, who had retaken her seat.

He hadn't thought about how difficult it must be for a young girl—growing into a young woman— living with only her older parents for company. She was too shy to venture into Society herself, even though their village was small enough to tolerate a young woman going about on her own, since everyone knew her.

So she must spend her days here, her only respite her writing, both the column she'd gotten, and the letters to Thomas.

If he were to fail at his goal he would have to find a way to make Alice's life more tolerable, no matter what.

Not that he was going to fail at his goal. Jane was seeing to that by inviting so many eligible young ladies.

BACK ON THE train the next day, Alice already seemed as though she'd blossomed.

"How bad is it?" he asked, after they'd settled themselves into their seats.

She shrugged, looking pained. "Bad enough. But things will be better soon?" Her voice was so hopeful it broke his heart.

As though it wasn't already breaking. Broken, once he'd proposed to someone else and been accepted. Which could be as soon as within a week.

"I believe so. My friends"—he paused as his throat closed—"my friends are assisting me, and I hope to secure someone soon."

Alice tucked her arm through his, leaning against his shoulder. "I hope your wife is kind to you."

Thomas gave a rueful smile. "I'll have to be very kind to her to persuade her to marry me."

She glanced up at him. "But you're so handsome and charming and good at parties already. What else could they want?"

As though that was all he was. Even though of course she didn't mean it that way—she no doubt envied his easy way of navigating Society, aware that it was near impossible for her. That her going to London to attend a party was the most daring thing she had ever done.

And he would be by her side the entire time to ensure she had fun and not terror.

"I would hope they would want for themselves what I want for you: a person who cares for them, who asks them how they are, who is thoughtful in all sorts of ways, big and small." He thought of his conversations with Jane, of how he'd spoken up for Miss Grosvenor to her father. How he hoped all the women he knew could champion themselves as Jane had.

"Two years ago," he continued, "my only goal was to find a lady with enough money to afford us. All of us. But now I want to be certain the lady will be happy with the bargain. I cannot trick her into marriage just because I happen to be charming and handsome. I hope there is something behind my appearance."

It struck him that he was replaying his first conversation with Jane, where they'd acknowledged the beauty of the other, both longing for there to be more to them than that.

There certainly was more to Jane.

Whether or not there was more to him, he couldn't yet say.

"You will make her happy," Alice said confidently. "Because you've changed in these two years. I wouldn't have said that before—before you were so fierce and single-minded in your goal. As though it was something to be conquered, not a life to be led. But now you're more thoughtful."

I have her to thank for that.

"I suppose I am," he admitted. He gave her a wry smile. "But you have to say I remain handsome and charming," he said, waggling his eyebrows at her.

She laughed, as she was meant to, and snuggled in closer.

But he'd meant what he'd said. He could not in good conscience marry anyone he didn't think would be happy with him for the rest of their lives. Even if she had all the money in the world.

"WE'VE GOTTEN REPLIES to the invitations already," Percy called out joyously as Jane walked into the dining room.

She'd come home late, and undone, and been relieved that Percy wasn't about. She'd managed to sleep a few hours before waking up, torn between exhilaration at what had happened the night before and despair that it—that this—wouldn't be able to happen again.

Unless he failed in his mission. And she could not allow that to happen.

She went to the server and poured herself a cup of coffee, then took it to her seat beside Percy. The replies to their party invitations were stacked to the right of his plate, and he grabbed one as she took a sip of coffee.

"This is from the Porters, Miss Porter would be delighted to attend." He dropped that letter and picked up another. "And this, from Lady Emily, which means all the rest of her gaggle will come, too." He surveyed the pile of letters with smug satisfaction. "We should have Thomas married off in no time."

Jane managed to give a vague smile in response, at which Percy's eyes narrowed.

"You haven't done what I specifically said you should not do, have you?"

Jane took a deep breath. Had she?

"You have!" he continued accusingly. "You went and fell in love with him. Oh, Jane, don't you know you'll just be heartbroken?"

Jane put her cup down with more force than she meant to. "It's not as though I chose to do that. You can't choose who you fall in love with."

Percy's face turned pale.

Jane immediately reached out to grab his hand to squeeze it. "I didn't mean it like that. I am so sorry."

He shook his head. "It's fine. I just—you're right." He took a few deep breaths and returned Jane's hand squeeze. "So what are you going to do?"

She shrugged. Given that she had just admitted her feelings to herself it would be remarkable if she had a plan, especially given that any plan that saw them getting together would mean his family would suffer.

"There's nothing I can do. I can't tell him—he did warn me not to. As you did." She took another sip of coffee. "I don't want him to feel sorry for me. I don't want him to feel obligated to do anything—not that he could do anything—and I don't want to have him know for all time, especially if he marries Miss Grosvenor, whom I happen to like very much."

"You're in a pickle, aren't you?" Percy remarked. He had recovered rather quickly.

"A pickle of love," she said with a smirk. If she could make light of it, perhaps it wouldn't hurt as much.

No, that didn't work. It did hurt as much.

Knowing he was hers for just a brief time longer made her heart ache. But there wasn't anything to be done for it—he had his course chosen, and so did she. She would just have to treasure whatever time they had left together.

And then see him every time he came to visit Percy, or if she and his wife were friends she'd see him even more. Never mind that they attended the same Society events, so she'd likely see him nearly as frequently as she did now.

Perhaps she should move to Australia. Or take herself off to some dark forest in Wales—not that she knew much about Wales, just that they had very few vowels and Society people were more likely to go to Scotland or Ireland if they left London at all.

"I promise I won't say anything to him," Percy said. His expression was soft, as though he knew just how Jane was feeling.

And perhaps he did.

"Is—is Daffy coming to the party?"

Percy nodded, his lips set in a straight line.

"Is something wrong?"

"I'm in as much of a pickle as you are," he replied, his voice melancholy. "Because I've fallen in love, too."

Jane immediately got up out of her chair to step to Percy's side, enclosing him in her arms. "I am so sorry," she murmured. Her eyes stung with sudden tears.

"Me too," he said. He patted her arm. "But at least we have each other."

"Forever," she said in a fierce tone of voice.

A WEEK LATER, and Jane had barely seen Thomas, which made everything seem so much more agonizing.

Oh, they'd been at the same parties, and exchanged greetings, but it seemed as though his tutelage of her was finished. It wasn't his fault; party planning was much more extensive than she had envisioned, and then Percy had gotten a cold, and required buckets of tea and soothing words. Thomas had sent word that his sister Alice was attending, so he was going to go to his parents' house to collect her, and spend a day or two there.

And now the party was two hours off, and she was standing in her bedroom trying to figure out what to wear.

"Something that will make you look exciting and dangerous," Lavinia called out from the corner of the room.

And Lavinia was here. She'd informed her husband that she was needed for party preparation, and had arrived earlier that morning, trailing her maid, a few changes of clothing, her dog Precious, and no baby.

"So nothing I currently own in my wardrobe?" Jane remarked.

"You can borrow something from me. That's why I brought so much—I knew you'd need something to wear."

Jane put her hands on her hips and faced her sister. "You are aware, are you not, that I am both taller and less . . . curvaceous than you are?"

Lavinia dismissed her with a wave of her hand. "It's a party all about exposing people to things they wouldn't normally see."

Jane wrinkled her brow. "So you want me to expose them to my ankles and lack of bosom?"

"Stop being so literal," Lavinia replied. She went to the door and poked her head out, calling for her maid. "Nancy, come in here, would you?"

Jane shook her head, bemused as always at just how much energy seemed to surround Lavinia even when she was just standing.

Her sister had always been the braver of the two, leading them into all sorts of trouble, even though she was younger.

She had tumbled headfirst into marriage, and then love, with her husband, the Duke of Hasford, and was as happy as Jane had ever seen her.

A husband who loved her. Children. A settled future.

All things that Jane didn't think she would ever have, at least not for many years. Yes, she and Percy could continue to live together, and yes, perhaps someday—perhaps even tonight—she and her mother would reconcile, but it wasn't the same.

Though she also wouldn't have to worry about marrying for the wrong reasons, or allowing herself to make a decision that was the easiest to make, if not the best for her.

"This one, I think," Lavinia said, plucking one of the gowns her maid was holding up.

Jane hadn't even noticed the maid's arrival—she was too busy thinking about her lack of a future.

But now was, well, *now* and she would enjoy whatever time she had left. With him, with her freedom, with her friends and her family.

Not that she was going to slip away after tonight, but it felt as though tonight was the culmination of everything she had wanted to do since moving out of her parents' house: taking charge of something and seeing it through herself, allowing other women like her to see something that they wouldn't normally see, supporting her friend as he tried to support his family.

And now that the door had been opened—now that she had opened the door herself and stepped through it, thank you very much—she was going to have to navigate her life after Thomas. But she would be navigating the world with much more knowledge than she had had previously.

"Jane."

"Oh!" Jane said, yanking her thoughts back to now, to gowns and parties and the dissemination of knowledge. "I'm sorry, I was just—"

"I know what you were doing," Lavinia replied in an arch tone.

"Hush," Jane said, her gaze flicking toward Lavinia's maid, Nancy.

"We don't have time for you to stand around and moon—we need to get you dressed." Lavinia gestured to the gown Nancy held with a flourish. "So, what do you think?"

Jane's eyes widened as she drank in the gown's details. It was black, but not the unrelieved black a widow might wear; it was ornamented with clear glass, as though someone had sprinkled water all over it. It shimmered in the candlelight, glinting as Nancy shifted to give Jane a better view.

Its sleeves were so tiny as to be barely worth calling sleeves, and it was made of black satin that also gleamed in the candlelight.

"You'll look like a mysterious creature who lives on the moon."

Jane wrinkled her brow. "That sounds like I'm a bug."

Lavinia waved her hand. "Or descended from a star, or whatever you wish. You'll look beautiful in this—it is striking and majestic and will ensure you stand out from everyone else."

"Why couldn't you have said that instead of the part about the moon?"

One eyebrow rose. "You do not appreciate an author's flight of fancy," Lavinia said haughtily. Ruined only by how her expression immediately turned mischievous. "Now, will you try it on and we can see what needs to be done to make it work on you?"

"We don't have enough time," Jane replied. "Remember the whole more bosom, less height thing?"

"Nancy can work miracles," Lavinia replied. "Can't you?"

"Yes, Your Grace," the maid said.

"And I've promised Nancy a generous bonus for doing the work. So stop wasting time."

"Fine," Jane replied.

Ten minutes later, Jane was in the gown, looking at her reflection in the glass. Twenty minutes later and Nancy had adjusted and pinned the fabric where it needed to be altered. Thirty minutes later and Jane was back in just her chemise, letting Lavinia do her hair as Nancy worked.

And then an hour and a half later—a half hour before the party's official start time—she was wearing the gown, now fitting appropriately around her bust with an extra length of fabric draped on the hem to make it reach the floor.

"You truly are a miracle worker," Jane said to Nancy, her eyes wide.

She didn't look at all like herself. The gown now fit her perfectly, the satin making her curves even more . . . curvy. And when she moved, the glass gems glittered and danced in the light, making it look as though she was lit from within.

Lavinia had dressed her hair simply, pulling a few strands out to achieve a studied messiness that was opposite to the way their mother had always insisted Jane's hair be dressed.

And of course the gown was literally as far from debutante white as was possible.

She looked—and now she felt—supremely confident, certain that the evening would be a success, and Thomas would finally find his bride.

Damn it.

She couldn't think about that now. Just that she

was doing something for someone she loved, even if her action would result in her losing her love.

She turned and smiled at Lavinia, whose expression was justifiably smug. "I don't think I look like I live on the moon, but I do look incredible," she said.

"Yes, you do." Lavinia gestured toward the door. "Shall we go to your coming out party?"

"I had a coming out party three years ago," Jane replied in confusion.

Lavinia shook her head. "No, your *real* coming out party. Where you reveal yourself to be the strong, wonderful person we know you to be."

"Oh."

Jane felt her eyes start to prickle, and then both sisters were in one another's arms, both crying as Nancy fussed around with handkerchiefs and water.

It was her coming out party. And she would enjoy every minute of it.

Chapter Twenty-One

$\mathcal{H}$e saw her as soon as he entered the building.

And felt his breath leave his body.

"Thomas?" Alice asked in confusion.

"I'm fine. Just—I'm fine," he replied.

She stood at the other end of the room, standing with Percy and her sister, the Duchess of Hasford, as though in a receiving line, though Thomas and Alice were the first to arrive.

Servants, circus performers, and various oddly dressed people circulated through the room busily, all intent on some task or another. It looked appropriately and delightfully busy, and he was confident that she would deliver the experience she'd promised.

To the guests, of course; to him she had already delivered more than enough of what she'd promised. Though she had promised him nothing beyond her influence.

Their eyes met across the room, and he saw her lift her chin and smile, then turn to speak to her siblings, indicating his presence.

Her gown was black with glints of silver strewn

on it. Her hair matched the silver, and she looked as though she was from another world, one where fairies and nymphs and pixies tempted humans into their seductive traps.

And the humans knew what they were doing, and were glad to go to their fate, certain they would be rewarded with infinite pleasure.

If only it were that simple. If only he could just step toward her and let her guide him to her secret home, a place where nobody could find them and all they needed to do was explore one another.

"You won't leave me?" Alice said, her hand clutching his arm.

He looked down at his sister with a reassuring expression. "I will not. Even if some lady wishes to have her way with me in the shrubbery," he said, waggling his eyebrows.

Alice looked so grown-up it was hard to believe she was the same girl he'd spent years protecting. She wore one of their mother's evening gowns, altered to fit her, a simple cream-colored gown with lace trim. Instead of wearing her hair down, like she usually did, she'd swept it to the back of her head, revealing her elegant neck. He had to stop himself from commenting too much on how lovely she looked, since he knew she would become self-conscious.

Percy strode quickly across the room toward them, his usual ebullient smile on his face. "I'm so glad you're first here," Percy said, sounding enthused. "This must be Miss Sharpe," he said, bowing to Alice. "I am Percy Waters, your brother's best friend. It is a pleasure to meet you."

He stuck his hand out and Alice took it after a slight hesitation. Percy met Thomas's gaze and gave a brief nod. Thomas had told Percy about his family, including Alice's painful shyness. "Miss Sharpe, if you find the party is too busy at any time, and your rapscallion brother is off doing rapscallionery, please know you can find me or my sister and we will take care of you."

"Rapscallionery?" Thomas said, raising a brow.

"Thank you, Mr. Waters." Alice leaned in close to Thomas. "I am excited to be here. And nervous," she admitted.

Jane made her way across the room to join them, and Thomas tried to school his expression so that neither she, her brother, nor his sister would suspect he had managed to fall in love with her, even though he had explicitly promised not to.

The introductions were made, with Jane smiling gently at Alice, who was regarding her with all the admiration Thomas hadn't allowed to appear in his own face.

Percy clapped his hands together. "As I was saying, I'm glad you're first here because we want to make it appear that you are also hosting the party so the ladies—the pertinent ones, that is—imbue you with that kind of authority. Not that you don't have authority," he added hastily, "just that it's best if you seem to have purpose."

"Purpose other than marrying a lady for her money?" Thomas said ruefully.

Alice glanced up at him. "It's not just that and you know it."

Jane put her hand on Alice's arm, a fierce expression in her gaze. "If it was just that you'd be no better than Lord Joseph."

"Who's Lord Joseph?" Alice asked.

"A gentleman who is on the same heiress hunt I am," Thomas replied. "Perhaps he has as many excellent reasons for his motivation as I do."

"You're being exceptionally generous. I highly doubt he is anything like you."

"I am trying to be a better person," Thomas said, catching her eye. *Better because I am not professing my love right here. Better because I won't compromise your future because mine is already determined. Better because I will watch you walk away from me when all of this is over.*

"You are already a good person," Alice said proudly.

Jane bit her lip as she looked at him. As though she wanted to say something, too, but couldn't. Wouldn't.

Don't say anything. It'll only hurt more.

"Someone will welcome us, I am certain."

The group turned at the sound of the voice coming from the doorway, Thomas recognizing Jane's mother, the Countess of Scudamore, followed by her husband and what he presumed was a random assortment of the Scudamore family.

He heard Jane's sharp inhale and wished he could touch her, reassure her that she had support for what was likely to be an unpleasant encounter.

Though of course she had Percy already, she didn't need him.

"Percy!" the countess exclaimed, making her way toward them, her gaze firmly fixed on Percy and not at all on Jane.

"Excuse me," Jane said in a quiet voice as the countess approached.

Percy grabbed her arm. "No, she won't make you run away," he said in a low voice. The countess was nearly upon them.

Jane swallowed, and Thomas could see the apprehension in her gaze. Then she lifted her chin and removed Percy's hand, turning her gaze to her mother.

IT FELT AS though this evening truly was her coming out party, as Lavinia had suggested. Coming out as a strong woman who could make her own decisions about her life.

Coming out as a woman who could walk away from the man she'd accidentally and entirely fallen in love with because it was the best thing for him. Coming out as a woman who might not know her future, but who would be in control of her fate.

"Good evening, Mother," Jane said as the countess joined them.

Her mother still hadn't looked at her.

Percy opened his mouth to speak, but Jane gestured at him to stay quiet. "Good evening, Mother," she repeated. "If you like, we can speak alone, or you can say what you want to in front of my friends and our family." She gestured to indicate all of them, including Lavinia, who'd just joined the group.

Then her mother did look at her. "You have the

temerity to host a party like this when you have scandalized our family!"

Jane took a deep breath. "The only thing I did, Mother, was refuse to have you trot me out again like a cow at an auction, waiting for the highest-bidding farmer to buy me."

Her mother frowned in confusion.

"I don't think Mother understands metaphors all that well," Lavinia said in a low voice.

"I chose not to try to get engaged again, Mother, because I realized I didn't know enough about myself, never mind about any potential suitors."

"What do you mean not know yourself? You're not a cow, certainly." Her mother's tone was triumphant, as though she had scored a verbal point.

"No, I am not a cow. But I am also not a sheep."

"Good one!" Lavinia cheered, albeit in that same low tone.

Jane felt her strength gathering, flowing through her body like an intoxicating spirit. Or like Thomas's kiss. "I do not wish to be at odds with you." She glanced over at her father, who stood slightly behind her mother, his expression both befuddled and sad. "Any of you. I love my family, but I also love myself." She took another deep breath. "I will not compromise myself any longer. I will make my own decisions."

The countess opened her mouth as though to utter a scathing retort, but it didn't come. Instead, she snapped her mouth shut again in frustration.

"Jane, dear, we love you. Don't we, Agatha?"

Her father emerged from behind his wife and

walked forward to take Jane's hand in his. "We just want what is best for you."

Jane smiled into his eyes. "That is what I want also." She shifted her gaze to her mother. "I hope you want that for me, too?"

Her mother's jaw tightened, and for a moment, Jane thought she might have lost. It would be heartbreaking to be estranged from her family, but the alternative was even more painful.

And then her mother flung her hands up in the air. "Fine! It seems I can't tell any of my children what to do."

"We're not children any longer," Jane said. "But we will always love and need our mother."

And then the three of them—Lavinia, Percy, and Jane—were enfolding the countess in a hug as she pretended she'd gotten a speck of dust in her eye.

Their father eventually joined them, and Jane felt a measure of contentment slide over her, as though there had been a part that had been missing from her life that she'd just realized.

Yes, her mother was controlling and wasn't particularly thoughtful, and played favorites. Tried to manage everyone and everybody. Did not like being told no.

But she did honestly believe she was doing the best for her children, and if Jane and the other siblings could push back, then eventually her mother would realize that her children—now adults—actually knew best.

But she could navigate all that later. Now she had a party to host.

More guests had arrived while she and her

mother had been engaged in their contretemps, and Jane extricated herself from her family to check that the servers had enough food and drink.

Miss Grosvenor was there, looking around with her usual excited expression, while her stepmother and father appeared to be equally amazed.

A good sign for the success of the party.

And Miss Porter was there with her younger, more vivacious sister, the two ladies whispering to one another while glancing over at Thomas. At Mr. Sharpe.

Jane felt her chest tighten.

He had to get married, she knew that. He had made her no promises. If anything, he had discouraged any kind of promise, any kind of attachment.

At one point she'd vowed not to fall in love with him.

And look how well that had turned out.

"Jane?"

She turned to see Percy, accompanied by another gentleman. He was taller than Percy, with mousy brown hair and a sweet expression. He swallowed nervously, glancing from Percy to Jane and back again.

Daffy.

"You must be Percy's friend," Jane said, a warm smile on her face. She held her hand out. "I am Jane, his sister. One of his sisters," she corrected. Lavinia was at the other end of the room buttonholing one of the food servers. Apparently pregnancy made you hungry all the time.

"Yes, my lady," Daffy replied, bowing over her hand.

"Daffy wanted to meet you especially," Percy said.

"And I him," Jane replied. "It is a pleasure to meet you, uh—"

"Just Daffy," he said. "Nobody uses my real name. I don't know if I'd recognize it if I heard it myself."

"Daffy," Jane repeated. "So tell me, Daffy, what are you looking forward to seeing the most? I believe we have acrobats, and jugglers, and a performing dog. Plus there are card games and a medium to tell your fortune."

Daffy looked at Percy before responding. "I suppose the performing dog. I would like a dog—my father was allergic, and my lodgings now wouldn't be good for a dog."

"I like the dog as well," Percy said, sounding as if he and his friend had discovered some arcane thing in common rather than a mutual love of canines. "I want to introduce Daffy to Lavinia, if you'll excuse us?"

"Certainly," Jane replied.

They walked away, Percy talking enthusiastically as Daffy nodded gravely every few moments. It warmed Jane's heart to see him happy.

"Good evening, my lady," Miss Grosvenor said.

"Good evening." Jane extended her hand to Miss Grosvenor's stepmother. "I don't believe we have met. I am Lady Jane Capel."

"Oh, I know all about you," Mrs. Grosvenor gushed. "Millie has spoken of your kindness, and I know my husband and I are pleased she has made such a good friend."

Miss Grosvenor nodded, blushing, while Mr.

Grosvenor glanced between the two of them beaming proudly.

"We are so pleased you could join us," Jane said, turning slightly to gesture to Percy and Thomas. Percy was engrossed in a conversation with Daffy and Lavinia, and Thomas was speaking to his sister, so neither of them saw her, but the inference was clear that the three of them were hosting. "Mr. Sharpe was determined to show me things that young ladies in our position"—at which point she smiled conspiratorially at Miss Grosvenor—"would not normally see."

Which was absolutely true, though the scene she'd seen a few days ago would not be replayed here.

She smothered an embarrassed giggle at the thought.

"Mr. Sharpe is a good fellow," Mr. Grosvenor said. "We met on the train; he had some revolutionary things to say on the subject of ladies."

Jane's eyes widened involuntarily, though she knew Thomas would not have been indiscreet about anything.

"He told me to ask Millie what she wanted. Imagine that!" Mr. Grosvenor exclaimed, looking at his daughter with that proud expression again. "As though she would know what is best for her." He shrugged. "But it is an idea."

Miss Grosvenor's expression faltered, and Jane reached out to take her friend's arm, pulling her close to her side. "Miss Grosvenor is very sensible. I believe she makes good choices." She looked at both of the elder Grosvenors. "After all, she chose me as a friend."

Mr. Grosvenor gave a broad smile, and his wife uttered one of her delighted shrieks, while Miss Grosvenor squeezed Jane's hand as though to give her a silent thanks.

Perhaps between herself and Thomas all the ladies in London would be free to choose their own destinies.

If only a certain gentleman could.

THOMAS KEPT HIS attention focused on Alice, though he found his eyes drifting toward Jane every few minutes. He had been on edge during her conversation with her mother, but she had handled herself and her parents with remarkable skill.

He admired her even more for it.

And liked to think his company, and their adventures together, had contributed somewhat to her confidence.

"Thomas?" Alice tugged on his sleeve. Apparently he hadn't been keeping enough of his attention focused on Alice.

"Mmm?" he said.

"The lady over there. With Lady Jane. Who is that?"

He followed Alice's gaze, seeing Miss Grosvenor standing with her father, Lady Jane, and whom he presumed was her stepmother. "Miss Grosvenor."

"Is she one of the heiresses?" Alice said in a whisper. "She looks very nice."

Thomas's jaw tightened. "She is." She also wasn't Jane. Nobody was Jane except Jane, which was ridiculously obvious, but also painfully true.

"I will introduce you."

"Oh good," Alice replied. "I'd like to meet all of the heiresses tonight. I don't want you to get married to someone who won't suit you."

The only thing that will suit me is a massive amount of money, Thomas thought cynically. And truthfully.

He took Alice's arm and guided her over to the group, sharing a quick glance with Jane. He wished he could tell her how proud he was of her standing up for herself to her mother, but it wasn't the time, and she didn't need his approval, anyway.

She didn't need anything from him.

A painful truth as well.

"Mr. Sharpe!" Mr. Grosvenor exclaimed as they approached. "And this is—?"

"My sister, Miss Alice Sharpe," Thomas replied.

Alice kept her head lowered, nodding. Thomas kept his hand on her arm for reassurance.

"I am Miss Grosvenor," Miss Grosvenor said in a quiet voice. "This is all rather overwhelming. Is this your first London party?"

Another nod.

"Mr. Sharpe, would you mind terribly if I take your sister to find a quiet place to sit? I believe there are a variety of entertainments on offer tonight— perhaps your sister and I might discuss which would be most enjoyable."

Thomas gave Alice's arm a brief squeeze before replying. "Thank you, but my sis—"

"Yes, that would be pleasant," Alice interrupted,

still not lifting her head but managing to be heard nonetheless.

"Excellent," Miss Grosvenor said, shooting a quick glance toward Thomas. "Come this way." She held her hand out to Alice, who took it, and the two of them made their way to the corner of the room where some chairs were placed against the wall.

He blinked in surprise. Alice was always so shy, so anxious about being in public, but it seemed something she sensed in Miss Grosvenor made her comfortable. It was wonderful to know his sister could, perhaps, get more at ease among a crowd.

Meanwhile, most of the performers and other workers had found their positions, and it was still for a moment, most conversation having stopped as everyone adjusted to wait for the remainder of the guests to arrive.

Thomas made certain Alice was settled, then turned his attention to the rest of the room. In one corner there was a middle-aged woman in a booth with playing cards set in front of her, and she was shuffling them with remarkable dexterity. She glanced up to meet Thomas's gaze, and her face was round and cheerful, but he thought he spied a mischievous glint in her eye. The opposite corner held another booth, also manned by a woman, only this woman wore several scarves and bracelets, a jewel-encrusted turban on her head. Overhead, a sign read Madame Sophie's Mystical Magic, which gave the general idea if not the specifics.

The female dog trainer and her dog stood in the middle of the room, the dog trainer frowning at her dog with an adorably perplexed expression, while the dog lay flat out on the floor.

A wire had been strung across the top of the room with what appeared to be barely enough room for a short person to walk without hitting a head on the ceiling.

There were other tables, too, arrayed with a selection of food and drink, a servant behind each station. Sconces lit the room with a gentle glow, while candlesticks were scattered on some of the tables with blazing light.

Jane stood next to one of those tables, her upper chest and face lit from below, the light from the candles making it appear as though she was a constellation spread across the night sky.

God, he wanted her spread across his night sky. His bed. Wherever she wanted to be spread out.

"Thomas?" Alice tugged on his sleeve, her face turned up to his. She was looking up now, which meant she must be more relaxed.

If only he could persuade her she could be as confident as any young lady, then all of this—all of his sacrifice—would be worth it.

"What is it, dear?" he said, taking her hand in his.

Her mouth curled into a shy smile, and he felt a slow relief course through him at the sight. If she was smiling, that was even more indication that she felt moderately comfortable.

"Miss Grosvenor has asked if we might take luncheon with her tomorrow. I told her—"

"She said she's never had an ice, and I think we should rectify that," Miss Grosvenor interrupted. "I told Miss Sharpe how I have only been in London a few weeks now, and that when I first arrived, it seemed as though everything was terrifying, but now that I've been here some time, it all is wonderful. If also somewhat terrifying," she admitted, sharing a smile with Alice.

"That sounds splendid," Thomas replied, even though he felt anything but splendid. If Miss Grosvenor and his sister were already friends, and Mr. Grosvenor had indicated his approval, then what else was there for him to do?

Propose, yes, but that would be a mere formality.

His future, such as it was, seemed to be laid out for him on a road strewn with Mr. Grosvenor's money and Alice's happiness.

Which, as roads to one's future went, wasn't so terrible.

Except for his heart.

Chapter Twenty-Two

"Lady Jane, have you visited the medium yet?"

She'd tried to avoid him all evening. Not because she didn't want to see him, but because she'd wanted to see him too much. If any of the young ladies who were potentially interested in being Mrs. Thomas Sharpe were to notice her hungry expression, the want she knew lurked in her eyes, they would realize—if not consciously—that he wasn't entirely committed to them, that he had aroused hopes in another young lady.

But here he was, looking resplendent in his evening attire. His suit seemed to be far more expensive and elegant than any other gentleman in attendance.

Though the gentlemen in attendance were Percy, who was consistent at wearing ink stains, Daffy, who was dressed modestly, matching his appearance, her father, who had already spilled wine down his front, and Mr. Grosvenor, whose suit was definitely well tailored, but who lacked Thomas's handsomely muscular form.

His sister was standing a few feet away with

Miss Grosvenor, the two of them chatting as though they had known one another for years, and not met just this evening. That must be a relief for Thomas—he'd spoken of his sister, and it was clear he was very protective of her.

"I haven't. Miss Porter and I were watching Lady Emily get fleeced by the card sharp." She kept her voice low, since everyone knew Lady Emily hated nothing more than being embarrassed.

"A good thing I haven't tried my luck here then," he replied. "Or a good thing I haven't any money in the first place."

There it was again. The reminder of who he was and what he needed to do.

"The medium, Madame Sophie, seems to be making quite a splash." The two turned to look toward the booth, where Percy sat with his mouth hanging open, his eyes wide. As they watched, he leaned forward to clasp Madame Sophie's hand as though begging her earnestly for something.

She hoped Madame Sophie—whatever she was telling Percy—was being kind. Daffy hovered nearby, hopping from one foot to another.

"I believe I know my future," he continued, sounding weary, "but I would be very keen to hear yours."

"Mine?" Jane said, surprised. "I haven't given it much thought." Which of course was a lie. She'd given it a lot of thought—she just hadn't come to anything that remotely resembled a conclusion. Unless concluding that one could not be with the person you'd fallen in love with, but hadn't been supposed to, was a conclusion.

In which case yes. She knew very well her future would not include him. Which would inevitably make it less happy than the alternative.

Percy rose from his seat, shaking the medium's hand firmly, then walking swiftly away as though he had a purpose.

Meanwhile, it seemed the guests were having a good time—Jane could hear applause, gasps of surprise, and a constant hum of conversation. It was a success, and she wasn't needed for the moment.

"Fine, then, let us go see Madame Sophie." Jane felt suddenly reckless, as though she could and would do anything that struck her fancy.

And she had, hadn't she? She'd just managed to do something, however, that would resonate with her the rest of her life. Perhaps not the best of choices in that case.

He took her arm and she resisted the urge to melt into him, to lean up and kiss his jaw, right where the shadowed edge of his beard showed in the golden light.

She heard him make a noise, low in his throat, and then he spoke in a low voice, one that only she could hear.

"I wish we didn't have to—I can't—" And then they were at Madame Sophie's booth, that lady smiling up at them with flashing dark eyes, tapping impossibly long fingernails on an overlarge pack of cards.

Thomas seated Jane in the chair at the booth, then brought another round for him to sit on.

"It is not usual, you understand, for anyone else to be here during a reading."

Madame Sophie's accent was vaguely foreign, as though she had traveled many places and imprinted on each one, or just had heard someone from another land speak and was imitating them poorly.

"It is fine. We are friends." And she attempted a brave smile toward him, a smile that said, *We are just friends, nothing more, and no, of course my heart isn't breaking because you are about to propose marriage to someone else for a most admirable reason that I cannot possibly jeopardize.*

At least, she hoped it said that. Because if it didn't say that, it said all those other things, and he could not know how she'd gone against everything she'd promised him, herself, and Percy.

Madame Sophie shrugged. "It is of no matter to me. Payment please." She extended her palm, and Jane placed a coin in it, then settled back into her seat, wishing the exchange of money hadn't felt so fraught with danger.

But this was just a medium with a traveling circus—it wasn't as though the woman could actually know anything. Because Jane didn't know anything, and it was her life, goddamn it.

"You wish to know your future?" Madame Sophie's eyes flicked between Jane and Thomas and back again.

Jane shifted nervously. Why had she thought this was a good idea?

"Yes," she replied in a firm tone, not looking at him.

But she felt him next to her—his legs nearly touching hers, his strong, graceful hands folded in his lap. The heat of him seeming to twine around her like an insistent cat.

Madame Sophie didn't speak again, just began to shuffle her deck, a frown creasing her brow.

"What do you hope to learn?" he asked.

"Hush," Madame Sophie said sharply. "You cannot speak while the cards are thinking."

She and Thomas shared an amused glance. At least now she had a reason to look at him.

He was so beautiful it hurt. His strong, mobile mouth that she knew firsthand—or first-lip—was devastatingly delicious to kiss. His dark blue eyes, like a nighttime sky, holding all his emotions. That curl that dangled over his forehead, making her fingers itch to push it back.

"You have to concentrate on the cards, not on him," Madame Sophie chided.

Jane felt her cheeks heat as she snapped her gaze away from him, staring down at the table where Madame Sophie was still shuffling.

"Sorry for being distracting," he murmured, sounding not at all sorry.

"Hush!"

Madame Sophie glared at him, then returned her attention to the cards, which had apparently finally been shuffled enough.

She placed one with deliberate care on the left, then placed four more in quick succession.

The cards weren't a usual deck; instead of numbers, they had elaborate pictures painted on them with words written above.

"Oh, the Hanged Man," Jane said nervously. "That doesn't seem good."

"Hush."

Jane met Thomas's gaze, rolling her eyes at Madame Sophie's determination to keep them quiet.

"The Hanged Man," Madame Sophie said, touching the card, "does not mean death. Upside down like this it represents needless sacrifice or fear of sacrifice." The woman's dark eyes shot up. "Do not needlessly sacrifice yourself for anything." She tapped another card, this one reading Strength. "This card tells me you have the necessary tools to make the right decision for yourself." Another tap, this time on The Fool. "This indicates you will be setting out on a new adventure, one you never knew about before."

"Why is it 'The Fool'?" Thomas asked.

Madame Sophie glared at him, but didn't admonish him to be quiet.

"The Fool is innocent, he does not worry about where he is going—he just knows he wants to start again." She tapped the card once more. "When it is upside down it means the person is likely too reckless. But here in this case it is a good thing. If you are prepared for it."

"How can I prepare for an adventure I never knew about before?" Jane asked in a wry tone.

"These two cards—The World and The Chariot— tell me you have the strength to face whatever might find you."

"My mother already found me, so that's sorted, at least," Jane murmured.

Thomas smothered a snort of laughter.

"Do not make light of the cards!" Madame Sophie said, her tone fierce.

Jane straightened automatically in her chair. Then realized what she'd done and immediately relaxed her posture.

"You have an excellent future," Madame Sophie went on, moving the cards around on the table. "You will just have to make your mind up to take what is yours." The woman met Jane's eyes, her gaze softening. "You can do it, my lady. It can be done." Then her expression settled back into its stoic lines. "Now go. I have others wanting their fortunes told."

Jane rose, glancing behind her to see Miss Grosvenor and Thomas's sister waiting just beyond earshot. She smiled at both of them, then turned back around, dropping another coin on the table. "Thank you, madame," she said in a soft voice.

"Pssh, it's nothing," the woman replied, snatching the coin off the table. "Be brave—that is all you can do."

Jane nodded, stepping away from the table and gesturing to the two young ladies to be seated.

Thomas lingered to speak with his sister as Jane moved further away, her heart in a tumult. *Be brave, that is all you can do.*

Truth.

"YOU ARE ALL right then?" Thomas asked Alice, who was sitting in the chair he'd just vacated in front of Madame Sophie.

"I am, stop worrying," she replied.

"Miss Sharpe has promised to visit me tomorrow, Mr. Sharpe," Miss Grosvenor said. "I do hope you can bring her by?"

Thomas nodded, his chest tightening. If he

brought her by—when he brought her by—it wasn't as though she could go alone, and it wasn't as though he would deny Alice anything she wanted—he would see Miss Grosvenor, and it would be an ideal time to propose.

Alice already liked her. Mr. Grosvenor had already indicated his approval, and all it would take now would be to say the words.

Will you do me the honor of being my wife?

Ten words. Just enough to fill up the fingers on both hands.

Enough to fill up the rest of his life.

"Go away now, Thomas, I don't want you to hear what my fortune might say," Alice said, pushing him gently away.

He smiled through a clenched jaw, glancing around to see Jane a few feet away, a contemplative expression on her face.

He knew she could be brave, as the fortune teller had admonished her to be. He hoped, if he had done nothing else, that he had helped her confidence so that she would know it, too.

"Mr. Sharpe!" Lady Emily exclaimed, she and her phalanx of young ladies surrounding him. "You must come see the lady and her clever little dog! Miss Porter is most insistent on it." And Lady Emily gave a knowing look toward Miss Porter, whose face turned a fiery pink.

Thomas felt himself sliding into his customary role, his impeccable manners surfacing even as his heart continued to break, falling down into his belly with an inexorable unhappiness. "Miss Porter, you like dogs, do you?" he asked the young lady in a gentle voice.

Miss Porter nodded, her eyes lowered, and Thomas held his arm out to her. "Let us all go see this charming canine then, shall we?" he said, darting a quick look toward Jane, who still stood in that same spot, that thoughtful expression still on her face.

What are you thinking about? Are you thinking about me? About your future?

Two opposite things.

He spent the next hour or so with his Mr. Thomas Sharpe mask on, replying politely and occasionally wittily when asked his opinion on anything. Lady Emily continued to push him toward Miss Porter, while Miss Grosvenor kept Alice company through the evening.

At least now it appeared he actually had a lady or two who would welcome his proposal.

He could save his family by saying ten words. He could foreclose on love for himself with those same ten words.

He had no doubt but that he could forge some sort of happiness—either young lady was perfectly pleasant. It wasn't as though he would be condemning himself to misery.

And before it would have been more than enough. He hadn't believed he would ever fall in love, anyway, and he'd reasoned he might as well marry to bring himself the best advantage. It was his mission to do just that to save the people he did love—his family.

Perhaps there was some sort of universe come-uppance that wanted him to understand just what he was sacrificing—that it wouldn't be a sacrifice without something equal on the other side, so the universe had figured out a way to make him suffer.

Though that would mean thinking he didn't have free will, which he most certainly did. He'd had the will to enter into his agreement with Jane, the will to kiss her, to touch her, to show her the passion he knew she was capable of.

The will to fall in love with her.

The will not to tell her, even though it was tearing him apart.

It took an extraordinary effort to pretend everything was fine. And then, at last, the evening was winding down, and he was searching for Alice in order to take her to the ladies' hotel he'd booked for her.

To prepare for the next day, when he'd say his ten words and seal his fate.

"Mr. Sharpe."

He turned to face Jane.

"Yes, my lo—my lady?"

She lifted her chin, a definite challenge in her eye. And suddenly he was reminded of their first encounter at Miss Ivy's, where she proposed she assist him in finding a bride in exchange for his assisting her . . . in other matters. When she'd snatched his whisky and drunk it, despite never having had it before. How delighted she'd looked when she tasted it, despite coughing.

It had been only a few weeks since then, and already there was a marked change in her. As though the quiet debutante had been peeled away to reveal the glorious woman underneath.

"I want you to—that is, I know you have to ensure your sister gets home safely, but I am hoping you might come find me later?"

"Later tonight?" he replied. Immediately cursing himself for questioning her, but also fine if his questioning her made her realize what she was asking.

What was she asking, anyway?

"Yes," she replied, a wry smile twisting her mouth. "Later tonight." She dragged her lower lip between her teeth, suddenly looking hesitant. "That is—unless you don't . . . ?"

"I do," he interrupted. He would do whatever she wanted. Even if it made his heart shatter. "Whatever it is, I do."

Chapter Twenty-Three

An hour later, Thomas was striding up the steps to Jane and Percy's house, the door swinging open before he could knock.

She stood as though framed, the low light behind her limning her form. She had changed out of her star gown, and now stood in what appeared to be a dressing gown—it was made of a soft fabric, wrapped around her and secured with a belt made of the same material.

Her hair was undone, flowing onto her shoulders, and her feet were bare.

"Should I—?" he asked, pausing at the door.

"Come in," she said, swinging the door wide. "Percy went to bed right after we returned. Mrs. Charing is visiting her sister. Cook is in her room, and—"

"I don't need to know where everyone in the household is," Thomas interrupted, smiling.

She returned the smile as he stepped inside, and she shut the door behind them.

There was a candlestick on one of the tables in the hallway, the only light in the room. The flickering light cast her face in shadow, and he desperately wanted to see her, see her expression, know if this was truly what she wanted.

"You know why you're here," she said in a low tone of voice. "I want—"

He waited as she hesitated, seeming to search for the words.

"I want you," she finished simply.

He took a step toward her. Now he was close enough to see her face, despite the darkness. Her eyes were wide and shining, her lips curled into a near smile, her gaze direct.

His fingers itched to touch her, but he had to make absolutely certain. "What are you asking me, Jane?"

She licked her lips, the action shooting straight to his groin. "I know tomorrow is—well, tomorrow. But tonight, I want you. I want to learn everything. I want to do everything, and I will deal with the consequences."

If she got pregnant, she meant. If that happened, could he bear to know that a child of his was out there being raised by the woman he loved?

He couldn't. Not when his heart was already shattered.

"So you agree?" she said. "I have fulfilled my part of the bargain"—meaning his finding a bride— "and now I want you to fulfill yours."

He moved forward another step. Now so close to her that when she breathed, her body touched his. He kept his arms locked down by his side, aware that if he let them move they would wrap around her and never let go.

"This wasn't part of the original agreement." He

paused. "But I am willing to negotiate to accommodate this recent demand."

She met his gaze, the honest determination in her eyes entirely undoing him. "Come upstairs with me, then."

She turned, and he followed, swooping to gather her into his arms. She giggled, wrapping her arms around his neck, her dressing gown sliding open to reveal a very serviceable nightdress.

Possibly the most erotic thing he'd ever seen, that sensible nightdress.

Because it was her wearing it, and she was inviting him into her bed.

"You don't have to carry me—I am perfectly capable of walking up the stairs myself," she said in a mock chiding tone.

"I want to. I want to teach you how to be swept away up the stairs by your lover." Saying the word aloud—*lover*—made it feel even more real. "I am supposed to teach you, remember? So just relax and enjoy your lesson."

Her breath hitched at his words, and she clutched him tighter around the neck, putting her head down on his shoulder, and then whispering into his ear.

"Teach me all of it, Thomas. I need to know everything tonight."

He sprinted up the rest of the stairs.

JANE FELT ALMOST gleeful now that he was here. Tomorrow, she would be heartbroken and devastated, but that was tomorrow.

Hadn't the fortune teller told her she should be brave and fearless? Or something to that effect.

And so, while she was watching him circulate effortlessly through the party, tossing a smile here, a clever compliment there, she was thinking.

About how this—their partnership—would be finished when he had persuaded an heiress to marry him. And judging by how quite a few of the ladies were looking at him this evening, he would not have to work that hard to persuade one of them.

And how she had no idea what her future held, just that it would be hers to decide.

So she was going to decide it.

And she'd decided she wanted to experience all of it, do all the things she'd watched in that illicit house of pleasure.

This time, it would be her on the bed receiving Thomas's attentions. He'd slide that remarkable appendage of his—his cock—into her, filling her completely, and she would take it, take all of him.

If he wanted that, of course.

And then they would part ways, knowing their partnership had truly been completed, that they had become joined in sexual congress.

She'd have something to remember when she was doing whatever it was she was going to do.

Thankfully, he had been just as wanting as she, even making certain it was what she truly wanted. Always a gentleman, even when doing things a gentleman would not do with a lady who was not his wife.

He was carrying her down the hall to her bedroom, his arms strong around her, as she lowered her mouth to his neck and began to kiss him.

He growled in response, walking more quickly,

until he flung the door to her bedroom open and tossed her the bed, kicking the door shut as he advanced toward her, a deliciously predatory look on his face.

He was already removing his jacket, and she held her hand up. "No, stop."

He froze, waiting for her instruction.

Oh, and wasn't that delightful?

What could she order him to do? She hadn't realized that kind of power was so alluring until she'd seen the two performers—Miles and Hattie—and how the stronger of the two had totally acquiesced to whatever it was the other wanted.

Kiss me. Kiss me there. Kiss me everywhere.

She squirmed as she thought about it, and he raised a knowing eyebrow. "Are you going to tell me what you're thinking about?" he asked, still not moving.

Jane sat up on the bed, undoing the tie of her robe, sliding the heavy garment off her shoulders. She'd pondered wearing a shift or nothing at all underneath, but had decided to wear what she normally wore to bed—a plain cotton nightdress. Because she would likely be wearing the same nightdress, or a similar one, to bed every night for the rest of her life, and she wanted to know what it was like to wear something so common, so usual, when she was doing something quite unusual.

"You are so damned beautiful," he said in a hoarse voice. His eyes drank her in, roaming all over her body like a caress.

"As are you," she replied. "Take your jacket off," she ordered, imitating Hattie's commanding tone.

He gave a wolfish smile, removing the jacket quickly, then returned to where he'd been. Understanding he wasn't to do anything without her telling him.

God, but the absolute power of it. It was intoxicating, as though she'd drunk an entire glass of champagne in one swallow—bubbles fizzing through her, lighting her senses up.

"And your neckcloth," she continued.

He complied, tossing the fabric to the floor.

"No," she said, "bring it over here."

He bent down to retrieve it, walking over to her with it in his hand.

She took it, then lifted her chin. "I will do the rest," she said, indicating his shirt and trousers.

He inhaled sharply, and she bit her lip, his eyes tracking the movement.

Her fingers went to the buttons of his shirt, undoing them one by one as she kept her gaze locked on his face.

His hands moved, as though he was going to touch her, or touch himself, and she shook her head. "No," she said simply. "Not until I tell you to."

His beautiful mouth curled up into a wicked smile. "Of course. I am here to serve."

She was already wet, her nipples hard and aching. But this was her only night, she wasn't going to rush through it.

"If I did allow you to touch me," she continued, pushing the fabric of his shirt aside to run her palm over his bare chest, "what would you do first?"

Her fingers brushed his nipple, and he hissed.

She glanced down, seeing the evidence of his arousal. All of that for her.

"You would be lying down, and I'd yank you to the edge of the bed, your legs dangling down, and then I would slide this nightdress up your legs."

She raked her nails over his skin, then pulled his shirt from where it was tucked into his trousers.

"Continue," she said, lifting the shirt up and over his head.

She buried her nose in it, inhaling his scent.

"And then," he said, "I'd lick my way up to your sweet pussy and put my tongue on you and lick you until you screamed."

"And then?" she asked, her hands at the waistband of his trousers. Her fingers went to work on the buttons as his breathing got unsteady.

"And then I would ask you to touch me. Beg you to touch me. And I'd straddle you and you'd take my cock in your mouth and suck me."

His voice was strained.

She finished the last of his buttons and dragged his trousers down. His cock thrust out from his smallclothes.

She bent down toward it, putting one hand on it as she brought her mouth there.

He gasped.

She licked the head, sticking out from the fabric of his smallclothes, holding on to the base of his shaft as she played, licking and sucking his cock.

"Oh fuck, Jane," he groaned, and she looked up and smiled.

"Yes, that is what I want to happen. I want to fuck," she said, squeezing his cock in her hand.

"Get your nightdress off now," he ordered, and she suppressed a smile at how fierce and demanding he sounded.

She drew it slowly up her body, his eyes watching every movement.

And then she tossed it over her head, where it landed on the floor, and she was naked.

He removed his boots and then his trousers, joining her on the bed, prowling toward her as though she was his prey.

She did want him to devour her.

"I think you should take over now," she said, sliding down to lie on the bed.

He smiled that wicked smile again, and he reached for her hand and put it on his hard cock.

"Gladly. And you're going to do everything I tell you to, aren't you?"

"Yes," she said, sliding her hand up and down his shaft. "Yes, and more."

YES, AND MORE.

He wanted to ravish her immediately, thrust home into her wet, willing warmth.

But he knew this was their first, last, and only time together, and he wanted to savor it. Savor her.

He ran his hands over her body, relishing her curves, her soft skin, her trembling responsiveness.

He brushed his palm over her nipple, and she gasped, and then he lowered his head and took one stiff peak into his mouth, licking it, while his other hand went to her other nipple, rubbing it gently.

She squirmed underneath his touch, and her

hands went there, but he grabbed her wrist, holding her back.

"That is mine to touch right now," he said. "Not yours." He licked her nipple again, then lifted his head up to gaze into her eyes. They were darkened with passion, a stormy blue that was the most beautiful color he'd ever seen.

Because it was her, and he loved her.

"Tell me what you want me to do."

She whimpered in response. "Please—just—please," she said, sounding as achingly wanting as he felt.

"Please what?" he replied. "Please suck my nipples until I come? Please bury my fingers in your sweet pussy preparing you for my cock? Please lick me there until I'm screaming your name?"

She gave a fervent nod. "Yes, please, to all of it. I want everything so I can remember."

So I can remember.

He couldn't let himself be distracted by the surge of emotions that welled up inside at her words— later, when this night was over, and he was contemplating the rest of his life, then he could think about it. But not now.

Instead of doing any of the things he'd said, he captured her mouth with his, sliding his tongue in to tangle with hers. She made a soft noise in the back of her throat, sliding her hands down his back to clutch his arse, shifting him so his cock was right up against her clitoris. He rocked against her, and she gripped him harder.

It took an immense amount of willpower to break

the kiss, but he had other things he had promised to do.

He slid down her body, blowing air on her, watching as her body shifted, searching for release.

And then he pushed her legs apart, burying his face in her, licking the bud of her clitoris as his fingers played with her nipples.

"God, Thomas, please," she said.

He chuckled, moving one hand down to where his mouth was, placing his finger right at her entrance. He kept licking her, slow, long licks that made her tremble as his finger began to slide in. She had thrust her fingers in his hair and was gripping it tightly, not so much to make it hurt, but enough to make him feel it.

He stroked her, then added another finger. Her hold in his hair was tighter, and she'd begun to move against his mouth, making him match her rhythm.

And then he felt her start to shake, her hands stilled, a low cry beginning in her throat. She arched off the bed, her inner muscles gripping his fingers, her whole body now shaking as she climaxed. She uttered an inarticulate noise that ended in a scream, and he kept up his rhythm until she settled down, making soft pleased noises.

He looked up at her, and he had never seen anything so beautiful—her eyes heavy and sated, her lips red and swollen from where he'd kissed her and where she'd likely bitten, her cheeks flushed.

Her body naked.

"Oh my," she said, giving him a satisfied smile.

"Oh my," he echoed, smiling back at her.

"That's not all I want," she said, after a long pause of just looking at one another.

"So demanding," he said.

"I am," she replied. "I demand that you show me everything. That you—" And she waved her hands in the air in a vague gesture.

"That I fuck you, Jane?"

Her eyes fluttered shut, and she bit her lip. "Yes. I want you to fuck me."

He pulled himself back up so he could kiss her, devouring her mouth, mimicking the action he'd soon be doing with his cock.

She had hold of him again, and was rubbing him up and down. He drew back, meeting her gaze. "Show me where you want me," he said. His voice was rough.

She nodded, then guided him to her entrance. He clasped his hand over hers and began to slide in, going slowly as she grimaced.

"Don't stop," she said. "I want all of you."

I want all of you.

That was the most romantic thing anyone had ever said to him—usually they wanted only part of him, the handsome, charming part. Not the part that was loyal to his family, not the part that got weary of always being the perfect gentleman, adept at any social situation.

He'd shown himself to her. Revealed himself as their relationship grew into so much more than either one of them could have expected.

I want all of you.

And she wanted him.

He nodded, then thrust in further, going slowly until he was fully seated, his body pressed against hers.

She wrapped her legs around him, making her tilt up to him, making him go even deeper.

She gave a hesitant smile. "And now what?"

"And now," he replied, sliding his hand underneath her body to hold on to her arse, "I fuck you."

Chapter Twenty-Four

$\mathcal{I}$t felt so odd to have another person inside her. Odd, and slightly uncomfortable, and entirely erotic.

He began to move, stroking in and out of her, one hand wrapped around her body, the other gripping her head.

His breathing was faster and she could feel his muscles flexing as he moved. She wished she could see what he was doing—perhaps, if this were to continue, she could think about hanging a mirror on her ceiling.

But it wouldn't continue.

This was it—this was all she could expect from him. Because tomorrow he would likely go get himself engaged to a young lady who could afford him.

She wished she could tell him how she felt, tell him she'd done what she'd promised not to—fallen in love.

But she couldn't put that burden on him. They both knew what he had to do, and it wasn't be with her.

She cast those thoughts aside and concentrated on what was happening here and now: him, thrusting into her in an inexorable rhythm. Their skin touching, the sound of their intercourse an erotic accompaniment to the movement.

She held on to his body as he increased his pace, feeling his muscles clench everywhere as he moved. It was erotic to feel that, even, to know all of him was entirely engaged with what they were doing.

And then he buried his face in her neck as he kept thrusting, faster and faster as she held on, knowing she would be sore but also knowing it would be well worth it. The memories would have to sustain her for the rest of her life, after all.

And then he tilted his head back, his eyes closed in concentration, his jaw tight, and then he gave an animalistic yell as he withdrew, spilling onto her belly.

He immediately collapsed to one side of her, his breathing rapid, his nose pressed into her shoulder.

"Mmmph," he groaned after a few minutes. She already ached with wanting him inside again. It just felt so right, she never wanted it to stop.

But of course it had to.

She stroked his back, sliding her palm over his skin.

He began to bestow gentle kisses on her neck as he murmured inarticulate noises against her skin.

It felt so perfect. So right. This was what she wanted for her future.

And this was absolutely what she could not have.

She bit her lip, unable to push aside the feelings of loss, despite his being right here.

Because tomorrow would be here in a few hours, and all of this would be over.

THOMAS LEFT JANE'S room right before dawn, creeping down the hallway as he could, holding his evening shoes in one hand as the other held on to his jacket.

He hadn't allowed himself to sleep, not when he could be enjoying his time with her.

Or counting the minutes they had left together, which was the exact opposite of enjoying his time.

She'd murmured sleepily when he was finally able to get up, and he'd spent a few more precious minutes kissing her, holding her warm, relaxed body that had welcomed him a few hours before.

His throat tightened as he thought about the future. His future.

It seemed clear that he had his choice between Miss Porter and Miss Grosvenor. Lady Emily and her entourage preferred the former, while it seemed the Grosvenors—and likely Alice—preferred the latter.

He'd check with Alice before going to pay a call to Miss Grosvenor.

But at the very least, his—and by extension his family's—problems would be on their way to being solved by that afternoon.

Of course he needed to bathe and dress in something other than last night's evening wear. That would delay the inevitable. And then there was fetching Alice, and making certain she was fed, and comfortable, and they'd planned on when she would return to their parents' house. More delaying tactics.

But the thing about the inevitable was that no matter how much you tried to delay it, you couldn't. Because it was . . . inevitable.

He swung the front door open, closing it softly behind him. Closing his heart, too.

The sky was just beginning to lighten, and there were a few carts carrying foodstuffs clattering by, but the streets were mostly empty.

It was unusual to walk through a quiet London— only the noise of the occasional cart, a few workers walking blearily to their jobs, stray cats darting out of the way as Thomas approached.

It left him alone with his thoughts, which was both good and bad.

He wouldn't be alone for long, though—soon he'd have a wife, responsibilities, his family to care for as well as her family to accommodate.

He gave a rueful smile as he realized this might be the last time he was truly by himself, at least for the foreseeable future.

And here he was, walking home to clean up after spending the night with the woman he loved in order to propose to a woman he didn't love.

What did that make him?

He heard the voices of the people in his life assuring him he was doing the right thing.

But could he reconcile himself to marrying someone purely for their money?

Before, when he'd been just a charming dilettante, it had seemed the logical thing to do. But now he knew—thanks to her—that he was more than that. He'd fallen in love with her, too. She'd shown him what it was to make a choice about one's life. How important it was, how it was the only thing one had control over.

Though if he made the wrong choice . . . it wouldn't be just him who would suffer. It would be everyone and anyone he loved.

Goddamn it.

"Ah, Miss Sharpe, Mr. Sharpe!" Mr. Grosvenor's booming voice echoed through the hallway. He seemed to have been waiting, emerging just as the butler opened the door when Thomas rang. Alice had talked of nothing but her new friend on the ride over, and was already bouncing on her toes, ready to find Miss Grosvenor.

"Good afternoon, Mr. Grosvenor," Thomas said. "I am—"

"Alice!" Miss Grosvenor exclaimed as she ran into the hallway. "I was just making sure Cook set out my favorite lemon tea cakes. Come with me, please," she said, extending a hand to Alice, who took it, barely glancing back at Thomas.

"Come into my study—I will ring for some sherry," Mr. Grosvenor said after they had left.

"I will fetch some, sir," the butler said.

"Oh yes, thank you, Parker." Mr. Grosvenor gestured to Thomas. "This way, Mr. Sharpe."

Mr. Grosvenor's study appeared to be used for much more than studying—there was an enormous desk piled with paperwork, while many of the chairs held boxes of even more papers. He frowned as he removed boxes from a few chairs, drawing one particularly massive one toward his desk. "There," he said, pointing. "You can sit there."

Thomas sat, folding one leg over the other.

Mr. Grosvenor pushed a few of the piles of papers to the side, giving Thomas a clear view of his face across the table. "So you're here to ask to marry my daughter." He didn't pose it as a question.

Thomas took a deep breath as he answered.

"No."

JANE WOKE LATER than usual and sorer than usual.

She gave a sleepy smile as she patted the bed beside her, then opened her eyes to confirm what she'd felt—or hadn't felt.

He had left already.

Her heart clenched in her chest, and she sat up swiftly, the sheet falling away from her body.

She'd slept naked, something she had never done before.

As well as doing other things she'd never done before.

Yet she didn't feel that different from the day before—she was still Jane, still determined to chart her own course in the world. Still in love with him, even though she still recognized she could not be with him, not without doing harm to him and his family, and she would not do that.

The whole experience had been wonderful, had been revelatory, but it had not irrevocably changed her life.

She had taken care of that herself two years ago, when she'd refused to follow what her mother wanted. And then taken care of it again when she'd entered into her agreement with him. She was in charge, no matter who she took to her bed and who she loved.

So her heart hurt now, and would hurt more when she heard of his engagement. But it would not wreck her.

She took a deep breath as she got out of bed, glancing down as something caught her eye.

A small stain of blood on the sheets, proof that what had happened had indeed happened.

It was a good thing, she thought wryly, that their household staff was small enough that her stripping her own bed wouldn't be a momentous occurrence.

Half an hour later, her bed was stripped and in the wash, and she was clothed, sitting down to breakfast, a bleary Percy sitting perpendicular to her, nursing a cup of coffee.

"Did you have a good time last night?" Jane asked, then immediately flushed as she realized he might ask her the same thing, and she had no idea how to respond.

Though yes, she did have a good time. To put it mildly.

Percy nodded, staring into his cup. "It was successful. And then Daffy and I went out afterward, and—"

"And?" Jane prompted, as he hesitated.

Percy lifted his gaze to meet Jane's. And then a sweet smile began to spread over his face, and Jane couldn't help but smile in return.

"I hope you don't mind, but I've asked Daffy if he wants to come to live with us for a while."

Percy's cheeks were bright red. Jane reached out to pat his hand, then took it in hers. "Forever, if I'm being honest." He smiled. "And we're going to get a dog."

Jane took a deep, swelling breath, tears beginning to spill down her cheeks. "I am so happy for you," she said. "Of course I will welcome Daffy here. We have plenty of room, though we might have to hire more staff," she added, thinking of the bed-stripping incident from that morning.

Percy gave an absentminded nod. "Yes, of course." And then his eyes narrowed. "But what about you? I saw you speaking with many of the ladies last evening, presumably letting them know that Thomas is devoted and loyal." Jane began to sigh in relief, until he followed that up with, "The only problem is that he is devoted and loyal to you."

"Uh—?" Jane said, feeling herself stiffen all over.

Percy rolled his eyes. "It's obvious you've fallen in love with him. And him with you." He shook his head as though it was entirely obvious and he was annoyed at her obliviousness.

"He's not in love with me," Jane replied, not addressing the other part.

Percy gave an audible harrumph, and shot her a look of disbelief. "We both know it's true, so what are you going to do about it?"

Did she know it was true? He hadn't said anything, but—but perhaps he didn't have to. The way he'd opened up to her, the way he'd taken care of how she felt and what she wanted—perhaps he was just being a good friend, but she strongly suspected there was more to it than that.

"Goddamn it, he has fallen in love with me," she muttered. "And me with him."

Percy slapped his palm down on the table, making her jump. "Yes! So what are you going to do about it?"

Jane shook her head. "There's nothing I can do about it. He has to marry to save his family—"

"No," Percy interrupted. "Just think for a minute—don't accept what everyone thinks should or will happen."

Jane gave a wan smile. "I know I've been bolder lately, but I'm not so bold that I will jeopardize a person's family just because I love them."

Percy slapped the table again. This time, Jane glared at him. "The two of you are smart and capable. I am certain if you talk about it you can come up with a solution."

Jane began to shrug, then froze as her mind raced. "They need money. Do you know how much?" she asked.

Percy shook his head. "I can only guess that it's more than what we have between us and less than what our brother-in-law the duke has."

Jane felt a glimmer of hope begin to kindle within her. "Thaddeus. Would he—do you think?" she began.

Percy slapped his hand on the table again.

"You really need to stop doing that," Jane said in irritation.

"He would. If Thomas would accept it."

Jane's shoulders slumped. "I don't know if he would accept."

Percy raised an eyebrow. "Really? If it meant he

could be with the woman he loves rather than the woman who can afford him? Is he a debutante whose only job is to marry well?" He emphasized the last sentence so pointedly it was impossible to miss.

Jane held her hand up. "He should have a choice. Just like the choice I made for myself."

"That you took," Percy said in a proud tone.

"But he is likely on his way to wherever he is going right now. It is probably too late," she continued.

She glanced at the clock, her heart beating faster. "I'd have to go to Thaddeus and Lavinia's house, speak to Thaddeus if he is there, and then find out where Thomas is." She took a deep breath, trying to calm herself. "Why couldn't you have thought of this sooner?"

Another table slap. "Because I didn't know you two were in love! But I saw Thomas sneaking down the hallway this morning—"

"You saw him?" Jane interrupted, her voice squeaking.

Percy gave her an exasperated look. "I just said I did, didn't I? And then I started to think about it, and if it would make you happy—"

"It would."

It would. It would make her joyous. She didn't need it to be happy, she would manage on her own, she knew that, but if she could have him in her life? It would be much easier.

"Then I think you should do whatever you can to make it reality." His expression grew thoughtful. "You don't have to go to see Thaddeus first. I am certain he'll help. Especially when Lavinia understands what it might mean to you."

"But the Sharpes, would they—?"

Percy shrugged. "Does it matter? They were willing to sell their son off in marriage. Like so many debutantes, I might add. If they have scruples about accepting a gift from a very wealthy duke then they might not deserve to be helped."

"That's harsh," Jane remarked.

"Harsh but true," Percy retorted.

Jane rose, smoothing her gown in a nervous gesture. "I suppose I'll have to go find him, then."

Percy stood also, reaching across the table to enfold Jane in a warm hug. "That's right. You go find your gentleman and tell him what he needs to hear."

Jane felt her eyes begin to tear, and she squeezed Percy. "Thank you."

Percy withdrew from the embrace, wiping his own eyes. "Hurry up—you don't want him to get engaged before you can find him."

Jane half laughed, half cried in response. "No. No, I don't."

Chapter Twenty-Five

$\mathcal{N}$o?" Mr. Grosvenor repeated in disbelief.

Thomas squared his shoulders, lifted his chin, and met Mr. Grosvenor's stare. "No."

Mr. Grosvenor tilted his head, regarding Thomas with a baffled expression. "Do you want to speak to Millie first? I understand it is perhaps old-fashioned to ask the father's permission first. If you want I can ring—"

"No," Thomas said again. He took a deep breath. "I don't wish to speak to your daughter because I cannot marry her." He uncrossed his legs, resting his elbows on his thighs and leaned forward, speaking earnestly. "Do you remember when we spoke on the train? I advised you to ask your daughter what she might want out of her life."

"I do," Mr. Grosvenor replied slowly. "Did you ask? And she doesn't want you?" He shook his head. "There can be no objection to you. I have looked into your family, and it is not as though you are not pleasing to look at."

"Thank you," Thomas replied with a slight smile. "But that isn't what I meant. I haven't spoken to your daughter, but I have spoken to myself. I have been thinking about what it means to make a choice, and I realized that I haven't given myself a choice about my future." He spread his hands out in explanation. "My family and I believed that marrying for money—pardon me for speaking so bluntly—was my only option. But I don't think it is. The way out of our troubles might be more difficult than standing in front of a clergyman and saying 'I do,' but I want to explore those possibilities before foreclosing on my happiness."

Mr. Grosvenor frowned. "Now see here, you would be very happy with Millie!" he protested.

Thomas nodded. "I do believe I would be. But would I be the happiest I could be?" He shook his head in answer. "Your daughter has much to recommend her, and it is not a judgment on her that I cannot offer for her at this time. I want her to have the same opportunity for the most happiness that I plan on giving to myself. Why should she accept the first offer that is made when she can review her options and make the best choice for herself? If she even wants to marry at all," he added in an aside.

"She'll marry," Mr. Grosvenor said grimly.

Thomas straightened in his chair. "Mr. Grosvenor, the world is different. Your daughter has everything in her favor: she has a lively, kind spirit, she is pretty, she is curious, and she has enough money to live on for the rest of her days, does she not?"

Mr. Grosvenor acknowledged that with an incline of his head.

"So shouldn't she live her best life? Shouldn't she explore all of her opportunities?" He thought of Jane, of her warm, quiet smile. Of her gentle mocking of him and his suppositions. Of how she made an effort to get him a bride, though he knew she had developed feelings for him—one couldn't be with her for longer than five minutes and not know how she felt about someone.

"I suppose she could. I'd have to ask her, and I hope she hasn't got her heart set on you," Mr. Grosvenor warned.

Thomas was opening his mouth to reply when the door shot open and Miss Grosvenor ran in, her cheeks flushed, an eager expression on her face.

"Father, Mr. Sharpe." Her eyes sparkled with pure delight. "I need to speak to both of you, since this concerns you, too, Mr. Sharpe."

Thomas felt a prickle of alarm start to crawl up his spine. Had she fallen in love with him? Or believed that she had?

And would he be consigning her to the same misery he was hoping to escape, the misery of not being with the person you loved?

"Well, Millie, what is it?" Mr. Grosvenor said impatiently. "Mr. Sharpe and I were just discussing"—he shook his head as though confused all over again—"many things," he finished vaguely.

"Mr. Sharpe," Miss Grosvenor said, addressing Thomas, "do sit down." She took a seat in a sofa set to the right of her father's desk as Thomas returned to his chair. "I only met your sister yesterday," she began, a wide smile on her face, "but we get along so famously, I feel as though I've known her my entire life."

Thomas couldn't help but return her smile, delighted that someone outside of the family had recognized how wonderful Alice was. She usually didn't feel comfortable enough with other people to reveal herself, but apparently Miss Grosvenor was a lively exception.

"And she said just now she has no plans to stay in London or to have a come-out, or any of those things."

No, because their family couldn't afford it, and Alice would loathe it all anyway.

"That is true," Thomas replied slowly. Where was this going? It didn't seem as though she was about to profess her undying love for him, at least.

"So I got to thinking, and I know we have just met, but I was wondering if you thought she might want to travel with me? My great-aunt Helen, my mother's aunt, is going to Rome in a month, and she asked if I would like to accompany her. I would, very much, but it would be even more fun if I could bring a friend, since Aunt Helen tends to nap often." She looked stricken, then added, "She is quite old. She does need her rest."

"Of course," Thomas murmured. Not only did she not want him, it appeared she did not want London or marriage, since leaving so soon would thwart plans any gentleman had to offer for her.

But she did want his sister, which made him profoundly glad.

"I would not want to even ask her unless you thought she might be open to the idea? I left her in the library—she doesn't know anything about this. She said last evening she is quite shy, but she also said she is curious about so many things she's read in books and never gotten to see. Rome has the Colosseum, you know," she explained.

"I see," Thomas replied.

"You would leave town in the middle of the Season, Millie? We came here to get you a husband, only—" And then Mr. Grosvenor made a vague gesture that somehow managed to indicate Thomas, only not really.

Miss Grosvenor flushed red. "I was thinking about that, Father, and thinking that I have seen too little of—of everything to make a decision." She raised her chin. "I would like the chance to do things now that I am grown without having to wait for a husband, because then he would likely want me to stay home and start having children, and I would never get to see the Colosseum!" She ended her words in a tone of despair, but she was so dramatic and frankly adorable Thomas had to suppress a smile.

He didn't want her to think he was laughing at her, after all.

Mr. Grosvenor glanced between Thomas and his daughter, then back again a few times. Eventually, as both Thomas and Miss Grosvenor waited, he exhaled and shrugged. "Why not? You will get married eventually, and since it doesn't seem as though you will be spurning anyone's intentions now," he said, shooting a glare toward Thomas, "I suppose Mrs. Grosvenor and I can spare you for a few months."

Miss Grosvenor hopped up and down, a huge smile on her face. "I'll go ask Alice if she'd like to go to Rome then!" Miss Grosvenor ran to clasp her father around his neck, kissing his cheek, before turning to sprint out of the room, giving a last, cheery wave toward Thomas.

"Well, young man, it seems that you and my daughter are both wishing to make your own decisions. I cannot say my parents would have been as understanding as I, but"—and then his face broke into an expression of warmth—"I trust Millie to decide things for herself. I have to. If I have done my job she will make the right choice." He held his hand out to Thomas. "Thank you for making me understand."

Thomas shook Mr. Grosvenor's hand, already anticipating what he would do next—find her, share his feelings, hope she reciprocated, and then—?

"Thank you, Mr. Grosvenor." He paused, keeping the other man's hand in his. "And may I say, you have done well raising Miss Grosvenor."

Mr. Grosvenor turned pink, giving Thomas's hand another vigorous shake. "Thank you. And I hope you are able to make the best decision you can."

Thomas drew a deep breath. "I hope to."

JANE RACED THROUGH the streets, holding the skirts of her gown up so they wouldn't impede her progress. Quite a few people gave her odd looks, which made sense—she didn't think young ladies of quality were often seen running through the streets of London with so much speed and without any accompaniment.

But, it seemed, she was set on a course of doing things her own way.

She had run first to his lodgings, but the person behind the front desk said he wasn't in, and they had no idea when he was expected.

Please don't let me be too late, she chanted in her head as she ran. If she got there after he'd proposed, and been accepted, could she even speak the truth to him? Would it be unnecessarily cruel to share her feelings only when it was too late?

Because if he'd proposed and been accepted she'd be ruining another lady's life, if that lady cared at all about him.

She'd had time to think on the way to his house where she would go if he wasn't at home. It wasn't to her house, because obviously he had just left there, and he could have just stayed if he'd wanted to.

Though that would make for awkward conversation at the breakfast table.

But he wasn't there, anyway, so it didn't matter.

He might be at Miss Porter's, but Jane thought he had made better progress with Miss Grosvenor, who was altogether the better candidate for the position.

Which meant even more that she hoped she was in time—Miss Grosvenor was a lovely person, and Jane considered her a friend, so she wouldn't want to jeopardize her friend's happiness.

But then again, if she didn't, she'd be altering her own happiness for the worse, and she wouldn't know how he felt about her or if there was a chance for them to be together.

She had no choice but to run faster.

Please don't let me be too late.

Her lungs were burning as she tore through the

streets, narrowly missing a few strolling pedestrians who turned to yell at her. Rightly so, she'd nearly knocked them over.

Apparently today was the day she was rude. And the day she was going to express her feelings to the man she loved.

And the day she might rudely interfere with the hopes of someone she truly liked.

Please don't let me be too late.

She slowed as she turned onto the street of the house the Grosvenors were renting.

And then slowed more as she saw him descending the stairs.

She was too late.

She'd waited too long to say anything, and now she was here, but he was leaving the house, which meant he'd at least spoken to Miss Grosvenor. Jane had no reason to suspect that lady would decline his proposal—she'd been quite effusive in her regard for him. Even if it didn't sound as though Miss Grosvenor had more than an affection toward him.

Goddamn it.

Her throat closed over, and she pondered just turning on her heel and slinking away, but that wasn't what she had promised herself she would do.

She was going to say what she wanted, and that was that.

Her whole life, until two years ago, she'd denied what she'd wanted. Denied herself even the option of considering what she wanted.

No, that wasn't quite right. She'd thought she'd wanted Mr. McTavish, but that was only because that was what she was told she would want. She'd never questioned it, never questioned anything.

Until she'd questioned all of it, and had realized that she was the only person who could possibly be in charge of her life. She could make her own decisions, and she would.

"Jane!" he exclaimed, rushing forward when he saw her.

Besides which, he'd seen her, so she couldn't exactly turn around and run home now, could she?

"Thomas, I mean Mr. Sharpe," she replied, glancing around. Nobody was in their immediate vicinity, thank goodness. "You've just been paying a call?" Her voice sounded unnaturally high and strained.

He nodded, folding his arms over his chest with a smug look. Was he looking that way because he'd secured his heiress?

"And—?" she began.

"We should talk," he replied, uncrossing his arms to take her hand.

We should talk.

Am I too late?

Is everything ruined?

"Yes. We should," she said, as firmly as she could manage.

"Not here," he said, glancing around the street. Of course they couldn't talk here—they were on a sidewalk in front of the Grosvenors' rental house, for goodness' sake. If Miss Grosvenor happened to be standing at the window and happened to glance outside, only to see her likely betrothed standing there with another woman?

Well, that would not be good.

Though a part of her—a tiny, not very kind part of her, she hastened to add—would be pleased if the engagement was broken, because then she could speak her truth with the fewest amount of people hurt.

"Where should we go?" Jane asked.

He didn't answer, just tugged on her hand and led her down the sidewalk, walking quickly. Not as fast as she'd run, but fast enough that it was hard to catch her breath.

He slowed a few streets later, tucking her hand into his arm and glancing about, clearly looking for an appropriate place to have their conversation.

Whatever their conversation was.

He frowned, then sighed in exasperation and strode toward an alley between two shops—one a bakery, the other a fishmonger.

The alley smelled unfortunately like the wares of the latter, and they met each other's eyes before laughing, Thomas guiding her out of the unpleasant area.

"You take me to the most unexpected places," Jane said, determined to keep herself cheerful, no matter what happened.

"And—" And then he cleared his throat and Thomas Sharpe, Mr. Thomas Sharpe the Most Unflappable Man in London, actually looked uncertain.

"And—?" she prompted after a few moments.

He took both her hands in his. Pedestrians streamed by on either side of them, but Jane didn't care. Yes, they were likely being an inconvenience, but she was done being convenient. She wanted to be a presence, both in her own life and in others'.

Hopefully his.

"Jane," he began, staring down at their joined hands. "I have never felt so nervous in my entire life."

She felt her throat close over. He was going to tell her that he had been accepted. That Miss Grosvenor was going to be his wife, and Miss Grosvenor's money was going to be his wealth.

She unclasped one hand to put it on his shoulder. "Tell me. You know you can tell me anything."

He exhaled, nodding, his head still down. She wished she could see his face.

"I won't be marrying anybody, Jane."

"She declined?" Jane said in a hesitant voice.

He shook his head, making her heart stop. "No. I didn't ask." He lifted his head then, meeting her gaze.

"You didn't?"

Another shake of his head.

And then she felt such an enormous sense of relief her knees practically buckled.

Chapter Twenty-Six

Jane was speaking, but all Thomas could focus on was her lovely face. How earnest she was, how he couldn't believe he'd even thought for a moment of not seeing her every day.

If she'd have him. He hadn't asked that yet.

Could he ask?

He had less than no prospects; he was still going to have to figure out a way to support his family, and he couldn't do the one thing he'd thought would save everything.

"And Thaddeus would give you the money," she was saying, making Thomas frown in confusion.

"Why would your brother-in-law give me money?" he asked.

She huffed out a breath. "You have not been listening."

Accurate. I was too busy thinking about you.

"Because neither one of us thinks you should have to sell yourself when—when there might be something else. Someone else," she corrected, her cheeks slowly starting to turn pink.

"What are you saying, Jane?" he asked, squeezing her hands tighter.

She lifted her chin. "I am saying, Thomas, that I have fallen in love with you, even though I promised both of us I wouldn't. That I don't want you to have to do what I refused to do two years ago. I know how strangling that future can seem, looming over you, and I don't want you to have to live like that. I want—"

"What do you want, Jane?" He spoke fiercely, his heart thumping in his chest.

"The same thing I wanted last night. I want you," she replied simply. "What do you want?"

They stared into one another's eyes for a long moment, Thomas's mind reeling from her words.

"Well?" she said impatiently.

"I want you, too," he said, the relief of the admission coursing through his body like the best kind of champagne. "I come with so many responsibilities," he continued, needing to make sure she knew his intentions. "I cannot deny them, even if the solution isn't what I thought it was." His throat was choked with emotion. "I didn't think there was any other answer before, but now I think— now I believe—that if you are beside me I can solve this. All of it." He took a deep breath. "I am a better person because of you, Jane. I like who I am when I am with you. I like who you are when you are with me," he added, with a smile. "I want us to face the future together, but it isn't going to be easy," he warned.

"You foolish man," she replied. "Of course it

won't be easy. You've already had an easy life, now you get to have an *interesting* life. I've been doing that for two years now. I'm certain you'll be able to catch up."

He grinned like an idiot, staring into her eyes, both of them still standing in the middle of the sidewalk like two besotted rocks, the stream of pedestrians flowing around them.

"Well?" she said again.

"Well—?" he said, confused.

She rolled her eyes. "Well, aren't you going to kiss me?"

He chuckled, drawing her into his arms, heedless that anyone could see them. Kissing her with the knowledge that they would have a future. Together. A difficult one, an uncertain one, but one that would be happy because they loved each other.

THEY STOPPED KISSING—eventually—and began to walk slowly back toward Jane's house.

He wasn't so stubborn that he refused to even contemplate accepting money from Thaddeus. She was proud of him for that—it was one thing to say you wanted to change how you lived, and what you thought, and another thing to do it. Because ladies accepted financial support all the time—from husbands, brothers, fathers, and family friends. Why should a gentleman be any different?

They were discussing potential moneymaking opportunities as they approached Jane's house when they saw a carriage draw up in front of them, with Mr. Grosvenor hopping out.

His expression was joyful, and Jane wondered

for a moment if she had hallucinated the past hour. If Thomas had actually offered for Miss Grosvenor, and she was in some sort of fever dream.

"I was hoping to find you here," Mr. Grosvenor said. "Millie said she thought Mr. Sharpe here was sweet on Lady Jane, and it turns out she was right! She is so clever, that one." He frowned, a confused expression on his face. "But that's not why I am here."

"Would you like to come in, sir?" Jane asked, gesturing down the street to her house.

"Yes, splendid," Mr. Grosvenor replied.

She and Thomas exchanged puzzled looks as the three of them went into the house, Jane directing Mrs. Charing to serve them tea.

Fifteen minutes later, Mr. Grosvenor was sharing what he'd thought of.

"And I know Mr. Sharpe is the most charming man in London," he continued, barely drawing breath, "and having someone like that to represent our interests would be enormously helpful. We don't want to stay in London forever, my wife and I," he explained. "Millie will be traveling with your sister"—at which point Jane shot a querying look toward Thomas, who indicated he'd explain later—"so with her taken care of I see no need to stay here. The thing is," he said more slowly, "I've been thinking about our conversations, and I want you to decide things for yourself without having to worry too much about outside concerns."

He finally drew breath, and Thomas opened his mouth, only to have Mr. Grosvenor start again. "Of course I'd pay you a wage, plus a percentage of profits." He withdrew a piece of paper from his waistcoat pocket, handing it over to Thomas, who immediately spread it out so that both he and Jane could read it. "I did a few calculations on the way over here. I can afford to pay you that much."

The amount he'd written on the paper was enough, Jane thought, to keep Thomas's parents in relative comfort, especially if Alice was cared for. They wouldn't be able to do much beyond live on their estate, but at least they would be able to do that without worry.

And if Thomas was as charming and persuasive as she knew him to be, he would soon amass a healthy sum of money, enough to live on. Without taking Thaddeus's money, though she would keep that in reserve, just in case.

Thomas stared down at the paper, then back up at Mr. Grosvenor. Then at Jane. And then back at Mr. Grosvenor.

"Yes, sir, I would very much like to accept."

"Splendid!" Mr. Grosvenor exclaimed, getting up from his chair. "I'll expect you at the offices in a week. Plenty of time to take care of your most pressing business, wouldn't you say?" he said, glancing between them with a knowing look.

"Indeed, sir. Thank you."

Thomas went to draw Jane into his arms as soon as the door closed behind Mr. Grosvenor, but then it flung open again, revealing Percy, whose expression was a blend of excitement, concern, and anticipation.

"Well?" he said.

"Well," Jane replied. "I have told him how I feel,

and he has told me, and we have decided to feel our feelings together."

Percy yelped, running forward to fold them both into a warm hug. "And you'll live here still? With me and Daffy?"

"Daffy?" Thomas said.

"I'll explain later," Jane replied. "Since it seems my betrothed—we are getting married, are we not?" she clarified, realizing they hadn't actually said the words.

"We are," Thomas said. "If that is what you choose," he added with a wink.

"Since it seems my betrothed will be working in London, and we need to save as much money as possible, we will stay here with you and Daffy."

And then, at last, they were alone.

Jane tilted her face up to Thomas. "Kiss me again," she ordered.

One eyebrow rose. "Are you going to be this bossy when we are married?"

"Yes," she said, putting her hand around his neck and drawing him to her. "Yes," she murmured, when their mouths were barely an inch apart. "Yes," she said, right before their lips met and they were kissing one another with the promise that this was just the first day in their lives together.

Epilogue

Two Years Later

"Jane, can you come in here? I need your help."

"Of course you do," Jane said in a fond tone, shaking her head. She walked down the hall to the nursery, where her husband was currently trying to change a very active baby. Percival was about a year old and looked like a perfect blend of the two of them. He had blue eyes, blond hair, and was already insistent on making his own decisions.

His favorite person was his uncle Percy, much to his parents' amusement, followed by their friend, Lord Michael Hughes, whom nobody called anything but Daffy.

"What do you need, Mr. Sharpe?" she asked pertly. He didn't answer, just handed her a naked Percival, who was wiggling his legs as though he was dancing the polka.

"And I am supposed to do—what?"

He made a gesture of defeat. "I don't know. He

will not be still for changing, and Percy and Daffy are out."

Percy was the only one who could persuade Percival to be still when necessary. Usually by making up a song about equations, or deliberately messing up his hair, which Percival found hilarious.

"How was work today?" Jane asked, grabbing a blanket to wrap the still wriggling Percival in.

Thomas's work for Mr. Grosvenor—persuading wealthy people to invest in a variety of Mr. Grosvenor's business interests—was hugely successful, even more than either Thomas or Mr. Grosvenor had envisioned. It utilized his charm, and he'd discovered he liked being charming when it didn't require he get married at the end of it. Mr. Grosvenor paid him handsomely, which meant that he could send enough money to his parents and still support his own family.

"It went well," he replied, taking a seat in the nursery as Jane began to jostle Percival up and down the way he liked. "And yours?"

Jane had found work also, teaching etiquette lessons to young ladies from families eager to secure their children better places in Society. The ladies were mostly the daughters of wealthy merchants, eager to take London by storm. Jane had also founded the Girls' Adventurers Club, an alternative for young ladies who wanted something other than a husband.

"Fine," she said with a shrug, continuing to bounce Percival up and down. "Miss Jenkins decided that she does not want to enter Society if it means she cannot express her opinion." She shot Thomas a rueful look. "Miss Jenkins has many opinions."

He chuckled, folding his arms over his chest. "As though that doesn't delight you to the tips of your toes," he replied.

She nodded. "It does, I will admit. She is planning her first Adventure."

They both turned at the sound of the door opening downstairs, followed by Percy's and Daffy's voices. Percival immediately began to express his keen desire to see his uncle.

Footsteps sounded on the stairs, and then Percy and Daffy both appeared, Percy holding his arms out to take his nephew.

"Come here," he crooned. "You are a very smart baby—you know who is the best one in this house to be held by." He gave a gleefully mischievous look at Jane and Thomas, both of whom rolled their eyes.

"That is just because you never have to take care of the things young Percival doesn't like, such as changing nappies," Daffy said in a dry tone.

Jane, Thomas, Percival, Percy, and Daffy continued to live together, even though they could all afford separate residences. But they had decided not to, since they were perfectly happy where they were, and they didn't see the need to change anything, even if Society thought their living arrangement was a bit odd. And, honestly, that all of them were a bit odd.

"Hush," Percy chided, but he gave Daffy a warm look when he spoke, belying his tone.

Percy still worked for the government, while

Daffy was training with Thomas since it seemed Mr. Grosvenor's business would be expanding. Daffy was the complete opposite of Thomas— quiet, modest, and extremely earnest—so they thought his personality would be an excellent foil.

"We've got Millie and Alice coming for dinner tonight, don't forget," Jane said, easing Percival out of Percy's arms and back onto the changing table. Percy peered over his sister's shoulders to entertain Percival with a variety of faces as she quickly did up his diaper.

"Oh good," Daffy said. "I was hoping Miss Grosvenor could share some tips on handling Mrs. Grosvenor." Millie's parents had kept their home in London, since Mr. Grosvenor's work required his presence there, and Mrs. Grosvenor had found she very much liked "dabbling in business," as she called it, which mostly meant going from desk to desk and asking basic questions about what each worker was doing.

Miss Grosvenor and Alice, meanwhile, had spent time traveling and had then discovered they liked their newfound freedom, spending lots of Mr. Grosvenor's money to rent a house right down the street. The seven of them spent many evenings together, handing Percival from one to another as they ate, drank, and laughed.

It wasn't what Jane had dreamt of as a white-garbed debutante, but it suited her infinitely better. But more than that, this was her choice. And his.

Keep reading for a
sneak peek at the next book in
the Hazards of Dukes series
by Megan Frampton

Coming soon from Avon Books!

Chapter One

*I*t's very simple," Octavia explained, taking a deep breath. The carriage chose that moment to hit a rut, and so she fell against the side, grasping the edge of the velvet-covered seat. "I'll take care of everything." She spoke with her usual confidence, though she did not *feel* her usual confidence. But perhaps that was just due to the shaking carriage. "I'll arrange the selling of the house and its contents. We should be able to get a substantial amount of money."

No response from her companion. To be expected, she supposed.

"The money will go toward paying what I owe Mr. Higgins." She scowled as she thought about him; she'd done research when she was considering borrowing money, and he did offer relatively reasonable interest rates (for a moneylender), but he also offered extremely prompt retribution if his funds were not paid in full on time.

She'd already received two visits from the gentleman himself, assuring her he would break all her limbs and ruin her life if she didn't make up for the payment she'd already missed.

Or perhaps it was the other way around—ruin her life and *then* break all her limbs.

"And which of my limbs did he threaten?" she asked. Again, no response. "If he means to break one of my arms, then that would be difficult, but not impossible. The leg, now, that would be more problematic. I can learn to write with the opposite hand, if need be," she explained. "But moving about on only one leg could prove problematic." She gave an annoyed huff. "But what was I to do?" she said, holding her hands out in supplication. "I believed I saw an opportunity, and if I see an opportunity, I should take it. Despite the risk."

Since Octavia was part-owner of and ran a gambling house, it stood to reason she would take a risk—a gamble, if she was being coy—when she was so certain the reward would be worth it. Hence the debt.

"It should be simple," she repeated, lifting her chin defiantly. Which made her bonnet hit the back of the carriage, sending it tilting over her eye. She straightened it with a fierce gesture. "Father left a will, and with a little searching, I should be able to find it."

It was at this point that Ivy, Octavia's sister, would usually point out some flaw in Octavia's plan.

That she hadn't considered that they hadn't seen or communicated with their father for over five years, so they had no idea what the house and its contents might look like; that Octavia shouldn't bother about their father's holdings because they were doing all right on their own; that they wouldn't even have known that their father had died unless Ivy had chanced to see a paper from their village in Somerset that shared the news.

If Octavia was currently speaking to her sister, that is.

But she wasn't. And it wasn't that there was a disagreement between them; Ivy and Octavia got along exceedingly well, remarkable considering that both women had strong opinions.

No, it was because Ivy was not there. Instead of being in London, where the sisters had lived for the past six or seven years, Octavia was sitting in a well-appointed carriage bouncing on the road to Greensett, a place she hadn't been to since she was fourteen years old.

"You are a much better listener," she said in a soothing voice to her companion. If Ivy had been there, Octavia would not have been able to speak at length for such a long time. Ivy was presumably safe at home with her husband, unaware of Octavia's departure.

Her companion was Cerberus, her Italian mastiff, who slept on the opposite seat, a distinct circle of drool marking the velvet upholstery. Theoretically, she was speaking to him, but since he was asleep as well as being canine, she couldn't expect a response. Though she would have welcomed one.

She *had* spoken to Ivy earlier that day, but she had not said anything she was saying now. Her sister had arrived early that morning to share the news about their father's death—discovered by accident in a newspaper Ivy had intended to use for her and her husband's dogs—and Octavia had listened, which was rare.

Usually, Octavia spoke and Ivy tried to interrupt.

The sisters had cried together, remembering a time when he hadn't put his own passion for gambling ahead of his family. Long before the estrangement. When he'd promised them he'd always have a home for them, even when his fortunes were low.

They'd cried because of what they had lost, and would never have now: a father who loved them. Who cared for them.

And then they'd wiped their tears, and a plan had begun to unfurl in Octavia's mind. He'd promised them he'd always have a home for them. That had to still be true.

Their father had died just a month before. Although he and his daughters were estranged, Octavia's fellow gambling club owners and workers kept her apprised of her father's activities. Just a few months earlier, she'd heard he'd bet on a race between a cow and a frog—she hadn't heard who'd won, but the very nature of the wager made her appreciate her older sister Ivy's taking her away from it all. But perhaps his luck had changed; there was no telling what might be in the house. Never mind that the house itself was also valuable.

What if, by his death, he was finally able to do something good for his daughters?

What if she were to go to Greensett herself and see what he'd left to her and Ivy? It would remove her from London, out of Mr. Higgins's reach, and it would definitely yield some money, hopefully enough so that Ivy might never know of Octavia's risky venture. She'd pay Mr. Higgins back without anyone being the wiser.

Octavia had originally wanted the money to make improvements to the gambling club she and Ivy co-owned. The club was making money, true, but Octavia believed it could make so much more, given proper investment. And at first the new tables, expanded playing rooms, and additional personnel had increased revenue.

But then the business faltered thanks to a combination of horrible weather and a distracting political crisis, and Octavia was staring at the possibility of being broken-limbed and ruined.

Or the other way around, she wasn't certain.

"It will be fine," she assured her still-sleeping dog. "Father must have left a will. And we will inherit everything. I'll be able to scrape up enough to pay Mr. Higgins. Just the house itself should take care of it. Ivy never has to hear of this." She spoke with a confidence she told herself she felt.

Cerberus opened his eyes, looked at her, and promptly went back to sleep.

"I would have thought feeding you would count for some loyalty," she said with a smile, leaning forward to pat Cerberus's head. He only made a snuffling noise and shifted on the seat.

She leaned back against the seat cushion and gazed out the window, wishing she could be there right now rather than in five hours.

Patience was not her strong suit. Nor was caution. Nor, for that matter, doing anything but being her obstinate self.

A benefit when it came to being a woman in a

field usually reserved for men, but not so much when it came to navigating life in a rural village.

Thank goodness she had been able to get out of London so quickly—she had recalled that her frequent, and frequent losing, customer Lady Montague was sending her carriage to fetch her niece from school. It was only a matter of asking the good-natured lady to have her carriage make a tiny detour.

Which meant she had no way of returning if she needed to get back just as fast.

But she didn't anticipate any trouble once she arrived.

She never did.

GABRIEL RAKED HIS hands through his hair as he surveyed the chaos that was his new house.

Mr. Holton had died close to a month ago, but Gabriel had been busy sorting out the details of his own father's estate.

Like Mr. Holton, Gabriel's father, Mr. Fallon, was a gambler. Unlike Mr. Holton, however, Mr. Fallon was very, very lucky. He'd transformed his modest holdings into a vast network of property, liquid assets, shares in a variety of companies, and several items that couldn't be assessed properly because they were unique.

Something brushed against his calf, and Gabriel looked down and smiled. "I know you're hungry," he said to Nyx, one of the unique items. She yipped in reply, then trotted off to sniff the leg of a chair whose upholstery had faded to an unpleasant brownish-gray color.

A tiny, fluffy Pomeranian, Nyx had been part of a parcel his father had won four years earlier. Mr. Fallon hadn't wanted to keep the dog, but Gabriel had hidden her in his satchel and brought her back to school. By the time Mr. Fallon discovered his son's duplicity, it was too late—Nyx was already a favorite at Gabriel's boarding school, and Mr. Fallon valued his access to Gabriel's schoolmates' parents so he couldn't just get rid of her.

"Those lords are always easy to fleece," he'd confided to Gabriel during one of the rare occasions he'd spoken to his son. "Think they will win just because of who they are." He snorted. "When it's what they do and how they play that makes all the difference."

As parental advice it wasn't much to go on, but Gabriel had embraced it, determined to make himself into someone who would succeed by his actions, even though his origins were merely respectable, at best, and infamous, at worst, thanks to his father's machinations.

And the final machination before he'd died had been to win Mr. Holton's house. He'd tried for years to best the other man, at one time even winning his daughter in a bet, but losing to that very same daughter only a few hours later.

Gabriel's father had been so triumphant about finally winning the house that he'd drunk more than usual and tipped over a candle, setting his house ablaze with him in it.

Thankfully, no one else was in residence at the time; Gabriel had gone to inquire about a rare manuscript, and Mr. Fallon's servants didn't live in the house because Mr. Fallon didn't trust anybody. Not even his son.

Gabriel had mourned his father, as anybody would, but he had been most sorrowful of what the elder Mr. Fallon had missed out on—his father had been so busy playing cards he'd never played with his son. Hadn't risked opening his heart to another person because he was risking pounds and pence in stakes.

Gabriel had been happily surprised when he'd gone through his late father's papers to find the scrawled piece of paper declaring Mr. Fallon was now the owner of Mr. Holton's house.

Thanks to the fire, Gabriel didn't have anywhere to live. He'd taken rooms in the village, but three weeks of the innkeeper's meat stew was an exquisite torture he thought Prometheus would have refused in favor of the whole "bird pecking out an organ" torture.

He'd arrived that morning, dropping the satchel containing his books, linen, and other items of clothing in the main hallway. It sent a cloud of dust into the air, making him and Nyx sneeze.

It was clear that if Mr. Holton had had any servants, they hadn't spent any time cleaning.

But Gabriel wasn't afraid of hard work—he liked manual labor, it kept his hands occupied as his brain sorted through his research.

"This place would make Hades flinch," he told Nyx, who had given up on food and was lying on a crumpled piece of fabric in the corner of the room.

Gabriel had walked through the entire house, assessing what needed to be done.

Everything.

In addition to the dust, it seemed a robust family of mice had taken residence in the library. The bottom bookshelf's books were uniformly marked by teeth, and when he'd entered, he'd heard a frantic scrabbling indicating the mice were retreating to wherever they lived.

There was a hole in the roof in at least one of the attic rooms, and the upstairs bedrooms were competing with one another as to which one was the worst.

The kitchen was an equally disgusting mess, streaks of grease on the walls and a dubious-looking stove.

But unless he wanted to endure more of Mrs. Packham's beef stew, this was where he would be living.

Having a house to himself, turning that house into a home, would be deeply satisfying. His father had sent him to school, then hadn't cared when Gabriel wanted to continue his studies. Gabriel had lived in rented rooms near the British Museum in London, poring over ancient texts as he worked to create a more lively, more modern version of a slew of Greek myths.

He saw the promise of the house, of what it had been when Mr. Holton's wife had been alive and their two daughters had lived there as well.

After her father staked his oldest daughter in a wager against Gabriel's father, the daughter, Ivy, had had the audacity to challenge Mr. Fallon to a wager, staking her younger sister.

Gabriel's father had wanted the sister, Octavia, to marry Gabriel, even though nobody had consulted either one of them. Why his father had wanted him to marry the younger Holton girl was a mystery, but then again, most of what his father had done was a mystery to Gabriel.

Thank God Ivy had won.

And promptly left that very night for London, taking her younger sister with her.

"Enough of that, though," Gabriel said to Nyx as he strode from the kitchen back to the main entrance. He undid the buttons of his shirt as he walked, yanking it up and over his head as he stepped outside into the early evening air.

The day had been warm, and he hadn't been able to resist moving a few pieces of furniture, making him sweat.

He'd spied a small pond in the back of the house when he'd looked out a smoke-smeared window.

"We're going for a swim, girl," he told Nyx as he circled around to the back. He dropped to the grass, sliding his boots and socks off, then stood back up to remove his trousers and his small-clothes.

Nobody was here, nobody would come here, and he'd be damned if he'd walk around in damp underclothes.

He plunged into the water, a blessedly cool relief on his heated skin. Nyx followed, her little head bobbing up and down in the water as she paddled.

It was peaceful. He was alone, which he relished.

He had a purpose, which he craved. And he now had plenty of time, funds, and a house, all of which would further his work.

He wanted and needed nothing else. He wanted and needed nobody else.

He floated onto his back, stretching his arms out to his side, when he heard an enormous splash, and lifted his head to see a gigantic black dog barreling into the water, with a woman running behind, yelling at the dog to come back.

"Cerberus!" she shouted, her attention focused on her dog. Gabriel jerked upright and grabbed Nyx, holding the tiny dog to his side as the other dog— Cerberus—continued his quest toward them. He instinctively thrust Nyx nearly behind him, protecting her.

And then the woman saw him.

Her eyes widened, her mouth dropped open, and she yelped, making an "eep!" sound. As though *he* was the interloper, and not she.

Gabriel gritted his teeth, keeping a wary eye on her enormous dog, who could have swallowed Nyx as a snack.

"I don't know who the hell you are," he said in a fierce tone, "or what you are doing here, but you need to control your dog."

Her eyes narrowed. "Cerberus wouldn't want to have anything to do with your dog. Would you, Cerberus?" she said to the dog, who was steadfastly ignoring her, now sniffing at the edge of the water, thankfully far away from Nyx.

She turned her gaze back to him. "*You* are the trespasser," she said in a firm, righteous tone. "What are you doing here?" she demanded. "And who are you?"

"I could ask the very same of you," Gabriel replied. "Since you are on my property."

"Your property!" she echoed. "It is most certainly not." She raised her chin. "This is my house."